THE WHITE KUDU

To Jo
Best wishes
Gus Hoyle

THE WHITE KUDU

GISELA HOYLE

picnic

First published in Great Britain in 2009
by Picnic Publishing
PO Box 5222, Hove BN52 9LP

All rights reserved
Copyright © Gisela Hoyle, 2009

The right of Gisela Hoyle to be identified as the author of this
work has been asserted by her in accordance with the
Copyright, Designs & Patents Act, 1988.

A catalogue record for this book is available from the British
Library.

ISBN: 9780956037060
Printed and bound in Great Britain by
CPI Antony Rowe, Chippenham and Eastbourne
Designed by SoapBox, www.soapboxcommunications.co.uk.

All rights reserved. No part of this publication may be
reproduced or transmitted in any form or by any means,
electronic or mechanical including photocopying, recording
or information storage or retrieval system, without the prior
permission in writing of the publishers.

This book is sold subject to the condition that it shall not by
way of trade or otherwise be lent, resold, hired out, or
otherwise circulated without the publishers' prior consent
in writing in any form of binding or cover other than that in
which it is published and without a similar condition being
imposed on the subsequent publisher.

Acknowledgements

I was born and grew up in the Northern Cape of South Africa, and spent some time there with my partner on Exploration sites; nevertheless the places described in the novel are a work of fiction, rooted as much in the imagination as they are in reality. For the reality I am indebted to probably countless teachers, experiences, books and papers, but in particular to the following:

Laurens van der Post (1961) *The Heart of the Hunter*, Harmondsworth, Penguin Publishers

Laurens van der Post (1964) *The Lost World of the Kalahari*, Harmondsworth, Penguin Publishers

J. David Lewis-Williams (2002) *A Cosmos in Stone*, Oxford, Altamira; (from which the quote on p71 in Chapter 3 of the Abbe Breuil is taken)

Richard B. Lee and Irven DeVore, eds (1998) *Kalahari Hunter-Gatherers, studies of the !Kung San and their Neighbors*, Cambridge Massachusetts, Harvard University Press

J. David Lewis-Williams and Tomas A. Dowson (1990), *Through the Veil: San Rock paintings and the rock face* in *South African Archaeological Bulletin 45*

Edward B Eastwood and Geoffrey Blundell (1999): *Rediscovering the Rock art of the Limpopo-Shashi Confluence area, Sothern Africa* in *Southern African Field Archaeology 8*

Edward B Eastwood and Catherine Cnoops (1999): *Capturing the Spoor: towards explaining Kudu in San Rock art of the*

Limpopo-Shashi Confluence area in South African in *Archaeological Bulletin S4*

Land Restitution in South Africa: our Achievements and Challenges by the Commission on Restitution of Land Rights in May 2003

Heartfelt thanks go to Corinne Souza and Rena Valeh for their patient editing, to Rod Duncan and Andrew Sharp for their encouragement and to my family for their great forbearance.

1
Abelshoop

'Pniel, you say it's called?'

'Yes, Pniel.'

'An odd name.'

'It's biblical – named by missionaries.'

'And how do I find this place, this Pniel, then?'

'You head north-west out of Kimberley.'

'North-west? Could you be a little more specific? Which road do I take?'

A pitying look: 'There is only one road.'

So Joshua Hunter found himself heading north-west out of Kimberley in late August, with little idea of where he was going or what to expect when he got there.

Somewhere beyond Upington the Kalahari truly begins, but on this route the veld begins a shifting, wavering transformation from Karoo to Kalahari, from Vaalbos to red sands beneath the graceful arches of camel thorn trees. And for a while the land is neither, and both. The grey hard bushes of the Karoo give way to the seeming-soft, sparse, yellow grass; the earth becomes increasingly red and uncertain as soil turns to sand, loose and light and glittering; and, with the sudden alertness of a meerkat, you think you have reached Namaqualand, only to find yourself in the grey sloot of an ancient riverbed or the green belt of the river, which, since its beginning in the Drakensberg, has been always unpredictable and restless.

Coming upon this place called Pniel, where Jacob wrestled with an angel, is an experience that does not lose its wonder with repetition: the world opens up and the desert engulfs you, transforming what you thought you knew into a wide and open emptiness, which watched attentively for long enough, will reveal a life beyond imagining in that heat-shimmering world. And in such vast openness, it seems that everything will go on forever.

And why would an Englishman be driving through this timeless wilderness, through a landscape that is as desolate as it is beautiful? Well, because he is a geologist, seeking treasure. Not gold for his own transformation, not an alchemist, but for a mining company – mopping up the loose ends on old, but unfinished projects. Joshua Hunter drove north-west out of Kimberley in the inevitable white 4x4 Toyota of the exploration branch of the Lefika Mining Company, towards a camp already set up for him by his field hands, on a farm called Pniel by missionaries long ago. Perhaps their faith had been challenged by the semi-desert, he thought, or maybe the name expressed a surprised joy at finding a piece of land, a patch of this vast earth where God touched the lives of mortals after all.

The camp on Pniel, with the dam and the three trees – peppercorns and a eucalyptus – and the windmill with its constant not quite regular clanking, and the accompanying wind in the leaves, sometimes the splash of water so welcome in this semi-desert, was one of the best he had had. It was raised slightly, with a view and not too far from the river. The peace of the camp, with its non-invasive sounds, was to be a minor oasis on a difficult project for several months: the caravan, the half-wild cats, the theodolite, and every day the sand, quickly became the only certainties in his life.

It had seemed at first just another routine double-checking project. Paul had said as he handed it to Joshua, 'It's worth checking over: a few anomalies in the findings of twelve years ago; it might be an interesting project.'

'And anyway, everyone ought to have done a stint in the near Kalahari,' he added heartlessly. When Joshua demanded more details, Paul responded in his usual calm way, 'According to head office, these anomalies are "worthy of another look, you never know". And sometimes Joshua, it is best to know no more, in order to find what others may have missed.'

Joshua had become suspicious, 'It isn't just another minor project for a greenhorn to cut his teeth?'

'We don't know until you've looked, Joshua,' said Paul, trying to placate him.

But Joshua, already leaving the room and sulking, shot out over his shoulder, 'A few years in the desert will chill him out?'

Smiling, Paul watched him go and muttered under his breath, 'Well perhaps they will, perhaps they will,' and was glad to have this intense and impulsive young man off his hands for a while.

Joshua remembered this conversation and he could feel irritation beginning to well up in him as he drove out to camp, leaving Kimberley with its looming diamond sorting house, and the open wound of the big hole behind.

However, the further he drove, the less the office seemed to matter with its sense of self-importance and its rude numerical approach to the discovery of precious metals. Above all, its corporate thought patterns receded and lost their power to irritate, their essential pettiness clearly revealed in a pan's simplicity. As he left the last smoky shanty of Galeshewe behind and the neater more solid houses of Homevale on the outskirts of Kimberley, and entered finally the uninhabited veld, he was struck by its endlessness and capacity to make even time go on forever.

The sky was pale blue, a perfect bowl tipped over the far round of the earth. The horizon was almost white and only rarely broken by small rises in the ground but otherwise leaving a vast space for eye and mind to wander, to contemplate the self, its smallness and the many potential faces of God. Nearer by, the sand lay baking and still in the heat, making the air above it shift and slither, a silent mesmerising dance of glittering air. The yellow grass was of course not soft as it looked from far away, but brittle and dry and by midday no longer waving, exhausted as everything else was at the end of winter and the dusty August wind.

The world stood stark and broken in the midday sun – metallic, bright, red and gold, and strangely beautiful. In the vastness only shade was thin and hesitant beneath the huge but insufficient umbrellas of the still acacias with their delicate curling silver green leaves. The birds too were silent by midday and the light now so bright it seared into the very back of one's brain, which longed for the relief of darkness, of the sun gone down. Everything seemed huge, overwhelming and endless here – except humankind.

Not even the small people who alone, according to van der Post, were truly native to it and had lived so lightly, so harmlessly in its vastness, perfectly adapted to this landscape, could survive: not when History joined forces with the climate. But Joshua did not know any of that then; he simply marvelled at the wide sky, the red earth and the searing stillness of the midday heat: an August day, still smelling of burnt veld in the lip-cracking clarity of the air here at the meeting place of Karoo and Kalahari.

He stared moodily out at the landscape, and took to daydreaming about what he would find. A sickening lurch and the sudden crunch of gravel rather than tarmac brought him awake as the huge car veered momentarily out of control and off the road. His hands closed convulsively on the slippery, hot black steering wheel, while his foot sought frantically for the brake pedal, as his mind, soporific with the heat, struggled to make sense of what was happening. It was all over before he could react and the car came to an abrupt stop against a sturdy fence post.

'Right,' he said to himself, embarrassed, non-nonplussed, 'wake-up! Focus!'

He turned on the radio, drank some tepid coke and, to keep awake in the hazy wavering day, focused on what he knew of the project ahead and what he had read of it over the past two weeks since receiving the assignment.

Once accepted, he had set about getting the options and permits for renewed sampling and exploration, beginning with the two neighbouring farms, Wonderfontein and Pniel, both with long river boundaries and therefore more prosperous than those deeper into Vaalbos or Kalahari. So far he had not spoken to the farmers themselves, only the lawyers, who had been gruff enough, but had seemed eager for more exploration activity. He'd thought that it must bring in more money for them, which the quiet lives of semi-desert living farmers themselves presumably did not.

He had been a little puzzled by the pitying looks of his colleagues about the project. And puzzled still more by a polite and well-expressed letter from Adam Vermeulen, offering him and the company, once again, a campsite for the duration of the project and every success with their search. The community was delighted to welcome back a geologist into their midst, the letter ended. It seemed so unlike the usual response of the farmers to having geologists on their land, who in the eyes of farmers only left gates open for stock to get lost and churned up the good earth without planting anything in it. And the paltry discoveries were no compensation for the invasion. Still, he supposed the puzzle would make it more interesting.

When all the preparations were in place, he set out to that area of red sand and dolomites and grey river beds, on his maps already covered with hopeful scribbling, hints of wonders to be found, criss-crossed with the marks and annotations of previous geologists, who had, however, come away empty-handed. His head was filled with data, maps, grids, and lithologies, and he was eager to give substance to these Delphic numbers, to see the reality behind the fiction of figures, which conjured wealth perhaps, but no landscape and no ore.

The puzzles, hints of rich findings, kept him awake now and focused, and looking forward to the next few weeks in the field. Tunelessly, he whistled snatches of jumbled melodies as he sped along happily on company petrol. Despite this speed and long, clear, straight roads, it was late in the evening and dark by the time he got to camp. He had by then stopped whooping at the rare sight of interesting outcrops and exciting rock formations or sand patterns, as Karoo met and then gradually became Kalahari, only to shift back, with just the dolomites beneath the soil remaining certain. In the still and almost complete darkness, after the brightness of the 4x4 headlamps, he could not see much, except that Josef and Ben had already set up both tent and caravan. He could dimly make out a clanking sound and a looming darkness to the left of the campsite. So he stopped the noisy engine of the 4x4, scrambled out, made up his bed in the caravan by the light of a torch and sank thankfully into it.

Morning brought the excitement – remnants of his days as a boy scout no doubt – of taking stock of the camp. Of finding a rusty but entirely serviceable shower set up beneath the wind pump at the side of a small, concrete dam, with shoulder high reed screening. Seeing the three beautiful large whispery trees, in whose shade the camp stood and setting up his office in the tent, the floor of which was covered in pink, crunching, peppercorn berries. The slightly bitter, tangy smell of these small, sour, crushed berries and the sharp scent of the thin, long eucalyptus leaves soon became unmistakable, and would always be Pniel to him after that: a farm, a camp lost now forever.

His office tent stood a decent way off from his home tent, nestled beneath the more looming bank of an ancient earth-built dam the size of a small lake. The office contained a large, rather shaky trestle table and core boxes stacked hopefully in the corners that made the tent wall bulge. Maps of various sizes lay on the trestle table, rolled and unrolled and somewhere in between, with several of his interesting, but desultorily collected rock samples as paperweights. There was space for the many bags of sand, which would soon cover the groundsheet. Back outside, he explored the looming darkness, which kept his tent cool – the dam wall sloping gently, the sides ravined and uneven with the roots of the large weeping willows, which surrounded the dam. He climbed the wall and was surprised by the peace of the lapping, shimmering green water – the beginning of the farm's intricate irrigation system. On one side a large concrete pipe opened its gaping mouth into the dam, with water pouring copiously from it, splashing above the hum of the motorised pump, which brought all this up from the river. This powerful squat engine seemed to mock the slim wind pump, which stood mournfully clanking beside the smaller dam at the other end of the field, pumping more slowly a trickle of water from the large dam to the thirsty livestock in the nearby kraals. A lifted sluice gate sent a rush of it along the furrow out into the arable fields, and red weaver birds flitted industriously from one swinging branch to the next. Then he saw the head of a water bird, snaking out of the shining green, briefly cutting a dark pattern through the still water. As he walked around the top of the dam wall, he looked out across the fields facing the camp and farmhouse and was blinded by a fierce bright flash. He looked away quickly and moved into the shade of the willow tree, but looking up, could see no source for the bright light.

Joshua climbed down towards the tent of his field hands Ben and Josef, on the other side of the dam. He was always puzzled by this distance, which they kept so carefully. But in a socio-political context beyond his grasp in its complexity, he feared to query it and did not know whether it was respect, a remnant of apartheid or simply keeping him at arm's length. Just as he got this far he saw Ben come stooping out of his tent.

'Mornings,' he called, as he squatted down near the fire burning between the two tents and over which the kettle had begun to boil.

'Mornings,' Joshua said smiling, glad to be away from the city, 'it looks like a good camp, this.'

'Ja-nee, it is going to be quite lekker here,' replied Ben.

'You set up beautifully, again. Thank you,' Joshua said.

'Thank you,' Josef too had come out now and was ready for that first enormous enamel cup of strong and sweet boere coffee with which he started every day of his life.

'How are the people here? Will we get on, then?' Joshua asked tentatively.

'Ja-nee, it's looking good. Looks like they are pleased to see us. Even the farmer himself.' Josef indicated the farmhouse some 200 metres away from Joshua's side of the camp if one followed the irrigation channel. A beautiful white house, with a grey roof, flanked as the camp was by two huge peppercorn trees, though the gate was guarded by softly whispering poplars and a little bridge to cross the irrigation canal, which surrounded the garden on this side like a moat. Along the sides of the moat grew figs. Joshua stared at the house, the beautiful garden, rockery and roses and a lovely pond. A veritable squandering of water here in the dryness of the Northern Cape, he thought. Ben and Josef smiled encouragingly, half-mockingly, nodding their heads towards the house.

'I'll go,' Joshua said, 'just give me a chance to get supplies first.' And he made his way to the caravan, but watched that little bridge and the moated house carefully all the way.

After a morning sorting through the maps and notes, finding the correlations, it was time to head into Abelshoop to buy supplies and food, and of course this was more important than meeting Adam Vermeulen. Abelshoop seemed a dreary dorp to Joshua as he rolled that word "dorp" about in his mind's mouth, thinking of its cousin, "village", but the word contained none of the cosiness of a village. And Abelshoop, despite its name, lived up to the bleak emptiness, the contempt of the word "dorp". In the midday brightness, the one main street seemed lifeless, despite the many listless bodies to be found scattered about on it: walking in a dreamlike way, talking, loud and shrill, or sitting long legged on the dusty pavement, having succumbed to the stupor, surrounded by plastic shopping bags that should have melted, but persisted in their noisy rustling existence.

Typically it had only one dark, dingy little general dealer store, which despite the lack of sunlight within, did not offer any relief from the brittle dry heat outside. A constant flow of Abelshoop's Black and Coloured population wandered aimlessly in and out.

The woman at the till, at first clearly wary of a stranger and an Englishman at that, could not stop herself chatting after a while; asking about the camp and how long Joshua was going to stay this time and so on. She, like the butcher's wife and the "oom" at the "kooperasie", was greatly interested in the "geoloog op Pniel". It was clear that the news of his coming had far preceded him and in such a small community, he was, of course, instantly recognisable, for not being recognisable.

It felt a bit like running a gauntlet – answering all these questions, which, when they quickly ran out of geological knowhow and laymen's mineralogical speculation, became unashamedly personal: Was he married? How did he find the new South Africa? Did he have trouble with his labourers? Did they bring women into the camp? The questions were punctuated by yelled commands to the back of the shop where shadowy figures climbed up to the high shelves or rooted underneath them in response to her words as he asked for various items. He received said items with suitable gratitude and answered or failed to answer as best he could. Then left reeling.

Joshua swore to himself that this would be the first and last time that he would buy supplies at the Abelshoop General Dealer. The prices were ridiculous, the company disturbing. Not that this held true for very long. Beautiful as the Kalahari fading into Vaalbos and the sudden green of the river was, and city born-and-bred as he was, Joshua was overtaken with a longing for "civilisation" (or its semblance) at least once a week and made the dusty trip into the darkness of Abelshoop commerce again. It became a cycle, part of the rhythm and routine of his life, to loathe the "dorp" and its inhabitants, the typical racist rural poor of South Africa, and yet to be drawn towards the exchange of goods which claimed him as more than a mere nomad or crazy rock tapper. A link tenuous but precious with a world he had thought himself glad to leave behind, when he opted for exploration over mining.

When all was finally sorted at the camp that could be done, he grudgingly made his way up to the farmhouse to announce his arrival, as courtesy required. He always dreaded the encounter with the farmer, who had such a very different attitude to the soil, the land, and its people. Most of the farmers he had met were angry and suspicious, stuck in attitudes and a culture which no longer matched the facts of their lives. This only increased their resentment about his activities beneath their soil, ruining their pastures, leaving gates open, even though he was always careful not to, and the new improved sampling methods were quite sophisticated now and did not ruin many pastures at all. The worst one had pulled all his marking pegs out of a grid, up on the banks of the Limpopo river, because he thought they were potential landmine markers, placed there by the inevitable "swaart gevaar" lurking just beyond the river, beyond the South African border with Zimbabwe.

But good manners required that he make this visit and try to get on well with the farmer – and the puzzle of the letter also remained. As he had walked him out to the car at the Kimberley office during his briefing for this project, Paul had been very clear about fostering good relations with Adam Vermeulen, 'He could be a difficult candidate this Meneer Vermeulen,' he said, 'be sure to get him on your side, invite him for a braai at camp, do whatever you have to.'

So there he was walking through the hot afternoon, across the burning red sand, in the middle of windswept August towards the farmhouse of Pniel farm. It was one of those old, colonial houses with white walls, surrounded by a deep, square pillared veranda or stoep all around. The roof was dark grey slate, and the steps up to the veranda and front door gleamed red in the afternoon sun. The bridge crossing the "moat" was cracked, but steady nonetheless and the water flowed only sluggishly now, heavy with mud. The garden was a green soft peace, in the sparse shade of the winter-bare poplars at the gate, after the white glare of the Kalahari veld. Encouraged, he approached the house, though the windows looked in darkness at the world.

On the steps sat a slim child of perhaps ten, wearing a wide-brimmed hat and playing with quartz stones, a complicated game which absorbed him completely for he did not look up as Joshua approached. When his shadow finally fell on the child's game, the boy gathered the stones protectively and clutched them to his narrow chest and only then looked up at him with wild, frightened, pale grey eyes.

He slowly stretched out his hand towards the child, not wanting to frighten him any further.

'Hello, I'm Joshua Hunter. I'll be living on your farm for a while. Can you tell me, are your parents in?' he said in his pidgin Afrikaans, which he knew required more practice. But the reaction of the child still seemed a little extreme. He ignored the proffered hand and simply propelled himself up and ran off down the steps past him and into the garden, all in one fluid swift movement. His hat fell off in his haste and Joshua was shocked by the absolute whiteness of the soft curls beneath. Even sweat soaked, they remained a perfect white. A child again by the surprise of it, Joshua had to remind himself not to stare.

He heard a soft chuckle from the pleasant darkness of the stoep and a voice said, 'Nee, Meneer, that's just Thomas daai, he doesn't talk, but we think he can hear.'

Joshua peered up into the stoep and now could make out the figure of a rather beautiful coloured woman coming towards him with a slightly wary smile. She had the golden colouring of the Bushmen and the slightness and lightness of step, too. For a moment her eyes rested on the jewel bright garden and the warm eyes took on a mournful look as she scanned it for sight of the child.

'Oo' he said, with the longer intonation of Afrikaans, not sure what else to say to such news. He stepped up the steps towards her, holding out his hand again, 'I'm …'

'You are the geologist, coming to scratch in our ground again, looking for the things K'xwai left behind in his mischief.' The voice was not unfriendly, though the way in which she said the unpronounceable word cast a shadow over it. Still he was rather taken aback and involuntarily stumbled down the steps again.

'Who?' he managed at last.

'Oh, he is a devil; he makes mischief and destruction.'

'Why would a devil leave treasure in the ground?' still rather inept at the mythical way of speaking, he felt.

'Because it can only be him that sends strangers here to us, lets them make holes in our land, that the miesies falls into, falls dead, as the jealous gods reach for her beauty, and take her away from those who need her. Leaving not even the promised rain in return for her death.'

This was a piece of the puzzle of the Pniel project of twelve years ago that Joshua had not read in any of the reports. Of course it had nothing to do directly with the findings and was undoubtedly a terrible accident and not the company's fault, but he could also see how it was going to make him cursed in the eyes of the farmer. This was not the kind of situation he had come prepared to face and he cursed Paul silently for his cryptic warning and failure to explain this complication. Till now, he had always managed to keep the natural hostility of the farmers to the exploration teams at a fairly neutral level, but this did not bode well at all. His image of the harmless, slightly eccentric English rock-tapper was not going to go down well here. And then he remembered the letter he'd received, that supremely courteous, elegantly written letter. It made even less sense now.

Once again this project seemed overshadowed with forebodings and histories he felt he would never understand. From the beginning it had none of that safe impersonal, temporary nomadic feel, with which geologists are so comfortable, and which sets them so proudly apart from the mine geologists who have given in and succumbed to the petty backbiting of company politics. Joshua swallowed, tried to regain his composure, mumbled something about how sorry he was and that he had not known, then introduced himself and asked whether Mr Vermeulen was in.

'Yes,' she said, he was in the office at the back.

'Thank you,' he said, 'er . . .' he paused looking at her expectantly.

'Janine,' she smiled and as he held out his hand, she brought both hands forward to take his in one, and cupped her own wrist in the other in a gesture which would become so familiar to him. She led him through the house and his discomfort was momentarily dispelled.

Inside the house was cool and quiet, the wooden floor was dark and though the walls were as white as outside, the deep green curtains kept out the bright sunlight so the house seemed as cool as the dam, glowing eerily. There was a square of light on the passage floor, where a door led into the kitchen, golden in the full light of the afternoon sun. It smelled of coffee and warm bread. A younger, black girl was at the sink, washing and singing quietly to herself. The corridor turned past the kitchen in a sharp L and as they walked down, he saw that the walls were hung with etchings of Bushmen rock paintings, beautifully done, delicate and brown as a duiker or the Bushmen themselves. Facing them as they walked down the first arm of the corridor was the largest of them all. A dark rock surface glittering with mica and the green smudges of copper glowed with the central luminous figure of a kudu, clearly recognisable by the large round ears, though only one horn spiralled from his head. Unusually the kudu was white, standing with his face towards the viewer, delicately stepping from an apparent crack in the rock, with crossed legs. Joshua could not help but stare at this oddly, hauntingly beautiful rock painting.

The dark wooden floorboards creaked as they walked and he hastened to catch up with the woman again. As they passed another room, somewhat lighter than the others, he could hear the soft tinkling of piano scales.

'Dis onse Nellatjie' his shepherdess volunteered. 'The miesies also played piano, but very beautifully. And these are hers, too,' she said, pointing to the pictures on the walls.

'But these Rachel made and Violet,' now pointing to two tapestries on a similar theme, hanging at the end of the corridor where there was a dark door of the same wood as the flooring. 'The baas chose them himself,' she said, before knocking on the imposing door. 'And then he sent them to school. They're living in Kimberley, now, got good jobs.'

'And that,' pointing to another door, 'was Jongbaas Abraham's room. He's out of the house now.'

Was there a faint note of relief in her voice as she said this? Joshua could not quite make it out.Feeling rather overwhelmed by all this information he stood and looked dumbly at the door on which she had just knocked.

A voice answered, 'Ja, Janine, what is it?' it was deep and sounded old and tired. Janine simply replied to Joshua, 'Go in now, it's okay,' and turned away, no longer talkative as she hurried back down the corridor.

So he went through that sombre door into a room, likewise dark with many books and those same heavy curtains. From behind a large desk a man rose and came towards Joshua.

In the dim light it was not easy to make out his features but his handclasp was firm and warm and his voice was friendly.

'I'm Adam Vermeulen, pleased to meet you,' in excellent English.

'And I'm Joshua Hunter, glad to make your acquaintance.'

Too formal, he kicked himself and swiftly added, 'Thank you very much for your kind invitation. It is a beautiful camp.' The farmer smiled at this, sadly it seemed, as they both sat down in the large dark, worn leather armchairs standing at slight angles on this side of the untidy desk.

Adam broke the silence first. 'So, you people are here again, and what are you looking for this time? Gold? Diamonds?' laughing at his own joke, knowing very well what they sought on his land. 'Or base metals again?' the irony palpable.

Joshua valiantly tried his usual approach, smiled his apologetic smile and claimed lamely as always that he could not tell as it was confidential etc. etc. And like too many of the farmers, Adam apparently simply accepted this. Mostly they were not interested in what lay beneath their soil as long as it provided good crops or grazing. But he knew he was wrong if he thought that about Adam. Adam spoke of the possibilities of a mine with a kind of hopelessness.

He knew already that the white farmers would probably lose the land claims feud that would soon burst into open battle. Yet it was not as if he did not care – he had given up on the land, but still loved it. A farmer's lot, Joshua hazarded a guess, to love the land, to lose it, but to be unable to leave it and so become an exile in one's own home. Adam smiled as if Joshua had spoken aloud and said: 'A white South African is always an exile, no matter where he is, even at home. It is our fate. Perhaps it atones for many things we have done as a nation.'

"Is there an appropriate response to a remark like that?" Joshua wondered.

'Ja,' Adam said, returning to the topic at hand, 'there are some nice rocks here, under all the verdomde sand. I have some here in the family room. Maybe you would like to see them?'

Surprised, yes he would. So Adam led him down the corridor, back the way they had come to the bright family room, where 'Nellatjie' was still playing the piano, Schubert now, and singing softly. She stopped and jumped up as they came into the room, blushing.

'Toemaar, Nella,' said her father, 'come and greet our guest, Mr Hunter. We won't be long then you can go on practising.'

She seemed to Joshua, who did not understand this family yet, an apparition from another time when girls had been held on such a tight rein by their parents and their communities, until they became teachers or nurses for a while, then married and became large ungainly women with a brood of wild children and a farmer for a husband. This one was very pretty, with softly wavy blonde hair, tied loosely back and her father's big blue eyes.

She gave him a smile with her hand for polite shaking and said simply, 'Hello, Meneer.'

'Hello, Nella,' he replied, 'I'm Joshua.' Her smile widened. Her mouth was pale but her Cupid's bow unusually full, which made the mouth already generous and warm in her still childish face.

'Over here, Mr Hunter,' Adam's voice was suddenly sharp, 'and Nella, ask Janine to bring our tea in here. You can practise this evening.'

Joshua turned his attention to the rocks on the wide and well-lit windowsill, behind the opened curtains. There were some excellent specimens there: delicate rose quartz and white quartz shot through with perfectly formed tourmaline, agates, garnets and a wonderful desert rose.

'These come from all over Southern Africa – Namibia, the West Coast, but these are from here,' he finished proudly, as he handed him two beautifully preserved fossils. There were also some Stone Age tools, clearly San. He spoke about each find with knowledge and understanding of its formation and location. Joshua was deeply impressed and ashamed of his earlier assumptions about the farmers. Adam Vermeulen seemed to know some of the rocks better than he, the professional.

Soon Janine brought the tea and beskuit and not long after that he left, not as he had expected, simply relieved at having 'got it over and done with' but having met an interesting person, a potential friend in otherwise alien territory. Over tea they had discussed many things, or rather Adam had talked and Joshua had mostly listened, as he was woefully ignorant of South African history and current affairs.

'Ja,' Adam was saying, 'we have come a long way from the days of old Smuts and his ideas of peaceful co-existence.'

'Ah yes,' Joshua hazarded a guess, 'Smuts – he was at the Versailles treaty, wasn't he?'

'He walked out, yes,' Adam said. 'He thought it would only bring more war. And here in South Africa he was just as unsuccessful, that old Voortrekker spirit dies hard in us – and we would rather be ostriches with our heads in the sand than face necessity.'

'Necessity?'

'We must lose the land now.'

'We?'

'The farmers,' Adam paused thoughtfully, 'but also the blacks – the New South Africa is not living up to its promises.'

'Ah – land returned to the original owners?' Joshua had heard of these disputes.

'Yes – even when no one can tell who they are any more.'

They drank their tea in silence for a while.

'You know,' Adam said then, 'the old states of emergency were bad and I am glad that violence has gone. But in its place is a random violence now – less predictable. No longer directed at a hated government, just anger and fear and loss; they are a terrible combination.'

'You have that even here?'

'Well yes, so many people claim this land: the farmers who have worked the land for so long, the Bushmen, who have buried ancestors here and the coloured people, who have nowhere else to go and know no other home. The Batswana, the Koranna and the Griquas have their claims too, and those who sought refuge when they became Christians so long ago.'

'And now you have to deal with a mining company again!'

'That is different. We all think of this land as home, and as ours, but we cannot all live here in peace. A mine,' he continued thoughtfully, 'would change all that, would offer a new focus and bring in enough money so that people could be compensated for the loss of their land, could start again, or stay and get work on the mines.'

'You think it would be a solution?' Joshua asked.

'Perhaps,' he said, 'though of course, it would ruin much, too. Perhaps that is the price we must pay.' That fatalistic tone again.

Thinking of the high walls of Johannesburg and the guard dogs, of the neighbourhood watches of Monument Heights in Kimberley, Joshua asked, 'Don't you think that money would make the situation more dangerous?'

'Life has never really been safe here,' he said, 'not even in our little Abelshoop, so far away from everywhere else. But now it is ugly as well as dangerous. There is no money, lots of the whites are moving away, leaving their farms to squatters and criminals, needing to lie low and hiding from the police in the city. How can we keep order?'

Joshua shrugged and raised his eyebrows, indicating that he was listening.

'Only the other day it was in the Diamond Fields Advertiser, three coloured men raped a white girl, a child of fourteen, about the same age as my Nella. And then, in retaliation, three white boys (not even the girl's family) broke into the house of old Mary near the back of the station and killed her. What are we coming to?'

But they did not only talk politics, so inevitable in this country and a topic Joshua usually studiously avoided with his farmers, as they did not and could never, he thought see eye to eye on this. Adam also told him a good many things about himself. Indeed he was a little taken aback at the readiness with which he opened his personal world to a stranger. Very unusual in a South African farmer, especially when talking to an Englishman. But Adam knew that it was no use to hide this history from the new geologist. Knew the town too well, knew they would talk and whisper again. So he made sure this geologist heard his story first. He told him very simply that the researches of Joshua's predecessor, a John Shackleton, had led to the death of his wife, as certainly as if she had simply fallen into one of the pits his predecessor had dug, but failed to mark clearly enough to make it visible in the dark.

'Surely, it was an easy oversight,' Adam said, his eyes desolate.

"Yes," Joshua thought, "one would not expect anybody to go walking at night around the open trenches."

'You see,' Adam said, 'Miriam, like Thomas, loved the impossible whiteness of the quartz under the red earth and couldn't keep away from it.' Joshua imagined a woman looking at the quartz in moonlight and in sun; its white a source of wonder. He saw her kneeling at the edge of a trench, leaning down, reaching out to the stone and then tumbling in, hitting her head perhaps on its sharp, newly trenched up edges. The image filled him with horror and he lost track momentarily of what Adam was saying.

Adam then also told him of Thomas, who had been only a baby when Miriam died and who did not speak, so that many thought him either stupid, 'vertraag' or touched by the devil.

'But he is not. It's only that he lives in his own world, because so much is sad around him. He is very sensitive you see,' Adam said.

Janine came in at that point with Thomas, who smiled now at Joshua and shook his hand in that well-brought-up way of Afrikaans children. Joshua told Adam of his brief encounter with Thomas on the steps of their house.

'Yes, he is a little shy always with strangers. We are so isolated here; he does not know people very well. But he trusts Janine completely and they can communicate. Nella also, a little bit. With me – it is more difficult.'

Joshua, faintly embarrassed by so much personal information had picked up a book, lying open and face down on a stool next to his chair.

Adam saw and taking the book firmly out of Joshua's hands, explained, 'I read to him, mostly his mother's old books – Rilke's *Stories for God*. They are about a very different world to this one.'

He paused and then turned his face, his whole body towards Joshua in a pleading posture. 'Please, Joshua may I ask you a favour? Thomas loves the quartz so, the way it sparkles, its whiteness. Will you bring him some nice clean pieces from underneath, when you start to dig again? There's so little to make him happy. I would like to send him to a psychologist, or find a doctor, who could get to the bottom of his refusal to speak. Ou Smitty says there is nothing wrong with his body, but he can't tell what it is. It needs an expert. They are expensive and far away.'

'I will do what I can,' Joshua assured him, not knowing what else to say.

Adam, realising this, went on in a lighter tone, 'And then there is Nella, the only child who does not make trouble for me, so far. Good at school,' he said, 'and no trouble with boys – yet.'

Smiling, the platitude about fathers and daughters restored the ordinariness of the moment a little.

'She's a quiet girl, good at music. Like her mother, but not so wild.'

"Oh dear," Joshua thought, "what do I say to that?" and he must have looked surprised, because Adam went on.

'Wild, you know, shy like a kudu, you try to come anywhere near, and they leap off into the bush, where no one can see them anymore. And they leave you then with just the memory of their grace and beauty. Her mother was like that, she did not like people much, most people. She preferred the silence of the veld.'

Finally, Joshua also heard about Abraham, his eldest, a son and the manager now of Wonderfontein, the neighbouring farm.

'He is angry: about his mother, about our dying community, about the girl that was raped and about the government. Angry, always angry and he will not listen to his father any more He is what I am frightened of, and what will happen to our country. I would not tolerate that kind of language on our land. We fought all the time, so I sent him away. He is a good farmer though and so he takes care of our neighbour's land – Wonderfontein.' he gestured vaguely to the right.

'Oh yes,' Joshua said, 'I will have to go talk to him then – or the owner. Probably both.'

'I'll take you one day, but you will find that like many others he will not be friendly. You are foreign, an invader he thinks, who represents the corporate mining houses, the English, the colonisers once, now merely money – either way still stealing the land from those who merely sweat over it – all the things we as a people have feared all our lives, instead of learning to make peace with them.'

'And you,' Joshua could not help himself, 'are you not frightened?'

At this point Janine could be heard calling the children to supper and Adam got up indicating that he would need to go. But he walked Joshua to the door and answered as they walked.

He smiled slowly, sadly, 'When the worst has already happened to you, and you have lost what you should have valued most, you are no longer afraid for yourself, only for the land, for everybody else and that they should forget to love one another.'

Joshua was moved by these sentimental words, at their generosity and pain, which remained private, yet changed the world. And as Adam opened the front door and Joshua stepped out, he glimpsed again that flash of blinding white in the evening sun.

'What is that?' he asked on an impulse.

'It is Witkopje,' Adam answered and a shadow passed over his face.

'Witkopje? What does that mean?' Joshua could see only the child's white head in his mind as he heard the word.

But Adam said, 'It's a large exposed wall with a quartz intrusion on a hill. The sun catches it often and it is a landmark in these parts. It has quite a good Bushman painting on it. You should go and have a look sometime.' Studied carelessness.

'I will. Thank you, Mr Vermeulen.'

'Adam, please.'

'Adam, then.'

'Joshua,' they shook hands and Joshua turned to go.

'But,' Adam said, coming back suddenly to the painting and the quartz 'the Bushmen believe it is a doorway to the world of the gods.'

There was no answer to this, and Joshua gave none.

He walked back to his camp, deep in thought. For, despite their apparent openness, the conversation had left so much unexplained. He was puzzled and continued to wonder at the strange events at the time of his predecessor out here in the middle of nowhere, but also to its inhabitants: the entire world, with all its harshness and beauty intact.

He tried to feel irritated still with Paul and the others who had let him rush in once again where all the other geologists clearly feared to tread, but he found himself instead puzzled, even intrigued. "Where," he wondered, "is my usual concern only for the rocks, my avoidance of the stories of people? I used to find them dull."

He cooked his rice and some or other tinned slop and ate it quietly in the dark under the myriad stars of the Kalahari sky, feeling the earth cool down at last as the windmill's song rang reverberating into the evening and the water splashed slowly into the dam. Far away he heard the last barking of the baboons in the krans by the river and then closer, the call of the hunting owl and the eager Spring-awaiting singing of the mating frogs in the irrigation canal. He wondered whether he would ever be able to sleep with this chorus. As he sat watching the dying embers of his fire, cradling a cup of tea in his hands, he found he could: a deep and dreamless sleep that first night.

2
Dances in the Night

Several weeks were dedicated to getting to grips with the concrete reality of the data Joshua had been poring over during the past few weeks in the basement, the strip-lit vaults of the somewhat dingy Kimberley exploration office. Joshua walked out at dawn into the crisp cool of a semi-desert winter with Ben and Josef to re-grid the area. He hoped to establish the relationship of the chemical analyses of the sand and what lay two to three meters underneath and discovering exactly where the core, which had lain dust covered in the sheds of the disused dairy farm (where all the core and sand samples eventually ended up, having been analysed and mostly found wanting) had come from. It was an enjoyable walk, though he had to stop to double check things he saw against his maps and grids of the area.

Ben and Josef were on good form, quick to spot old sample markers and so able to establish with great accuracy the old lines of the grid across both the red sand and the grey hard cracked earth nearer the river, where the flat expanse was relieved. So he felt he was making some headway and had finally begun the real work of the project, rather than simply reworking old data. He could begin to see where more drilling would be in order and where new trenches might need to be dug in order to find out what had happened to the ore body, which had such promising values. This body was either too tiny to care about (the previous geologist's hurried conclusion, after several months of arguing the opposite) or had been faulted, broken out of view by intrusive dykes and so was simply elusive – a far more interesting perspective and one, which Joshua for the moment chose to believe.

He decided to try and do some float mapping for a comparison and in search of sub-outcrops, as possible structural indicators of what that ancient and wily ore body was doing, or rather had been doing several million years ago.

There would not be much time before contractors arrived and he needed to be ready to make decisions about where the excavators should begin their work. Paul had warned him about that, also that there might soon be renewed interest in this project from head office. Joshua uneasily wished he had more time to get a feel for the area and its geology before having to decide on the exact placing and direction of trenches. Of course strictly speaking, this was not necessary, his predecessor had been thorough in his geology – if not in his safety precautions – and if it were not for the odd conclusion, Joshua would simply agree with him about the next series of trenching: it was logical and clear. But Joshua was new and wanted to be sure he was right. He had been able to read up a good deal about the area and he and Paul were fairly certain that they knew what they wanted (as much as a geologist ever knew that). But there remained always the odd hasty decision that the ore body was too little to warrant further interest, and the strange and eager letter from Adam Vermeulen, and there was his gut feeling that somehow there was more to this project than met the eye.

There was uncertainty: the geology, the people and the landscape seemed to shift in and out of focus too easily. So Joshua felt as unsure of this earth, as he did of its people, who had taken him so much by surprise in the form of Adam. Once he had made some of his own decisions about the geology, he knew he had to get to Adam and explain to him, which kamps would be trenched, so that he could make plans about where his sheep and cattle could be put, and life remain bearable for all concerned. This was always a tricky situation and sod's law dictated that one of the kamps had to be the only one with a big dam in it, this side of the road, he thought! He began to head back to the farmhouse, when he saw the khaki-coloured old ford bakkie pull up at the gate of the kamp where he was working. He went over to investigate and Adam came forward to greet him. They fell to talking about the land, and how things would work out. Adam was most accommodating, the only concern being the absence of a dam in the alternate kamp and so no water for the sheep. Joshua promised to phone Paul about that and to ask him about financing a solution to this problem. He did so and Paul promised to get back with an answer as soon as possible.

As Joshua walked towards the farmhouse the next morning, Adam came to greet him before he had even lifted his hand to the gate. He had a slip of paper in his hand. It was a message from Paul at the Kimberley office and Joshua was to phone immediately. Yes, of course he could use Adam's phone. Joshua went back into Adam's quiet, dark, cool study and picking up the handset, turned the handle of the party line phone. The voice of Matilda responded promptly:

'Ja Adam and who are you phoning this early in the morning?' came a cheerful Afrikaans voice. 'Do you also want to phone your lawyer?' it continued in the same breath.

Joshua was surprised by the recognition of the line so easily: 'Good morning . . .' 'Matilda,' Adam supplied the name in a whisper and with a wide grin at Joshua's surprise. Clearly there was little privacy on the phones in Abelshoop.

'Matilda,' Joshua went on, 'I need a Kimberley number please.'

'Certainly,' she said in her rehearsed bits of English, 'and the number is?' Joshua gave it to her and listened to the ringing tone with some trepidation. Stephanie's voice answered. 'Lefika exploration office, Kimberley. How may I help you?'

'Hi, Stephanie, it's Joshua. Paul asked me to ring.'

'Sure. I'll put you straight through, he's in a meeting but asked for you to be put through anyway. What have you done this time?' She laughed.

'Don't even joke; I have no idea. I've only just got here and haven't yet met enough farmers to upset them.' Adam smiled again and left to give him some privacy.

'Hello Joshua,' came Paul's voice, 'Listen, before you begin trenching, I want you to diamond drill in the northern kamp, Doringaar, I think it's called, at these coordinates on the grid . . .' Joshua barely heard the rest so relieved was he. 'Shall I fax these numbers to you?' Paul asked anxiously. 'You need to do this with some urgency, the excavators have already been ordered. They're on their way from Nelspruit right now.'

Irritated by this urgency in his infant project, and by the typical muddle of Paul's management, Joshua only answered, coldly: 'And where do I find a diamond drill in Abelshoop?'

Paul, entirely unperturbed, 'Oh ask Josef, he knows the man.'

"Great," Joshua thought, "someone Josef knows. He's not even from this area."

'We worked with him before, Joshua,' Paul now sensed the irritation, 'it's part of the experience.' Joshua could hear the smile, and only remembered just in time to ask about the dam problem.

'Tell him to do whatever he needs to do, we will pay the bills,' Paul answered, 'the man needs water, after all.'

'Thanks,' Joshua hung up, unaccountably filled with a sense of doom about his project.

Adam looked back in as Joshua put the receiver down, eyebrows raised. 'Adam,' Joshua asked, 'do you know who has a diamond drill in this area?' Adam winced and said, 'Jaaaa,' in that long drawn out way one uses when one would rather be saying no.

"Better and better," Joshua thought, "this project is already heading for disaster."

Adam, seeing the young man's face, owned up. 'His name is van der Merwe, Danie van der Merwe and he lives just the other side of Abelshoop. I have his number for you.' He looked through his many, dirty, untidy bits of paper with a great sense of purpose that Joshua did not believe, until he produced a grubby piece of paper with the number and the name vd Merwe on it in a childish, ungainly hand. 'He wrote it down for me himself, in case I ever needed to drill again for water,' Adam said.

'Oh yes,' Joshua remembered, 'Paul said to do what you need to do for water, Lefika will pay.'

'Thank you,' Adam said.

Joshua got Matilda on the line again and asked her to dial the number Adam had given him. Joshua waited. And waited. There was no answer.

Finally, Matilda's voice again, 'There seems to be no answer,' she said proudly enunciating the strange English words with excruciating clarity and a thick accent. 'Shall I keep trying and ring you back when I have him on the line?' and without pause passed on the gossip. 'Do you know there is a land claims lawyer in town today? The whole place is buzzing; he has called a great meeting outside the church! I am sure we will have a riot, like they have in Jo'burg, before noon!'

Joshua struggled to maintain his focus and equanimity in the face of all this, knowing how such news might affect head office's perception of the project. 'Yes please, Matilda. Please ring me back once you have been able to contact him.'

Adam offered tea, a consolation prize for what seemed a wasted morning. It was that very strong tea with condensed milk dripped thickly into it, strangely pleasant in its sticky sweetness, especially with traditionally dunked boere beskuit.

Joshua asked Adam about the land claims story, but he was dismissive about Matilda's fears of a riot. 'It has been coming ever since the election,' he said. 'Of course the "people" – all of them – want the land. That is what they, who never lifted a finger in the years of the struggle, have been fighting for. We, the white farmers, will lose this land, if not to you, then to whichever claim is strongest.'

'How do you mean?'

'Well, the Basters, the Griquas, the Koranna and finally some remnants of the Bushmen – you probably call them the San – all have claims to this land. Also some Setswana tribes, it has been a busy part of the country, really. They all have ancestors buried here; they have all at some time in history lived here. Now they all want it, as was almost inevitable since fences were first put up and the nomadic life became no longer viable. Just as inevitably, it is not possible for all of them to get some, enough to make viable life sustainable. So it may get ugly if the lawyers do not find a decent compromise.'

Joshua waited half the morning during which Adam's affable company made the Africa time approach more bearable, before Matilda rang back and Joshua spoke to a gruff and bemused voice on the other end of the line. He'd been asleep, Mr van der Merwe apologised, but yes, certainly he could bring his machine out to Pniel today.

So Joshua went back to camp to wait some more. "Oh the joys of working with contractors" he thought, but only half bitter, having seen by now the humour of the situation, and not wanting to lose face before the laughter of Ben and Josef. They doubled up with laughter, when he told them about Paul's message.

'Mr van der Merwe?' they asked.

They turned to each other, eyes alight with some secret joke, 'Rommel and Strooi,' they said and dramatically slashed their throats in Joshua's direction, laughing all the time.

'Paul said you knew this guy!' he said to Josef and then, 'What was that you called him?'

'O ja, I know him and his drill,' Josef snorted, and would say no more.

Finally, at about midday the stillness of the veld was rudely broken by the most ridiculous noise: the gurgling of some giant creature's indigestion alongside a stampede and then the whooping of Ben and Josef as they came running towards Joshua's caravan shouting, 'Dis Rommel en Strooi.'

Joshua leapt up despite the lethargy of the day and went to the gate with them. Stopped at the gate was the most enormous, ungainly contraption Joshua had ever seen. A rusted red farm trailer bore on its tired and buckled back a giant yellow scorpion or praying mantis of a machine made of equally rusted metal. Crouching on four wheels, which had their steel ribs protruding through a threadbare rim, was a barrel of a belly, which on one side was wounded and displaying to the world its tortured innards, made up of the typically kabanga-ed engine held together unimaginably with bits of rusted wire, strips torn from tyres and that inevitable bright orange rope, fraying at the edges around knots that miraculously held together failing, fragile engines. Above it reared the shaft of the drill, bent at hideous angles like a broken limb, or possibly the threatening tail of a scorpion. From the grease and dust begrimed Ford bakkie drawing this contraption heaved a ludicrous figure: a belly barely contained in a bright orange t-shirt, first emerged from the swirling dust of their arrival, followed by a head of remarkably dirty blonde hair, which stood out in all directions like an unruly haystack. The name Strooi was immediately clear to Joshua.

He managed to repress a grin and walked forward with hand outstretched to greet this strange apparition, which, dust-covered and sleepy, seemed to emerge from the surrounding dust and sand.

'Middag, Meneer van der Merwe,' Joshua said

'Middag,' he said, wiping his hand to no great avail, on the backside of his greasy jeans, before offering the black-rimmed moons of his fingers. Joshua gingerly took the hand.

'Ja, you see, Meneer Hunter,' the apparition said, 'she only works at night. During the day it is too hot and she dies and there is never enough water out here to cool her down.' Josef was grinning wickedly from behind what was now to Joshua's sinking heart, definitely a scorpion, not a praying mantis.

Helplessly, Joshua replied: 'Right, well let me show you the way to the drill site.' He had forgotten the conventions of offering something to drink. Damn. But he recovered and offered to bring two cold beers for the journey. Ben obligingly fetched them and came back to find Strooi already squeezed in behind the sticky wheel of his bakkie and Joshua preparing, rather unwillingly to climb aboard, too.

He climbed in on the other side and in the side mirror saw the gleefully grinning faces of Ben and Josef making that oh too familiar African gesture of trouble: the rapid downward flick of the loose-fingered hand, allowing the knuckles to click together with the soft explosions of foreboding. And they were laughing.

Strooi was eating a polony and tomato sauce sandwich, which he washed down with a gulp of cold beer and no sign of embarrassment at the mess he was spraying all over the car and himself. He continued to talk through the mastication. It was difficult to make out a word of what he was saying but he seemed to be explaining the intricacies of the scorpion's breakdowns to Joshua. Joshua, feeling far out of his depth as he watched his decisive and efficient project recede before his inner eye, simply smiled apprehensively and nodded as they drove with agonising slowness towards the drill site, over the road knee-deep in sand or bare rock, interrupted by enormous dongas.

Finally they got to Doringaar, and Strooi stopped the bakkie so suddenly that the scorpion shuddered, as did Joshua, with the jolt. Joshua got out and showed him the marker for the drilling to begin. The man smiled comfortably, nodded vaguely and began unloading his tent from the back of his bakkie. With the slow movements of long habit, he began pitching it, ignoring entirely thoughts of the job at hand. Joshua, who had vaguely anticipated discussing the various possible depths to which drilling should be done, was nonplussed by this lack of concern, this complete disregard for the usual courtesies of a working relationship. Eventually he simply sat down in the shade of the scorpion and watched dully as the grimy tent materialised from the sand. Finally he stirred himself and the rest of the day passed in frustrating attempts to set up Rommel ('Rubbish,' he thought how apt) in the correct place and to mark out accurately the others where drilling would be necessary. Strooi and Joshua both knew that drilling would not even be attempted till much later so in the end, they both headed into town for another beer and Joshua decided he would see whether the new labels had arrived for the core. And so he found himself once again on that dusty pavement opposite the "stillte kerk" as Ben and Josef mockingly called it, thanks to the sign on the pavement outside that admonished silence to the noisy and unrepentant sinners not inside the church. He and Strooi were drinking an almost cold beer from an almost clean glass and watching the tiny world of Abelshoop go by.

All were heading for the piece of common open ground outside the church where a large crowd was assembling. Only then did Joshua remember Matilda's news of the morning, and paid a little more attention to the movements of the crowd. At the far side opposite the church, a kind of makeshift platform was being set up and people were stopping to watch, and to read the banners about "land of the ancestors". Promise of the freedom charter will come true was the rumour – "land for all", it read. Incendiary it would have been a few years ago, Joshua knew, but these people seemed more curious about the strangers putting up the banners and the platform, than interested in the slogans. Possibly not many of them could read well, he thought. Or experience had made them naturally suspicious of all government initiatives.

Now in the company of a local, to whom none of these people, mixed crew that they were, were strange, Joshua could take stock of the kind of community it was: white women went by in twos or threes, wearing faded flowered dresses and sandals made red by the iron rich dust. White men in safari suits and battered leather hats ventured out alone or stood about in groups discussing animatedly, despite the dusty glare, the wrong doings of these land claims commissions. They were constantly on their phones, which seemed oddly out of place in this town so apparently forgotten by progress. And the ever-present important issues of farming and weather seemed for the moment forgotten.

And then Strooi called Joshua's attention to the multi-coloured multitudes, with a disgusted snort, saying, 'Look at them run like sheep.'

'Who?' Joshua asked, not wanting to assume anything.

'The natives,' Strooi said with an ironic emphasis and a lifted eyebrow in the direction of the street.

'Yes,' Joshua tried to keep a conversation afloat, 'Paul said they were a mixed lot. Can you explain?'

'Ja, you see that tall man, leaning on the fence post of the church?'

Joshua looked to see a tall blue-black man lounging casually and watching, like him, the people passing by.

Strooi spat and continued, 'They are descendants of the Korannas. Haughty they are and they think they are handsome,' said Strooi, clearly irritated by the man's relaxed and confident demeanour.

Joshua distracted him, 'What about this man?' indicating a small smiling person, coming out of the off-license, hugging gleefully a brown packet.

'The small yellow oriental ones – they have Bushman blood.' And his voice was a strange mixture of contempt and awe. 'They are the oldest; they know the veld like no one else. But they're all drunkards now. The lowest of the low in the eyes of the other natives.' Strooi drank his beer reflectively, clearly inclined to be kindly.

He smiled patronisingly at Joshua, waved his hand at the street and said, 'Of course we also have all the shades in between' as if he were an estate agent, pointing out the particularly attractive aspects of a property.

And Joshua could not but be puzzled by this contradictory behaviour – this mixture of contempt and affection, of hatred and pride. He supposed in the end that it must be the result of a history of shared land occupation, despite everything that apartheid had done to prevent it.

'Ja,' Strooi was saying, 'we have an interesting history and I think we are about to see more. Watch, watch this. This is how we South Africans do it.'

And Joshua followed him only half reluctantly to the edges of the field where the crowd was gathering. If one had leisure, as Joshua did this morning, God and Strooi having decided that he would not have any core to examine until midnight probably, one could examine closely and in some detail the complex social stratification of this small but utterly divided community. And crass though it seemed as Strooi explained it to him, it was clear that colour still determined almost everything about social status in this world of racial mixing, so evident and yet so strenuously denied. It was so stark that it was almost humorous.

'But that's terrible,' Joshua protested, trying to maintain his liberal English self. 'I thought that would all be over now.'

Strooi looked at him with pity and said brutally, 'That is how it is – the black man hates the yellow man, and the white man hates the black man. That is how God made the world. And you had better not ignore that here.'

And he took Joshua by the shoulders roughly and turned him to face the people. 'Look and learn,' he said. 'Watch that Koranna girl.'

'The beautiful one?'

And Joshua found his eyes resting on a tall girl in a red dress who was extraordinarily beautiful. 'Watch,' Strooi said, 'the young men, they think so too. See how they flirt, how they show off to make her smile?'

Just at that point a young man did swing himself up onto the fence with ostentatious agility and grace. The girl knew it was for her, but only watched from lowered lids.

Then the young man's mother came up and pulled him angrily from the fence.

'Why was that?' Joshua asked bewildered.

Strooi chuckled brutally, 'Ja man, she is too black!'

'So the lighter you are the better?' Joshua asked, angry now at the stupidity of it.

'Don't be simple,' Strooi said, pronouncing the word in Afrikaans with some venom. 'Look over there. They are Batswana – see? Chocolate brown.' Strooi was clearly enjoying Joshua's discomfort with his classifications.

'They do better,' he said, 'look lighter, softer. They have round faces – they are more placid than the Korannas, who always want to fight. Even when they are not drunk. The Batswana only fight when they are drunk.'

'And now watch this,' Strooi's clammy hand grabbed Joshua by the arm and led him to the further side of the field where the coloured section of the community was gathering. 'Ja, your coloured man, he likes his girl pale. And the mothers – oooe – they like a coffee-coloured face, too. It is a good match for their daughters.'

'I think I'll go back now,' Joshua wanted nothing so much at that moment than to end this conversation. But he could not help noticing that the men did stop to look most often and whistle at the pale girls, with soft coffee coloured skin, straightish hair and large liquid eyes.

'See,' Strooi said triumphantly. 'The whiter the brighter.'

'Yes, Mr van der Merwe, thank you very much for an educational afternoon, but I really must get back to camp now.'

'What for?' Strooi asked. 'You have nothing to do until I can give you some core.' And with an animal cunning, sensing how overwhelmed Joshua felt by it all, and wanting a small triumph against this confident-seeming Englishman, he said, 'now watch the children.'

A group of them was playing a makeshift game of craps on the pavement. They were oblivious to the adults milling about them, and the adults indulgently stepped around them or clipped them if they got in the way. With a yelp, the stricken child would scurry back to the game. Then a particularly small and fine-boned boy tried to join.

'Haai, bushman, voetsek' and he was shoved roughly aside. But he was persistent, and tried again and again to take his turn. Finally the whole group turned on him. They yelled incomprehensible vilifications at him, 'blerrie boesman' and 'jou ma is a dronklap', at which point the poor, afflicted, too-yellow boy turned and fought. It was brief and brutal, and no one else paid the slightest attention.

'Why should they?' Strooi said, 'It happens every day. That is what you do not understand. This is what life is like here. It is not only us Afrikaners who are racist!'

And Joshua left it at that because he knew then that he did not understand the full implications of this behaviour. Even much, much later, when the social history of this desert had been explained and the long tradition of the persecution of the San by all new arrivals, he was not sure such behaviour could be understood.

Strooi finally took pity on him. 'Ja man,' he said, 'you must feel sorry for the kids,' and offered to buy him another drink.

So they passed the morning, philosophically watching the Brownian movement of the people on the dry and glaring main street of Abelshoop. The crackling dryness, loaded with static, remained oppressive as the day wore on and tempers grew more frayed. A thin and ragged woman, swollen about the face, came loudly crying to the platform, clearly the worse for drink. She was pleading with the strangers, leaning precariously towards them from their makeshift steps, with eloquent gestures and loud crying. Suddenly a man, brandishing a knobkerrie, burst through the crowd, and with colourful curses, began beating the woman. Her cries became bloodcurdling, and it took several men to separate them. Both were taken to the police station to sleep it off. The shocking part was not the violence, but the nonchalance with which it was accepted. There was a certain amount of laughter even, and Strooi simply said as he got up to leave, 'Yes, they're all like that: drinking, fighting, and whoring.'

Joshua did not think it worth arguing with him at that point, but remained disturbed by the brief scene and the response of the people.

They agreed to start drilling at 7:30, by which time everything would have cooled down enough for "her", as Strooi called his scorpion. Together they drove back to the creature, waiting on the sand for darkness to descend before she would begin her work. 'There is going to be trouble in town tonight,' Strooi said knowingly, as he lifted an enormous spotlight from his bakkie.

Joshua left him there, wondering what the next few days would bring. When he spoke to Ben and Josef about what he had seen in town, they only shook their heads and said, 'Yes, that is how it is now.'

'It's poverty, man, you don't know how it is,' Ben said, who had lived here as a child in a family of eight children – he was the only one who had a real, permanent job.

Joshua changed the subject. 'What about this van der Merwe,' he asked, 'what should I expect there?'

'Hey,' Josef replied, 'hey. That is a hard one to answer. It all depends – can he dance her right and make her work?' Cryptic answers always to questions they did not think he should ask. He was learning, slowly.

So he decided to expect nothing as the safest option, and walked back to camp with some agitation and the nagging awareness of the excavators, who were returning from Nelspruit.

The sudden interest of head office in this small, simple, mopping up operation of a geologist's project, remained a puzzle over which to while away the remains of the afternoon.

Back in town the lawyer from Cape Town – who turned out to be a woman to Matilda's hushed shock on the town's phone lines – set up her small stage with her entourage. She had no desire to cause trouble, only a burning conviction that what she was doing was right, that the people who had lost the land, in which their ancestors lay buried and on which their lives ultimately depended, had a right to have it back. It seemed so simple, so right. She was anxiously aware of the tangled nature of the claims, but hopeful that they could be untangled to everyone's satisfaction – that the truth, whatever it was, would prevail.

She was dimly aware that the mining houses were again exploring in this district and feared those most of all. The white farmers were defeated already by the climate and their own fear, many of them only too ready to sell their land, the quibble largely being the amount; but the mining houses wanted to do their exploitation in freedom, untroubled by thoughts of the shades dwelling in the land, which they hollowed out so ruthlessly; the shades of the people who belonged to this land and to whom therefore she felt the land should belong in turn.

What she didn't know, having lived in Cape Town all her life, far away from a life linked to the land, was that they too had been disconnected from their land too long. Removed from their "traditional" way of life, they had become urbanised and so unable to follow the call of the desert, except occasionally just before the rains in October. But following that call meant they lost what meagre jobs they had.

And so her rather romantic ideal of a simple return to the land might no longer be possible for them. Still, they came to listen to her and were moved by her idealism on their behalf and she was right, after all, the land and all its riches had been stolen from them. And like her, they all had had dreams once of a fair and beautiful world. Who had stolen it? In the excitement of the meeting, which stirred the tired and barren hearts to dreaming again, this question took on an importance, a burning urgency they had not known in years about anything. Long-forgotten dreams of sip wells in the desert, of herds of cattle grazing on a rich savannah, of villages untroubled by technology, welled up in confusion in hearts which no longer knew themselves. And the people were filled with longing at her words, a longing they could not name. And for the answers she was offering, they had no words, knew only that they longed at last to go home, to be who they were meant to be and to belong to the world in their own way. She was giving them that hope, they knew that much, but the words she used meant little to them. They understood only the need to fight.

When she finished talking, the people sat in silence, stunned and overwhelmed – would the dream of justice truly come down to walk amongst them again? They had waited so long that they had forgotten how to hope, and almost forgotten what it was they had been waiting and hoping for. Now her words brought back to their hearts all that was valiant and true and they felt they could stand a little taller and look any man in the eye again. Briefly the shame of the excess of violence, drink and despair looked to be lifted as the land, and they, returned to one another.

Then for Ruth de Jaeger from Cape Town began the long process of getting down accurate names and birth dates of the claimants so that the claims could be tracked and verified, and presented to the claims court. But it had been a good session, she felt. The people had responded well, which she had not expected with the occurrence earlier of the wife beating. When she had recoiled from the violence of it, a soft voice had said to her, 'Don't worry miss, they will not hurt you. They only need to feel the world is theirs again and they a part of it.' She'd turned to look into a handsome, fine-boned face creased with smiling, as a hard dry hand inserted itself into hers, and the man said, 'I am Dawid of the Bushmen around here.' She had shaken his hand delightedly and taken his details.

Joshua set out that evening, armed with a viciously strong insect repellent, a flask of tea, a reading torch and a book. Ben and Josef watched him pityingly, but not sufficiently so to accompany him.

'Jy sal niks kry vandag nie,' Josef said, mercilessly.

'Nothing,' Joshua said to himself, 'expect nothing.' But secretly he did not believe them and besides, he was still feeling virtuously keen and aware of approaching excavators. He got to the drill site to find that the scorpion had been taken down from the trailer and now crouched unthinking, and unblinkingly threateningly, sunk into the Kalahari sand up to its belly. The sand, Joshua felt, had not deserved such a burden, but then he supposed the earth certainly did not deserve the rape and ruin, which Lefika mining company was contemplating here in any case. Waxing philosophical, he thought of the times at various mines where the surface had collapsed and the media had called this "disaster", ignoring the fact of its man-made nature. He parked the car under the nearest Camel thorn tree and walked over the cooling sand towards the Rommel. Strooi was moving about her with a purpose and resolve that Joshua had not seen in him before. He became more hopeful again.

It seemed a bizarre ritual dance, a kind of desperate worship before an implacable god. He spoke constantly in a low flow of invectives and pleading and the machine spurted and spluttered in return, mocking the feeble antics of the small human creature. But finally, just as Strooi was on the point of giving up, it sprang to life. Having wiped his face innumerable times with the oil-stained cloth that turned his face a shiny black, which only enhanced the macabre and religious aspect of the work, he despairingly banged his forehead against the heaving side of Rommel – and lo – she began to work. His face transfigured with joy and gratitude, Strooi leapt up into the seat and steered the head of the hungry drill towards the marked place. Rommel bit eagerly into the sand, sinking her head in, and soon Rommel and Strooi disappeared in a whirl of dust and sand, which stung the eyes and shone eerily in the bright torchlight around which the mosquitoes and moths were dancing their own longing dance of death.

Once Joshua had retreated beyond the blinding sting of whirling sand, it seemed oddly beautiful, though unbearably noisy in the quiet of the desert night. The sand whirled up in an agony of twisted shapes as the bullet-headed drill point bit into it. Tight knots of sand boiled around each other in the intense light of the power torch, finally twisting in tightly-coiled torpedoes and reaching up towards the stars, away from the biting head, away from the harsh light. And once in the air, the wind soothed the twisted shapes and they fanned out, became almost languorous and floated gently into the darkness, winking out as the particles sailed beyond the circle of bright light.

It was mesmerising. Then Rommel sputtered and the night was shockingly still again, absolutely silent before the night sounds came back. With muttered curses, Strooi climbed down from his perch. Joshua too climbed out of the car, feeling rude not to show some concern for the ailing monster. Strooi heaved on a lever, and the head came up, streaming sand, but clearly unrepentant. He took it apart, shook the sand out of the delicate bits and with patience, replaced them. Joshua stood leaning against the hot shoulder of the great beast and watched. This new night time Strooi, this elegant and dedicated ritualist, smiled eventually, briefly returning to the ordinary world.

'It is difficult, drilling through the sand. Once we get to the rock it will be better.' he said with a confidence he clearly didn't feel, but felt honour-bound to express, close as he was to the wrath of his god. Joshua did not like to question it so soon, but his heart misgave nonetheless.

Strooi aimed the bullet head again, climbed back astride his ancient creature and started the machine. It sputtered unwillingly and he leapt back down. 'Oh, I forgot,' he said, and delved briefly into the innards of the machine. Back in the seat, he managed to start the machine and the sand leapt up in twisted agony to dance once more in the light and the dark as the head wolfed deeper and deeper into the sand in overwhelming noise and dust.

Then the noise changed, the rather high pitched whine turning into a darker growl. The sand dance slowed, became elongated, and twisted more tightly as the agony intensified. Against all expectations, Rommel's head had found the bedrock and the swirl of sand became the finer coiling of rock dust.

Joshua's heart leapt with excitement and he leaned eagerly forward, ready to spring to the earth, which at last seemed ready to relinquish its treasures. Finally near dawn he crept back into his camp, elated. He flung himself on his bed, looking forward to the faces of Ben and Josef when he showed them the core in the morning. Of course by the time he actually woke up, they had long found it, hosed it down and could pretend they had expected nothing less.

A week of hard work followed, involving a lot of walking and heavy sample carrying and at night that strange pleading with the beautiful and grotesque machine. An odd routine, but Joshua would not miss it for the world; there was something entirely captivating about the monster that produced the precious core. And this pattern, so removed from anything else he had experienced, could have been enjoyable for that very reason, had there not been so much pressure to get on. Added to the vague abstract pressure from an increasingly mythical "head office" came pressure from another quarter, more welcome in some ways, but also more disturbing.

Adam Vermeulen came almost every day to the sampling sites, always seeming to know where the geologist would be, and talked about the project. Joshua found it increasingly difficult to be confidential about it. Adam even advised, suggested sampling areas and talked Joshua through the one trench that had been made twelve years earlier, almost as if that trench had not torn his life apart, as if the only thing that mattered was the sparkling gems beneath this red sand.

So when the trenchers did come with their huge and ungainly machinery, in comparison with which Rommel – with her small bullet head and neat mouth – seemed a benign and mild deity, Joshua felt a little more familiar with his work. And thanks to Adam, in some cases even familiar and confident. Despite this he had nagging concerns. Would it be a good idea to spend so much money, to rip open this earth and peer at what it would reveal? What if again it revealed tantalising traces, but not enough to make it "worth it"? Would this strange community survive another fruitless invasion?

Ben and Josef seemed to feel little of all this, though they lived off the land and with the land in a way that Joshua knew he and the white farmers never could. But they were far more pragmatic about their lives, the land and their role in it all, than Ruth de Jaeger could have imagined. They did not question their jobs and their effect on the community. This was not for lack of concern, but they understood their own powerlessness and realised that it is good for families to eat. They went quietly about their work, patiently bringing in endless bags of sand samples collected accurately and neatly. Joshua knew that they were utterly reliable. They laughed and joked as they went, yet kept a sharp eye on their work too. At night they would often go "hunting" with a storm torch. The process involved blinding some small buck, and then driving into it, a kind of artificial road kill which made a gleeful braai on a Saturday evening. These would extend far into the night, with storytelling around the fire, dancing and laughter.

Joshua found it wonderfully peaceful to lie in his caravan and listen to those voices, which had been with him through several camps by now. The stories were of "heroic" hunts (car versus buck? Joshua had asked, to be met only with laughter – ja, man, what else?), of encounters with snakes, and of backbreaking work made lighter with laughter. They told them cheerfully and the listeners remained warm and appreciative of new embellishments on stories now as familiar as their old shoes.

He could hear Josef's voice and listened more carefully. Josef was quiet usually, as a stranger here, too, a migrant labourer, who had escaped the mines by being noticed as quick to understand the geology at West Driefontein. With some training, he had become a field hand in the exploration branch instead.

'Ja yous,' Josef was saying, 'in the Eastern Cape we hunt baboons, you know.'

'Baboons?'

'You, Josef, you and hunt? Ag man you a city boy aren't you? You from Jo'burg, the mines?' Laughter, but good-natured.

'Man, you only hunt rats in the dark of the mines.' Half mocking, half encouraging what was assumed at first to be a preposterous lie.

'Ja, but I was born there around Grahamstown you know. And there just by the Hellspoort pass is good baboon hunting country.'

'Oh ja, ja, I've been there – lots of baboons there in those mountains,' Joshua heard a voice as the rituals of storytelling and listening, of believing and doubt, settled around the fire for another round.

'There was this one look-out baboon who gave my grandfather trouble. Every day he would steal something from the shepherds – the goat's milk or the cheese, even the bread. And he would make the herds to go crazy too, barking alarms just to frighten them so he could steal from us.'

Murmurs of assent could be heard across the dark veld – yes, baboons were 'skelms', not to be trusted – tricky and difficult and clever. This one needed to be taught a lesson.

'We'd collect stones and wait for him, but he was too clever for us boys – he would always lure us away from them and then double back round to our stores of food. And when we did throw them at him, he didn't care – once he even caught one and threw it back.'

'Aish,' exclamations of disbelief.

'So my grandfather saved up for a gun and went out after this baboon,' the voice went silent.

Other voices filled in: 'Ja and – so did he get him? What happened?'

Josef's voice became anxious and maudlin with alcohol and dope, 'No one knows. That baboon never bothered us again, but also no one found my grandfather. We searched, but that mountain played with us and we kept getting lost. The mountain took him and would not give him back . . . then our cattle started dying.'

'We moved to town and from there to the mines. It put a curse on us, killing that baboon.'

'Ja,' Joshua heard an older voice, 'you never know what you are going to get if you go out with a gun – in the mountains or the desert.'

Joshua was invited to join them around the fire one evening. It was a big group that had come together. Several of the locals from the old Pniel Township that had been set up for Christian refugees a long time ago by the missionaries, had joined them – women and men, friends from Ben's childhood. By the time Joshua got there the party was well under way: the meat on the braai sizzling, alcohol flowing and already one zoll was doing the rounds.

They ate and drank, laughed at Rommel and Strooi's struggles, when in a sudden silence, the women who had gradually moved together on one side of the fire began to sing and clap their hands. It was beautiful in a chant-like unmelodious way and their clapping soon became mesmerising. One of the locals – by name of Klaas, Josef whispered to Joshua – a small golden and delicately made man, got up and began to dance. Underneath his overalls which he had shed next to the fire, he wore anklets of seed pods and shells. They made soft hissing sounds as he stepped and stamped rhythmically on the sand, which whirled gently around his feet in a dance of its own. One by one other men joined Klaas. Their movements were graceful and quick, despite the slow steady stamping of the feet, the gentle gyrations on an axle, which felt palpable as they turned. And through it all the women sang and clapped steadily.

Klaas' turning quickened and the slow gyration became a spinning vortex. His feet seemed almost still, yet his body whirled faster and faster. An agonised scream tore from his throat. Two of the others stepped in close, a small old man made insistent, firm hissing noises, "tsk, tsk" to keep them steady. They placed their hands on the small of his back and held his arms just below the shoulders. It slowed him down and the strain around his neck subsided, but he seemed to be in a trance. When he was calm and the screaming had ceased, the others let him go and the old man took up the slow clapping again. Klaas now danced alone: a graceful dance of leaping through the fire with arms stretched above his head. He leapt higher and higher. From standing quite still he would leap straight up into the air then over the fire to circulate round the people seated around it, nodding and smiling at them. He threw sand on the fire sending up a white smoke, through which he leapt repeatedly, calling out softly, 'Xai kovadi, Xai kovadi' with such unbearable longing, it broke one's heart to hear it, even without understanding.

But for the slow steady clapping, the singing had ceased and everyone was watching Klaas with awe and wonder. Gradually his leaping became subdued, the longing in his singing turning into an inconsolable sobbing, which finally brought him to his knees and he fell forward onto his elbows, and hid his face in his hands.

His wife, a beautiful young woman, stood up and knelt next to him, 'Toemaar,' she murmured, overcome with his grief herself, 'toemaar, my kudu, my liefling, toemaar, nou.'

Joshua felt exhausted, just having watched, and was surprised to see now that all eyes had turned to him.

'What is it?' he asked Ben and Josef anxiously.

But an old man smiled and said, 'Nee, jongbaas, don't worry. It has only been a long time since anyone danced the white kudu in these parts – a long time.' And in his voice swung gently a kind of jubilation, despite the obvious sorrow of the dance, and his eyes were bright with tears.

Again Joshua turned to Ben and Josef for an explanation. Josef backed down, he was Xhosa he said and not from around here, but Ben obliged. 'We have a legend and a prophecy. The legend is that the white kudu will return to bless the land in his final passing, when a stranger comes who can open the quartz door for him to pass through and then rain will come and the little people, the bushmen, I think,' gesturing towards Klaas and the small old man, 'will dance again on their own land.'

Joshua still didn't understand why they should look at him.

Josef laughed. 'You, you are a stranger, no?' pointing an unashamed finger at him. This startled the rational geologist in Joshua so much that he got up and walked away from the fire, from the round of smiling faces, afraid to be drawn into something he didn't understand.

He went to stand by the old willow tree, weeping the last of its slim brown leaves into the sluggish dam. And there beneath the tree he saw a creature. Tall and graceful he stood with quiet eyes, beneath the old willow tree and looked at Joshua. And the best he could do at that point was to look back. Unsteady, groggy with wine and cannabis, he only stared back, but even then there was something. Recognition he did not understand but felt in his body with a piercing certainty – so piercing, he almost cried out. A certainty he could neither place sensibly in his experience nor lose comfortably as he had hoped in the morning when the effects of the party had worn off. He tried dismissing his reaction, 'You're going native,' he said to himself.

A small wrinkled man with golden eyes had walked him back to camp after the braai and the dance and the silent kudu. 'One day,' he said, 'I will tell you the story and you will understand. For now only sleep and do the work the gods have brought you here to do.' Joshua wondered how destructive that work was going to be, remembering the trenches, which would soon be dug and could not help asking which god he was working for. He didn't know, but this strange old man only smiled and said much more about the white kudu, which Joshua did not know he would remember until much later.

The next morning, Sunday, as Joshua stumbled sleepily but oddly enough, not hung over from his caravan, a young man, with the same golden eyes as the oracular little man from the previous night, was sitting on his steps waiting for him. As Joshua came out he stood up and held out his right hand, the wrist clasped in his left hand.

'I am Klaas,' he said. 'I danced the white kudu last night, when you came to our fire.'

Joshua smiled awkwardly at the introduction; he did not think he would ever forget the strange evening – the encounter with the white kudu and then the old man with the calm golden eyes.

He shook hands.

Klaas said: 'Come, I will take you to Hendrik.'

'Hendrik?' Joshua asked.

'Yes, my grandfather. He will explain.'

'Explain what?' not entirely comfortable with these thoughts and memories in daylight.

'Go shower first.' Generous on Sunday morning, Klaas offered him time.

Joshua showered in a hurry, enjoying the crisp feel of the water under the open sky, trying to clear from his mind the cobwebs of dreams as he ought, but fascinated despite himself.

When he came out, Klaas smiled cheerfully, 'Mornings,' he said.

He seemed quite recovered from his traumatic dance the night before.

'Did you like our party?' Klaas asked companionably as they walked past the back gate of Adam's garden, where the windmill and the reservoir tanks stood high above them in the morning light, and followed a narrow track through the wag-'n-bietjie bushes and bloudoring. The veld was dry still but serene as though aware it was Sunday morning.

They came at last upon a strange round structure, which seemed to rise up from the sand itself, being made of the exact same colour, yet set apart from it by the surrounding sunflowers and mielie plants which formed a kind of natural wall around it. Sitting on his haunches watching something in the air invisible was the small, yellow man.

'Oupa-Hendrik,' Klaas called.

'Ssjt sssjt sssjt' the small man said, placing a finger on his lips without taking his eyes off whatever he was watching.

Klaas seemed to understand and simply hunkered down next to him, but like Joshua, also failed to see what Hendrik was seeing. Joshua joined them feeling foolish and ignorant, barbaric and not wanting to disrupt whatever it was that so rapt this little man's attention.

Finally Hendrik seemed to mark a spot somewhere far off in the distance and then turned his attention to his guests. His wrinkled face creased and wrinkled further as he smiled in obvious delight at this visit from his nephew and the young geologist.

Klaas and Hendrik began a rapid conversation in Afrikaans mixed with Nama, which Joshua could not follow, but understood enough to realise that it was about the dance the previous evening. Hendrik smiled knowingly at Joshua and then threw his head back and laughed with such delight, that he could not help but smile too no matter how uncomfortable this conversation was making the scientist in him feel.

Then Hendrik, no longer laughing, turned his eyes on Joshua – they were golden brown and quiet as animal eyes, and deep within them lurked such an odd mixture of pain and laughter that for a moment Joshua held his breath. Then he spoke and the moment was broken.

'Kom sit,' he said simply pointing to a stone, clearly worn and shiny from many such invitations. Klaas got up and excused himself, saying baas Adam had asked him to check on a pump at Ouma se Hek. He left Joshua with this strange little man with the words, 'vertel vir hom, vertel van die wit kudu.'(Tell him; tell him of the white kudu).

But Hendrik only smiled. When Klaas' footsteps had completely died away Hendrik said to Joshua, 'look at the moon.' Joshua looked up and saw the sickle moon pale and slender in the bright sky. 'Do you know what it is?'

Joshua squirmed, his mind filled with stories of mountains, which would not return lost hunters, stories his scientific education on the other side of the globe had simply not prepared him to face. He guessed that his geologically accurate answer was probably not what Hendrik was after. 'Green cheese,' he hazarded, trying to make light of it all, trying to restore his own perspective, feeling a spoil-sport all the same. But Hendrik just laughed, 'Yes,' he said, 'or more scientifically as you would say, it is a dead rock, mostly, is it not?'

Relieved, Joshua could only nod.

'It is also a beautiful thing to look at in the night,' Hendrik went on. 'Many find it comforting and wonder about how it changes its shape and even once they know – the beauty is not gone from the fact is it?'

'No' – anxious that answer, the lips pressed and the throat tight.

'Well and so people have also told stories about it. We have one too, in it the sickle moon is a feather stolen from the bird of truth – the ostrich. It is a feather flung up in despair by a lonely ancestor desiring light in the darkness. And the stars are the wood ashes strewn into the sky by a girl lighting the way home for her love who has gone hunting alone to find her a gemsbok, to make her beautiful kaross.' A pause, a searching look.

'Nonsense yes, these stories, but what do they do?'

Joshua didn't know and was afraid to risk another guess.

'You hear that story and then you look at the stars and you think of that girl, waiting and afraid in the dark. And you look at the moon and you think of the ostrich and you laugh because you know it is a foolish bird, why should it be called the bird of truth simply because it has beautiful feathers? And as you laugh you know now that you are at home here, the moon and the stars are no longer as far away, they have come down and spoken to you. You know their stories and you begin to think they might know yours and your heart can find rest then, because you know that you belong.'

Joshua was silent. Hendrik looked long at him in the stillness of the morning and said, 'The wilderness here has begun telling you its stories. The white kudu has come to talk to you.'

His kettle had boiled then and he offered a Joshua a cup of Rooibos tea with lots of honey. It was delicious, though Joshua had not been able to drink it before. He looked up at Hendrik from the huge enamel cup he held carefully in the fingers of both hands.

'Hendrik,' he said, 'don't misunderstand me, I am just a geologist, I am here because my job sent me here, no other reason. I am just working here. And when the job is done, I will leave.'

Hendrik shook his head softly, swiftly, a tiny movement from side to side, 'sjjt, sjjt, sjjt' was all he said and pointed carefully to a bee flying away from one of his huge sunflowers. He carefully put down his mug and beckoned Joshua to do the same, got up in one smooth silent motion and waited intently watching the bee. Presently it flew off and Hendrik followed. Joshua, less silently, followed Hendrik.

Hendrik was moving at a gentle trot, his eyes always intent on the bee as it flew, keeping up with it, his bare feet sure on the ground placed swiftly and certainly not on loose stones or the ever-present little 'duiweltjies' tiny thorns. They lost the bee just beyond the dam, but Hendrik was unperturbed. He searched up into the trees on the dam and then went towards a wag-n-bietjie. In the bush sat a small brown bird, a honey guide and it flitted from bush to bush. Hendrik followed, making soft tsk tsk noises, to which the bird seemed to reply. Finally the bird took them to a hollow ancient tree not far from the river bank and they could hear the buzzing of a swarm of bees. Hendrik tsk tsk-ed more loudly, reached in and his hand came out holding a large piece of honeycomb. He broke a piece off for the bird, another piece for Joshua and a piece for himself, which he popped straight into his mouth, the rest he carried home with great care, where he stored it in an earthen pot before returning to the fire.

'Ag,' he said, 'this is the best.' Carefully taking his cup from the side of the embers he drank his tea, which was still warm. Joshua too found it washed down the wild honey with a warmth and comfort which made one feel, momentarily, entirely safe.

Hendrik turned then with his golden eyes, like the honeycomb in the sun, to Joshua. 'The white kudu is like this honey: it is !kia – what we strive for in the dance. Klaas called to it: Xai kovadi – a plea for healing. The white kudu, we call him Ou Groote here, is a link to the spirits, which will show us how to heal what we are. He is patience and mercy. He is what makes life bearable – sweet, even. Now you must make of that what you can.'

Joshua remembered then the painting Adam had told him about and the beliefs of the Bushmen. In the afternoon, he tried to walk casually up to Witkopje. He found it was a sizeable hill for this landscape, and took some walking up. As he walked he glimpsed now and again Nella and Thomas with a group of farm children, clearly playing some elaborate game of hide and seek on the slopes. With its odd protruding boulders of dolomite and termite hills, its sturdy bushes rather than merely grass; it was an ideal place for such a game. He felt like an intruder and was about to turn around to come back later, when Nella suddenly burst out of the bush at him. Flushed, breathless and giggling, she stared at him a moment, caught still in the world of children and games. Then she recovered, remembered her manners and held out a hand.

'Mr Hunter, good afternoon. What brings you to Witkopje?'

'Hallo Nella, please call me Joshua.' He shook the proffered slender and rather dirty hand politely, 'I have come to see the painting, which your father said is here somewhere.'

On the actual hill itself it had become impossible to see the white blinking expanse of quartz.

'Oh yes, would you like me to show you?'

'That's very kind of you, Nella, but I don't want to interrupt your game.'

She blushed at being caught in such childish activities, but said with what dignity she could manage, 'Oh, it will take them ages to find Thomas. It always does. There will be time. This way.'

'Well, if you really don't mind, that would be most helpful.'

'Sure,' she said, 'everyone who comes to Pniel comes to see Ou Groote.'

'Ou Groote?' That name again. He began to feel the world conspiring against him.

'Yes, it is what we call the painting. You will understand why when you see it.' And she led him quickly and easily up the hill on which every patch was clearly familiar to her.

They stopped at last before a two metre high expanse of exposed rock. Closer to, it was difficult to see what caused the bright flash, though the rock was clearly flecked with quartz as well as mica, facets of which glinted even in the late afternoon sun. Of course it could not be white, he told himself, not with topsoil so rich in iron – it stained everything red.

Then they came to the painting. It was astonishingly white. Down the centre of the rock ran a deep crack and from this stepped expectantly a kudu bull. The artist had used a quartz intrusion for the main part of the kudu, added horns and ears and those curious large eyes. His hindquarters were not visible, but otherwise the painting was remarkably lifelike. One half expected the creature to move. The ears were pricked forward in interest, and the noble swing of the horn (just the one, he noticed, and wondered whether the other had been rubbed out with time) was entirely, unmistakably kudu.

'It's beautiful, isn't it?'

'Yes,' Nella said simply, 'it's Ou Groote.' And she let him stand quietly and admire for a while. Soon the other children trooped up noisily with Thomas in their midst. He was smiling and nodding at what they were saying. They spoke so quickly that Joshua found it hard to follow what was being said.

Then Nella turned to him. 'Do you want to play with us?'

Taken utterly by surprise, Joshua found himself agreeing to play hide and seek – and thoroughly enjoyed the afternoon on Witkopje. The game dispelled all sense of conspiracies and dreams and soon, like them he was calling out cheerfully "Hi, Ou Groote," every time he dashed past the painting, in order to call himself home when he was found.

3
Unrest

The combination of the various core sampling exercises from previous and current explorations, and the grid mapping Joshua had now completed, suggested that he needed to take up the contact with Adam's neighbour before the trenching could begin. Wonderfontein belonged to the Radcliffe sisters, two delightful old ladies left stranded on the banks of the Vaal River by a colonial past, which had long forgotten them. They lived in a dark and smelly old house with about a hundred cats, two huge and floppy Labradors undone by the heat, their fur and ten chickens, which terrorised both the cats and the dogs.

Rumour and village legend had it that they were fabulously rich and kept the family silver and jewels buried under the old willow tree, which wept beside the enormous lily pond in the centre of their wonderfully verdant garden. 'I am sure they were related to royalty,' said Marina of the Kooperasie, when she heard of Joshua's forthcoming exploration on the Radcliffe farm. 'That Rosalie moves as if she were a queen and her sister has all the delicacy of a princess.'

In better times they had searched and found a great deal of ground water and so were able to create a lush and green paradise here on the edge of the desert, before the river life began. Their green paradise of a garden really was the start of life here, the end of the desert, the beginning of the river country. And beneath this paradise, did there lurk gold and silver, already worked to perfection, already torn from the bowels of the earth and returned there now for safe keeping? The romance of the legend charmed all who heard it and no one was ever prepared to question it: the idea, the faint hope of treasure was enough.

Tant Rina of the Off Licence on the other hand, was convinced that they practised witchcraft, which they had learned from Hendrik, Adam's old Bushman gardener, she said. Apparently this included the power to call down lightning upon your enemies, to silence your ancestors and bring upon your children "luisiekte" so that they did not have the energy to go out and seek employment and would stay a burden on your life forever. When, with his usual liberal fastidiousness at such outrageous beliefs, Joshua expressed his doubt at this, Tant Rina heaved her bosom further across the counter and, grabbing his lapel, pulled him perilously close to her breath, smelling of beskuit and condensed milk, and said, 'Gaan vra die kaffirs! Hulle weet, hulle ken die soort,' (Go and ask the kaffirs. They know. They understand that kind of person). And after a hefty pause and an enormous breath, 'Jy sal nog sien as sy jou eers vaskyk met haar skewe oe en die swart kat wat altyd by haar is, dan sal jy my glo.' (You will soon see, when she first catches your eye with her squint and you see the black cat always at her side). Joshua found this harsh prejudice about two women living alone cruel and distressing. He untangled himself as quickly as he could and left the shop in a hurry, more than a little taken aback by the venom in that Christian voice. But he too was curious about these two people, who called forth such stories and such intensity of belief.

It was Adam who took him to meet them. He had worked their farm for years. As young women they had managed manfully on their own, he said, had set up a beautifully and economically sound business – a sheep farm, with a product of good reputation, for which he said, smiling in memory of it, the local farmers never forgave them.

'Except you, Adam,' Joshua said.

'No,' he said, 'except my father, who sent me to them to be foreman and later manager, to learn. And my brother, Gideon, who used to read in their library.'

Again Joshua was left staring at him, amazed at the far reaches of each person and how little one can ever grasp of them; how many-layered, how deep and true the core, but hidden. "We with our own monstrous Rommel," he thought, "our language merely scratching ineptly the surface of each other. Which perhaps is best, after all!"

The Radcliffe house was painted a burnt sienna with a deep green roof and nestled darkly amongst the peppercorn and syringa trees, the magnolias and of course the many roses. The deep veranda was overshadowed by the most magnificent bougainvillea. Adam and Joshua climbed up the steps into the peaceful shade in which sheltered white cane furniture, pristine and almost luminous in the cool darkness. They stepped into this silence, disturbed only by the far away, tired clanking of a windmill, refusing to give in to the afternoon's languor and before Adam had even knocked, the screen door opened and a small wrinkled face, surrounded by a halo of silver grey curls, popped around the door to greet them.

'Adam,' a soft but by all means firm voice said gladly. 'Adam, you have come to see us. How good of you.' And the large, burly farmer, usually so reserved in his dignity was bending down tenderly to accept and return a birdlike hug. 'You must come in and see Rosalie, too. She will be so glad to see you.'

'Cecilia,' Adam said, 'this is Joshua, a geologist. From England, like you. He is doing some exploration on Pniel again. And he also needs to have another look at Wonderfontein.'

Adam had warned him that there was no use beating about the bush with these two women and that he would tell them immediately what the visit was all about. But this, before they were even in the door surprised Joshua nonetheless. It was so different from the more or less agile diplomacy more usual in these interactions.

'Oh' was the only response he received. And the delicate little old lady turned and called in a tender and sweet voice into the house, 'Rosalie, Rosalie, Adam has come to see us and brought another geologist.'

From deeper within the dark recesses of the house came a rich alto voice, 'Coming Cecilia, just let me finish cutting these crunchies and I'll bring the tea.' By this time Cecilia had led the two men through the dark echoing corridor into the stuffy silence of the lounge that smelled penetratingly of cat. Cecilia went in ahead of them and made soft shooing noises in a couple of directions and they could just glimpse quiet shadows gliding off the chairs and sofas and into the darkness.

'Come in, come in,' she said, 'tea is just coming. I think we can open the curtains now.' Which she did, allowing enough light in to display a rather dilapidated, typically Edwardian colonial lounge. Once white couches with curly wooden edgings, claw and ball feet, and enormous roses embossed upon the upholstery crouched on the dark wooden floor. Scatter cushions and a few half-hearted doilies completed the furnishings. The coffee table had several copies of the obligatory *Reader's Digest* lying on it, some *Garden and Homes* and the *Fair Lady*. Also though, some beautiful books on Namibia and a Lawrence van der Post lying open. Centre piece was a fragrant bowl of roses. The wooden floor was only partially covered by the worn and threadbare rug and was polished to a lovely, muted dark shine. Along the walls, glass cabinets contained ostrich eggs and more books, a motley collection: a complete Shakespeare, Rilke's elegies and some Goethe, Walter Benjamin and several rock and mineral samples, the best of which was a large yet delicately shaped desert rose.

Cecilia saw Joshua's gaze resting on the rocks and immediately invited him to take a closer look. She opened the cabinets and handed him the samples with loving familiarity. 'Here this rose quartz is my favourite. Rosalie found it on Witkopje – Adam's place. She gave it to me for my birthday one year.' And as she held it out to him, looking up earnestly, he noticed for the first time the squint Tant' Rina had spoken of. It was not disfiguring he thought. It gave her the look of someone peeping into another world. Perhaps that is what people did not like about her, that appearance of seeing what others could not.

Carefully Joshua took this precious piece but saw in its rosy sheen nothing that warranted its favoured place. Perhaps here too her disconcerting eyes, green as the faraway sea, could see something that he could not in the sharp contours of that rock. And then he shook himself free of such superstitions, and remembered that it is often the manner of the finding that makes rocks meaningful, something that cannot be passed on to anyone else. So he simply looked at it carefully, remarked innocuously on its shape and colour, and handed it back.

Adam, in the meantime, had walked to the bookshelf, taken down the Duino Elegies, but was looking out of the window with a faraway look. Joshua glanced over his shoulder at a dedication in the front, "Dear Rosalie and Cecilia, thank you for everything, Miriam." It felt like prying, so he turned quickly to look at the cats, which wove themselves about everyone's legs and the legs of the furniture silently, not begging or seeking attention, simply there, part of the place and looking the guests over.

Then Rosalie came in. She was much larger than her sister and dressed in jeans and a t-shirt and with bare feet that still had the markings of socks and laces across the top. She held in her strong hands a white mesh tray with delicate, rose patterned china cups, and fragrant crunchies piled high on a plate, and smelling of oats and honey. She carefully put down the tray with a concentration that showed all too clearly that doing this silently and gently did not come easily. Then she straightened, wiped her hand on the back of her trousers and stretched it out towards Joshua.

'Hallo, and welcome,' she said simply, then turned to Adam with that same clear affection in her face and voice as she engulfed him in a bear hug that was entirely unlike her sister's delicate flutter. Adam returned the hug with just as much affection as he had her sister's. Clearly he had a lot of time for these two eccentric old English ladies, who, for all their delicate and otherworldly Englishness, no longer seemed at all out of place in this landscape. They drank tea, discussed the weather and the possibilities of good crops. Then briefly and to the point, Joshua explained Lefika's business in the area and where he would need to drill further. They were accepting in the same way that Adam had been, as if they knew only too well what the community needed regardless of their own feelings about it.

When all this was done, documents signed, hands shaken, Cecilia said, 'Come let's look at the garden. It's cooler now the sun is almost down.' Rosalie kissed her sister lightly on the top of her head and said she needed to go out again; there was an ewe that was not entirely happy. Cecilia smiled fondly and let her go. Adam too excused himself, Cecilia knew he'd rather look at sheep than flowers, and was gracious. She walked with Joshua through her fragrant kitchen and out into the back garden: a herb and kitchen garden such as Joshua had never seen. Cecilia wandered about in this garden, here and there touching a bush or plant, feeling the dryness of leaves and checking on the ripeness of the fruit. Clearly this was her home and not the conventionally presentable lounge they had sat in previously for the business part of the visit. Gradually she changed as they walked in her garden, her voice became warmer, softer, deeper and her arms now swung loosely at her sides, the hands extending gently to the plants, picking a leaf here for Joshua to smell or bringing a blossom within reach. She spoke of each plant as if it were a friend. 'They have a language, too, you know,' she said confidingly to the young man, 'and in times gone by humans understood that and were able to tell each other things that words could not.' And her roving eye seemed to Joshua alight with memories and possibilities. She smiled at him.

They had walked around the side of the house and found themselves in her rose garden, surrounded by roses of so many different colours, scents and shapes that it was quite overwhelming. At its heart stood a fountain, oddly familiar in its tall elegance beneath a young apple tree. Joshua stood still a while and Cecilia too fell silent as they let the simple abundance of the roses and the soft murmur of the water fill the afternoon.

Cecilia watched his face. 'Shall we sit?' she asked. Joshua could think of nothing he would rather do at that moment than sit beside the fountain amongst the roses and think of nothing. They sat, silent both as old friends would be. Joshua closed his eyes a moment and saw a monastery garden, enclosed and peaceful, watched over by the quiet peal of the vesper call from a high tower. Surprised by its palpable clarity, he opened his eyes and saw Cecilia smiling at him.

'You heard the bell?' she asked.

'I heard it yes. How did you know?'

'Our garden,' she smiled, 'we planted it to be like the garden of the unicorn tapestries, which hang in the once medieval cloister, the Musée de Cluny . . . or as near as we could get it. People often hear bells in it.' A shimmer of white amongst the trees then and a memory of golden eyes smiling, Joshua shook himself.

'Why?' He could not stop himself asking, disconcerted by this idea and the memory it awoke of the dance.

'Well,' she said, 'because they are beautiful and a dream of harmony rarely achieved. I wanted to be part of that dream, however small; however far removed.'

And as with Hendrik, Joshua knew that his own world had no answer to such dreams. The garden seemed serene and calm at that moment, not one ounce of gold or diamond or even core in the world mattered there.

The peace of the garden stirred. It was not immediately apparent whence the disturbance had come. The smells were too much, nauseating the senses, the sunlight seemed at once tired and too much, the evening breeze slowly coming upon them now brought with it the sharp smell of diesel and farm business. Joshua looked about, irritated, without understanding why.

The disturbance stood before them. A man had come up suddenly through the small white gate at the side of the garden. Abraham: Adam's son, manager of Wonderfontein for the Radcliffe sisters. He was a large man, without any of the grace of his father: a hard, clear-cut chiselled face, large capable hands swung from a strong neck and hard shoulders; legs like tree trunks standing firmly rooted upon the earth, ending in the inevitable woollen socks and veldskoene of all the farmers here.

'Hello, Tannie,' he said incongruously as they all did, briefly and without any of the warmth Joshua had come to expect between the two families, after watching Adam with the two sisters. He turned abruptly to Joshua. 'Ek is Abraham Vermeulen,' he said. Joshua shook that red, and in so many ways ruined, hand and replied 'Ek is Joshua Hunter.'

'Die geoloog,' the younger Vermeulen finished for him. 'Die geoloog wat weer kom soek hier by ons en alles weer omkrap wat ons an vrede gevind het (The geologist who has come looking again, upsetting all the peace we have found). What the hell are your head office people doing snooping around here already? Wanting to talk to my father and I am not invited to the conversation?'

"Adam," Joshua thought, "why didn't you warn me?"

And then realised the foolishness of it and berated himself – pathetic, really. How does one expect a man to warn a stranger about the violence of his son? A son in whom all the anger of a nation's long struggle against itself, all the pain of a family that has lost the battle with a landscape and a climate and an unravelling history, have found an explosive gathering point.

Rosalie and Adam returned and Abraham rounded on his father.

'There is a fax from the mining company. They want to talk to talk to you.' And he handed his father a crumpled piece of paper accusingly. Adam looked quickly, searchingly at his son, reached for the fax and exchanged a glance with Rosalie, excused himself and went towards his car. The others all sat down on the stoep where Eve had brought a tray of that wonderful colonial tradition, sundowners. Long cool drinks of gin and tonic, orange juice and vodka, or simply a sharp whiskey on the rocks. It honoured in its own exiled way the brief and splendid sunsets of Africa. Self-indulgent and decadent though it was, Joshua thoroughly enjoyed it. And it restored for the moment an uneasy peace, disturbed by father and son, between farmer and geologist.

Tomorrow they would begin drilling on Wonderfontein. 'Just stop off at my house,' Abraham said, as he drove Joshua back to his camp 'and Esther, my wife, will give you the keys to the Sandveld gate.' His voice sounded defeated and sulky, something was eating at him.

Early the following morning Joshua drove slowly and painfully ahead of Rommel and Strooi as they moved the delicate monster from Doringaar to Wonderfontein. Joshua found that he had become quite fond of the odd pair and their constant struggle to do the simplest thing. They stopped at the small, bizarre Cape Dutch style house standing bare and lonely on the desert landscape, and Joshua walked carefully up to it. It seemed so out of place without mountains to echo its lovely curves, no blue in the landscape to mellow the whiteness of its walls. He went up to the dark kitchen door, having already learnt that unless formally invited, these farmers don't welcome anyone to their front doors. The top half was open and he could hear a dark alto voice singing inside. Joshua knocked as loudly as he dared. A large Ridgeback immediately stirred and then stood up warningly. No need for anything fiercer, he supposed, when you were that size.

'Haai, Chaka, bly still,' the singing had stopped and a small woman, with brown hair swept back from a high forehead and almond shaped brown eyes, glanced briefly into the kitchen.

'O, goeie môre Meneer,' she said, 'Ek sal die sleutel gou haal, Abraham het gesê u sal verby kom vroeg.' (Good morning, I will fetch the key. Abraham said you would be early).

And disappeared again to reappear with the key, carefully marked on a coloured key ring, so different from the assortment of red string and bits of leather or feather, which Adam used to identify his keys.

'Thank you very much Mrs Vermeulen,' Joshua said. 'My name is Joshua and I'll probably be trespassing on your land for a while, though hopefully not again on your time.' Joshua babbled, anxious about this farm, not owned by the farmer, but angrily protected nonetheless.

She smiled and answered in English, 'That is all right Mr Hunter, it is very quiet here. You will not disturb us. Would you like a cup of tea and some beskuit?'

'Sure,' Joshua said, 'let me give the key to Ro . . ., to Mr van der Merwe – would that be OK?'

'Yes,' she said, 'Abraham knows him.'

So Joshua took the key out to Rommel and Strooi and came back to drink tea with Esther Vermeulen. It was the usual strong tea with the thick creamy milk and homemade beskuit. This beskuit had the added faint flavour of burn on it and Joshua could see where the edges had been scrapped. Esther was nervous. Joshua didn't think it was his presence in particular, she was simply habitually nervous, eyes never still, back and hands constantly alert. Still she smiled and spoke a clear and lilting English, with those strangely rolled r's, marking her clearly as from the Boland, far down in the mountainous and green south. How ironic that she should be in this house, which would remind her of her homeland and yet be as out of place as she herself seemed to be here.

They spoke of the morning, laughed about the state of Strooi's dreadful machine (he confided the name to her) and soon moved to other topics such as her abruptly ended, uncompleted studies at Stellenbosch university where she had begun a degree in psychology. She smiled, 'I tell myself it's interrupted not broken off, but I think I'm lying to myself.' Smiling, but tearing up too at the strange web her life had become.

'How long ago was that?'

'Oh, I've been here a whole year and a little more now with Abraham.'

'A year isn't very long,' Joshua said. 'Much may still happen.'

'Yes,' she smiled, 'much may still happen.' But her eyes remained bleak.

Joshua had a sense that here was a broken and unhappy person, whose suffering went well beyond the usual scope. The small daily cruelties of marriage, of daily and ordinary life together, seemed intensified here by the barely reined-in violence of Abraham and the vague and wandering anxiety of Esther.

Then a bakkie could be heard arriving and her alert back stiffened a fraction more, her hands flew about the cups as she cleared the things away and said, 'I must prepare breakfast now, Abraham will be hungry.'

'Of course, Mrs Vermeulen,' Joshua said, 'Thank you and I will see you around no doubt.'

'Yes,' a swift handshake, 'please call me Esther.'

And she was gone ahead of him into the kitchen to greet her husband coming in.

'Abraham, Mr Hunter came to fetch the keys,' she explained. 'Yes,' he said, 'Danie said I would find Joshua here. Where is breakfast?' he dismissed them both with this lack of interest.

'Bye Abraham,' said Joshua as he left to go out to the bakkie, feeling as though Chaka, the huge dog, was seeing him off the property.

Joshua thought there would be little social calling on that house. It was too tense, too anxious, too filled with a vague foreboding, and he wanted no part of it. So he left Strooi to set up Rommel in the river kamp and went back home to his camp – and it did feel like home now, he realised. He hoped to find what little sense there would be in the grids, when he looked at them in the thin shade of the peppercorn tress and wrestled in quiet with results that did not match. As he rested after lunch, an unread book lying open on his chest, and his eyes half closed, Joshua heard suddenly Nella's voice calling.

'Joshua, Joshua, where are you?'

'Here, behind the caravan.'

And then her lithe form appeared. She spoke to him cheerfully, her father's acceptance of him making his camp part of her world. The shyness, he knew now, was for strangers without names, not people who played hide and seek on Sunday afternoons.

'Joshua, there's going to be a slide-show night in the school hall. You must come with us. I've forgotten what my teacher said it is going to be about – something about art? But it doesn't matter, the whole town will be there, so we have to go.'

'Nella,' Joshua laughed 'don't forget to breathe,' as Thomas caught up with his sister and nodded enthusiastic agreement with shining eyes. He loved it when she was happy, though in his silent world the reasons for this must often remain a mystery. But for now he simply grabbed Joshua's hands, wanting to go to the river. Joshua went, what else was he to do? With Rommel and Strooi out of action in the daylight, the entire world of a fading childhood was there for him to enter again with these two half-wild children. Their imaginative stories were a delightful escape from grappling with handfuls of sand and data. And Ou Groote who played a part, had remained since the night of the dance, a half buried thought that tugged constantly at his mind.

Friday evening arrived. All afternoon, Nella and Thomas had been washing their father's old Chevrolet with much enthusiasm but little effect, in preparation for the "great outing". At noon Joshua had seen a company Toyota pull up briefly at Pniel farmhouse, then leave again. He felt bothered. Why did he not know what was being discussed? What was going on? But there was little he could do, and didn't even know whose car it was as they all looked alike. So he simply went on with the core boxes, marking the smooth cylinders of rock and making notes.

At six, all assembled solemnly, suitably scrubbed and dressed for the occasion. Nella looked delightful in a new flower print dress and Thomas in a white shirt and brand new blue shorts. His grey eyes were larger than usual tonight and their restlessness betrayed all too clearly his anxiety. Nella too knotted her fingers even as she twirled in her dress to show Joshua. Soon the reason for the unease became apparent. Adam came round the front of the house from his office, and declared in a stiffly controlled voice that he would not be coming to the slide show. Esther came out the front door, eyes and face a little tear-streaked, and Abraham came after his father.

'Ja, maar Pa moet tog kan insien,' Abraham was saying, 'hierdie land is ons sin, dis nie vir die kaffirs nie, en dis nie vir die verdomde Engelse mining companies,' a vicious look at Joshua. 'Ons moet bly veg, Pa kan nie ingee vir die swartes se getjank.' (Yes, but father you must agree this land is ours, it is not for the bloody kaffirs or the damned English mining companies. We must go on fighting; we should not give in to the whine of the blacks.)

Adam turned and said in the softest voice, 'Abraham, you will not use language like that in front of your wife and my children.'

'Your children?' a mocking question, a desperate defence.

Adam's face turned darkest thunder as he rounded on his eldest, who stepped back, hands raised, placatory. 'I am sorry, father.'

Abraham was quiet then. Father and son seethed at each other in silence above the heads of the two youngsters, whose eyes were already watching their dream of an evening out disappearing.

Adam looked at his two youngest and his eyes softened momentarily. 'Joshua, do you think you could drive this old thing?' he asked, handing him the keys without waiting for an answer.

Joshua took the keys without another word and came round to the passenger side to open the door for Nella and Thomas. Esther made a sudden decision; she had been a bundle of nerves watching her father-in-law and husband, resigned to the need for loyalty, ready to sacrifice the evening in order to mollify her husband, to make him make peace with his father. But now as Abraham turned away from the entire family to kick viciously at a piece of the rock garden and curse murderously under his breath, a small long-forgotten part of her briefly raised its head and she darted towards the car with the other two. She turned to see what Abraham would do. Esther watched him fearfully for a while, with that absolute concentration reserved for events that are life-threatening. Then abruptly, shaking a little, she climbed into the driving seat of the car and said, 'Who's coming?'

Nella, with one curious glance at her big brother, climbed into the back seat and Thomas, who went where Nella went, climbed in too. Janine came out with a huge box of popcorn which she pushed this into Joshua's arms before he could get in the car and said, 'Meneer sal u dit voor vir Mies' Rina gee, asseblief?'

So before Adam's raised hand, the urgent glimpse at his son, and sharply indrawn breath could become a protest, and while Joshua looked about a little helplessly with the popcorn, the evening had been decided.

Esther drove in silence, too fast for the dark roads deep in sand, which shifted under the wheels. But suddenly Joshua too was angry, angry that he had not been told what the meeting earlier had been about, sure that it had something to do with Adam's tension and Abraham's defeated anger. He felt left out, treated as a minor by his colleagues and it seemed unfair to do this and leave him there to deal with the people involved when he was uninformed. And here he was, doing what he 'had to do' – socialising with the farmer – as he had been told and found himself in water too deep to see the bottom. What had the quip about the children to do with it, what had it meant? Esther's set face betrayed a similar anger at the ruthless self-importance of the men who had potentially spoilt the evening for everyone with their behaviour.

They arrived at the poorly lit school hall with a jolt. Nella and Thomas escaped as soon as they could, finding friends among the excited, quick young bodies playing murder in the dark, in the suddenly strange and adventurous schoolyard. Joshua stood patiently holding the box of popcorn while Esther gathered herself to face the other adults, the young mothers and the entire PTA, who had come to help sell the cool drinks and popcorn to raise funds for the school for some mysterious and eternal project only the PTAs of the world ever knew about or understood.

'Haai, Meneer, put the popcorn over here, please.' A cheery voice called out and Joshua moved off in that direction, acutely aware of the distress he left behind. He delivered Janine's popcorn, which was welcomed very happily – clearly a quality product. Rubbing his palms on the thighs of his jeans and smiling apologetically he bowed his way out of the overheated kitchen. Here urns for tea were being manhandled, and huge petrol drums filled with water and ice were standing with Coke and Fanta bottles bobbing cheerfully in their dark depths and kitchen goddesses made him feel awkward with questions about Adam.

When Joshua escaped, Esther had extricated herself from the car and was smiling in a strained way at something Tant Rina was saying. 'Ag you know what men are like, they're far too busy to come out and see something, aren't they?' She smiled a tired agreement and seeing salvation in Joshua, moved away with covert haste.

They stood together rather awkwardly, with neither able to forget the quiet intensity and barely disguised violence of the scene they had left behind, nor get their minds off the conversation that Abraham and Adam might be having. Finally the school bell rang to let people know that it was time to go in.

As they sat in the semi-darkness of the school hall, which smelt of gym shoes and chalk, Joshua, on the end of the row, had time to contemplate the faces of the Vermeulen family in the half-light. Nella and Thomas's faces expectant, still quite rosy and breathless from the games outside, clearly not entirely convinced that coming in for a lecture was a worthy exchange for the wild games in the darkness outside, but too well brought-up to cause trouble. Esther sat forward on her seat, perched really, with a painfully straight back, shoulders raised as if ready to leap up at any moment; wringing her hands in her lap and fingers that went constantly to her ring, twisting it round and round. Her lower lip was white with teeth marks as her eyes darted about anxiously – hyper-alert. Yet she too contained her agitation and gave the appearance of complete stillness to anyone sitting further away. She felt Joshua's eyes on her, turned briefly and sent him a polite, half-stranger's smile.

His contemplations were interrupted by crackling flashes of lurid light as the old projector in the equipment and boot room leapt haltingly into intermittent action, after several attempts. He could not help but think of Rommel and smiled, more familiar now with the bungled but game determination of outdated machinery to keep going. Only now did he think to look down on the piece of paper he had been handed on entering the hall beyond the foyer. 'The White Lady of Brandberg' it said in runic stick-like font and beneath in smaller lettering, 'the Bushman art of Southern Africa and possibilities for our town.' He glanced over at the children – why had they been excited about this?

Then he saw the not very covert passing of notes, sweets and other communications amongst the adolescents all seated on the last two rows, and grinned. He turned to concentrate on the lecture and slide show. The first slides were of the Mountain and the Namibian desert, and of the beautiful lodge and wonderful tourist accommodation and safari possibilities of holidays in Namibia.

They were accompanied by the voice of the headmaster, who had seen in this, real possibilities for Abelshoop. 'We have paintings, too,' he finished his part of the talk. 'We also could be a haven for tourists.' He paused and beamed at his flock and their parents.

'And now I will hand you over to Ms Shackleton, who will tell us a little more about the actual paintings and the stories they tell.'

A slide of The White Lady herself came up again; an elegant figure, half painted white, with red hair and taking a long stride apparently, arms energetic and wide. The young archaeologist turned the house lights down and began to read in a clear English accent.

Eternally she walks there, young, beautiful, supple, almost aerian in poise. In ancient times, all her own people also walked to contemplate her adored image and went on walking for centuries, not only Men but Oryxes, Giraffes, Elephants and Rhinoceros swayed by her magic . . . One day she drew me from the sombre gloom of our European caverns, and the great Jan Smuts sent me towards her, in the fierce sunshine of Damarraland. Across deserts, we walked towards her. I and my friends and guides, captivated by her incomparable grace.

'These are the fanciful words of the Abbe Breuil about this most famous painting, which on only slightly closer inspection turns out to be a man.' Appreciative laughter as she zoomed in appropriately. 'Yet his words express something of the power of these paintings,' she went on more seriously. 'And it is the source of that power I want to explore with you tonight. Professor Oelke states that this power can only be discovered if these paintings are taken more seriously than such romanticised projections of a repressed European psyche. They need to be looked at with care and scientific accuracy.'

Slide after slide of the delicate paintings came up, with pencils, key rings, and rulers laid alongside it on the rock for scale, and the young woman's voice spoke into the darkness. It droned a little, enumerating first, as the scientist in Joshua knew it must, to establish credentials of the theory, all the statistical results of findings: sizes, elevations, combinations, colours, animals – be they anomalous or a perfect fit to the pattern expected. Then the tone changed, lifted, as the speaker turned to the skill and detail of the artists.

Joshua sensed the restlessness of the audience. Like the youth, many of the adults had come largely for the social occasion, for the cakes and popcorn afterwards and to be seen too probably. Only one sat with eyes riveted onto the pictures coming up. Joshua watched her now. It was difficult to see what had caught her attention. He was not sure she was even listening to a single word, so intense was her faraway concentration on the pictures. Her tense back, her anxiously clasped hands, made him wonder whether her fascination was not part horror, though it was difficult to see why. But she was certainly spellbound by the event in some way.

Now the voice became warm with enthusiasm, speaking of shamanistic experiences, of the three-tiered world of the San belief. The slides scrolled backwards and forwards with almost dizzying speed as the voice explained with the deep excitement of enthusiastic conviction the significance of the "canvasses" chosen by the artists. How the rock was part of the painting, and how between then the rock and the painting represented a site of where potency had been found – a bridge between the worlds of pan-San belief. She explained that the White Lady was really a shaman ritual dancer surrounded by therianthropes. How the paintings recorded travels into the dream world where the shamans went as hunters to find the rain animals, and to fetch the rain for their land.

Joshua noticed that the audience, apart from Esther, remained unconvinced and were clearly ready for the refreshments now. They had been surrounded by these paintings all their lives – and had been taught mostly to think nothing of them. They were simply part of the landscape. But Joshua found himself thinking of Witkopje and the Kudu coming out the cracked rock. Of Klaas dancing, of Hendrik's honey-coloured eyes as he spoke of the white kudu and the blessing of rain.

The speaker, sensing the restlessness of the audience, now began telling stories of the activities of Kaggen a San god, often in mantis shape, and of his love for the eland, and his battles with the meerkats. The audience laughed politely but Joshua wondered how much of this remained incomprehensible or at least indifferent to the rural and mostly white South African audience.

The headmaster took over again to close the official part of the evening. 'So you see people: our white kudu of Pniel could become like the White Lady of Brandberg – a beacon to call tourists to our land. Tourists who will make it possible to go on living here as we have always lived.'

Someone called from the back: 'Ja Frans, we know your brother works for the Parks Board. Bloody let us get something to drink now.' This met with general approval. The audience clapped for the young archaeologist, boo-ed the headmaster and got up to get into the foyer where refreshments were being served.

Afterwards Joshua found the speaker. She was from Wits University and the lecture was a by-product of research for a doctoral dissertation under the supervision of Professor Oelke, international authority on San shamanic traditions. He smiled and thanked the woman dressed in khaki, even for such an occasion.

'It was an interesting lecture,' he began uncertainly.

She smiled back politely, used to this awkwardness, then suddenly paid attention to the man speaking to her.

'The paintings here are like those you speak of, but they are of a kudu.'

'Yes?' she said encouraging.

'Can they mean the same thing though? Can this kudu also stand for such an experience?'

'Quite possibly.' The scientist in her was cautious, wishing her supervisor were there to be asked, and to dispel the uncertainty with her calm methodical explanations.

'They have a dance they call the white kudu, too.'

'Then, very possibly! In the southern Drakensberg too it is occasionally the kudu – who the bushmen say smells like the Eland – that represents the potency being hunted. So yes – it is possible, but the paintings would need to be studied in some detail to be entirely sure. In Brandberg of course, the shaman is surrounded by Oryx, not eland.'

'Thank you again,' Joshua said, not sure that this was the answer he had hoped for. It dispelled not one of the cobwebs his mind was spinning about his experiences on Pniel so far. 'Shall we have some tea, then,' he offered, 'and drink to our sciences in the service of the miracles of modern tourism?'

Ms Shackleton grimaced, then laughed, 'Thank you yes,' she answered, switching her projector off and wiping its surface with solicitous movements not unlike those of Strooi, Joshua decided, and wondering why her name seemed familiar.

They moved back into the foyer, Joshua now talking of the rocks in the Abelshoop area, and describing the painting of the kudu, based on the quartz intrusion of Witkopje.

'Yes, the rock surfaces are often part of the painting,' the young archaeologist said. 'The sites were carefully chosen and were often meaningful in ways we do not yet fully understand.' She paused as he drank his tea.

'The paintings here must be among the last before we enter the Kalahari,' she added thoughtfully. 'Not much in the way of exposed rock surface in the Kalahari itself.'

'You should speak to my host about that,' Joshua said, thinking of Adam's collection of flint tools and the drawings in his hallway.

'Unfortunately he is not here,' Joshua added as he saw Ms Shackleton's eyes sweep the room. 'It is a pity, he would have enjoyed your talk, I think. How long can you stay?'

'I must leave tomorrow. I have fieldwork waiting in the Drakensberg.'

'Well, perhaps another time – I'll leave you his address and phone number.'

'Thank you.'

A child barrelled into Joshua and he remembered Nella and Thomas. He saw the time, said a rapid goodnight and went in search of Esther and the children.

Esther was relieved to finish a conversation about the ironing sins of cleaning women and turned quickly to Joshua. 'Come,' she said, amid the raised eyebrows of the surrounding ladies, 'we had better find Nella and Thomas and get home.'

'Goodnight, Tant Rina,' she added sweetly.

Joshua smiled at the ladies, calling for Thomas and Nella. There was no response. Finally they found them, hidden behind the shed, crouched together in the thorny bush.

'Nella, Thomas, what's the matter?' Joshua asked as he dragged Thomas out, 'why didn't you answer when we called?' Then he saw that Thomas had been crying and decided to get them home as quickly as possible before asking any questions.

A group of younger children had been stealthily following Joshua and Esther and now they were accompanied, from a safe distance, by calls of "Bushman's child" and "why don't you dance for the rain, Thomas?"

He turned to Nella to ask what this was all about, but she only glared at him to hurry up, her arms about the shaking shoulders of her small brother. He bundled them quickly into the car and pulled out of the drive too quickly, scattering the jeering children.

'What was all that about?' he asked as soon as they had put some distance between them and the school.

'Ag,' Nella replied, 'they always tease him because of Ou Groote and his white hair.' Joshua sensed that there was more to it, but did not like to ask right now, the child seeming terribly distressed. He drove as quickly as he dared in the dark on the shifting sand.

Esther too seemed distressed so he tried to distract them. 'What did you think of the lecture?'

She realised what he was doing and responded politely, neutrally, keeping an eye on Thomas who soon fell asleep and even Nella was nodding with exhaustion.

Then Esther turned to Joshua with a sudden intensity: 'I hate this world.'

'Which world?'

'This Kalahari, Vaalbos place – the world of the Bushmen. I hate the way it is everywhere, I am frightened by their stories – by the way everything becomes part of their stories – their dreams. Their stories about dreaming things into existence. And I hate the way our lives make no sense here.'

'But their stories are beautiful, aren't they?'

Now Esther was crying, too. Tentatively Joshua patted her shoulder, taking one hand off the steering wheel. 'What is it that got to you so much?'

'Ag,' she said, 'their world mad as it was, makes sense here in this desert. It is crazy but it all fitted and their actions all have a purpose, no, I mean, a meaning. Not like ours, not like the ordinary life of white South Africans, which seems always meaningless, mistaken, and stupid out here.'

Feeling a little out of practise with such conversations, Joshua hazarded a consolation. 'Perhaps it need not be,' lame, he did not know how to answer such despair.

She smiled then across at him, acknowledging the inept attempt. 'Perhaps not, perhaps we just have not found what it means yet.' But then the intensity broke through again. 'We are trapped here by things, by gods even, which we do not understand!'

After that they sat in silence on that dark drive, with the children nodding off in the back. Then Joshua asked again, tentatively, but needing to know now, 'Do you mean the stories about the white kudu, and the strangers everybody is waiting for?'

'Yes,' she said, 'yes I do. It is a story Abraham has been secretly fighting all his life.'

'Why?'

'Because he thinks it will mean that he loses this land.'

And then Joshua discovered what it was exactly which had caused the argument between Adam and his son Abraham. It had been a preliminary contract detailing the conditions of potential sale of the land and the mineral rights as well as the possibilities of mining, which circumvented the various issues of the land claims battle.

'Adam,' she said, carefully pronouncing the name, not used to calling her father-in-law that, 'has wanted to sell the land for a long time. He cannot bear it anymore and he thinks that is the most practical solution.'

'Solution? To the land claims battles? Or something else?'

'Both. He needs money also to take Thomas to doctors and their mother always wanted Nella to study something, maybe music.'

Joshua saw again fleetingly the photo of the woman on Adam's desk.

'Yes,' he said, 'I can understand that. Nella plays well, doesn't she?'

'I wouldn't know.'

'Abraham feels that the land is not his father's alone to decide over. By our traditions, he should inherit it and it is all he has ever known.' She spoke defensively of her husband.

'He knows land, he understands it. Not like the Bushmen do, but like a farmer does – to work it, to make it give something back. He does not know what he should do with money instead.'

'But I thought, from what Adam has told me,' Joshua began tentatively, 'that Adam knows that losing the land is inevitable and that he needs to prepare for that.'

'Ag, but Abraham will be lost without land. Why can his father not see that?'

'I think he can, but there is not much he can do.'

'He could fight! Abraham does. Why does he never fight? Not for himself and not for his land! What is wrong with a man like that?'

Joshua did not know then what had defeated Adam and Abraham, though the son did not know it yet either. But next to him, sat an unhappy woman who would soon be returning to her own troubled world from a night out and a lecture about the possible wealth of the tourist trade for impoverished rural areas.

'I think Adam would rather face the possibility of losing the land to a mining project, which could change the future positively. He hopes, I think, that it is better than losing money to fruitless land claim battles,' he said gently.

'What if we gain the land by that battle? Abraham thinks we still can. He has sweated blood and tears into that land. It should be his. No one knows it better than he does.' She was being stubborn now and Joshua could not tell how much of it was her own and how much that of her looming young-old husband. It made him irritable.

'I think anyone can see it is a losing battle!'

'That does not matter,' she cried then, 'it does not matter. He has fought it so long, he does not know what he would do without it. It has been part of him all his life.'

They drove on silence.

Joshua dropped the two children off with their father then drove Esther home as Abraham had taken their bakkie.

'Thank you, Joshua,' Esther said, conciliatory. 'I am glad you were there, otherwise we would simply not have gone and the evening would have been spent in arguments.' A pause. Exposed, she wanted to explain.

'Abraham and his father are alike in this one way: they are both as stubborn as each other and this stupid land they love.' And she leaned over swiftly and planted a kiss on his cheek before leaving the car and softly closing the door. Joshua put his hand up to his cheek. It was wet. She had been crying.

On Joshua's table back at camp lay a message from Paul – he was pleased to come back to the Kimberly office, some of his samples were showing very interesting results. Urgent – before the trenching. "Damn." Joshua had thought to start trenching as soon as the excavators, already too long delayed, arrived. They were due once again by Monday. Still he sighed, knowing that he would do as he was told.

4
The Journals

Lefika Mining and Exploration Company liked to do things in style. The name had been adopted as part of their new African renaissance image, which involved concepts like *slick, organised, downsized, efficient and eco-sound* as well as Politically Correct. The managers liked to think of themselves as leaders and motivators rather than managers. They wore bright ties and all had one golden earring in their left ears, the result of a communal bet over a certain high target. They were worn like trophies; the managers felt alive and young with them.

A meeting had been scheduled with one or two bigwigs from head office, who had come down specially, apparently more "specially", than Joshua himself had, leaving his precious project unsupervised. Paul did not think it was an apt comparison, or amusing. He was in a state of high agitation and said the project had suddenly become urgent, that the laboratory results were 'astonishing' and he hated doing this to his young colleague. So Joshua barely had time to shower and change; put on a fumbling tie and a white shirt before appearing cool and collected in the Robbenheimer Room of the Kimberley hotel, pretending to nurse a pre-lunch sherry. The lunch passed in a haze of endless congratulatory drinks, and all Joshua understood was that his project had suddenly become the focus of all the important people in the company because the chemical analyses of the sand samples, and one or two core samples, looked very promising.

'Promising for what?' Joshua finally managed to ask Paul in a whisper.

'Gold, you idiot,' Paul hissed back, half-affectionately.

'Gold? I thought I was looking for diamonds.'

Paul glanced at his bosses, who had not paid the slightest attention but were discussing the merits of some golf course. 'Ours is not to wonder why . . .' he grinned, 'anyway, they think it's very promising.'

Joshua emptied his glass. Some of the anomalies began to make a little more sense now.

Paul watched comprehension sink in and added quietly, 'And it has all become a bit high priority and hush-hush, before the government can nationalise the land; or any of the other land claims come through. I find it a bit tasteless, actually.'

So an innocuous "mopping up" geology project had become urgent as a result of the land claims battles raging in the district. If at all possible the company wanted results before the land changed hands. They had favourable agreements with both Adam and the Radcliffe sisters, and did not want to face the whole "the land where our ancestors lie buried" palaver – despite their image, Paul said wryly – which always ensued when mineral and mining rights were discussed.

Lefika Mining and Exploration Company, Paul explained, also wanted a show-case New South African mine. One which would bring employment to the locals rather than using cheaper migrant labour, and improved the life of the community. It would offer services while generating money and gain the trust of the shareholders in a sustainable small mining operation in accordance with all the rules of decency and the promises of the freedom charter – except Article 25: land ownership.

'So we will need detailed results soon to present to the decision-makers and the shareholders to convince them of the value of a possible mine at Abelshoop – in the romantic wilderness of Karoo and Kalahari.' Mr Redding had clearly found poetry at the bottom of the fifth glass of wine.

At best Joshua felt disgruntled; science and its discoveries were to be sacrificed to an as yet imaginary greed and pragmatism about land ownership that struck him as deeply flawed. Political expediency seemed to him then only another version of exploitation and disowning, of exiling people in their own land. In the midst of only a semi-scientific speech about the trenching and alluvial deposits with fractures marked by quartz, he suddenly remembered with painful vividness the face of the golden-eyed old man saying, "the little people will dance on the earth again, when the white kudu goes home."

"Where is home," he thought "for anybody in Abelshoop?" Only Paul noted this with any sympathy.

The next morning Joshua asked Paul, 'Why have I uncovered something like this in just over a few months, when my predecessor had failed in several years?'

In answer, Paul handed Joshua a box and said, 'John's logbooks are in here with some notes on the project.'

'John?'

'Your predecessor, he sent us everything, when he left the company. There's some personal stuff, too, which you can probably throw away. But the logbooks could be worth looking at.'

'Why has no one else done so?'

'Well, you'll see. They are not exactly light or always entirely useful reading. See what you make of them, there may be something useful in them. He was an odd man: good, thorough geologist, but some of his notes were quite cryptic and he was likely to quote Shakespeare in his reports – quite pompous at times. He also thought that reading Rider Haggard would be good preparation for exploration geology in Africa, and a little more appropriately, *'The Story of an African Farm'*. Still, he was a good geologist despite these aberrations and the journals and later logbooks should have some useful information for you. They might also make more sense to you now that you have seen the area.'

Joshua eagerly took the box, for there remained many mysteries about this fluvial deposit of an ancient river with such anomalous concentrations of various elements here in Kimberlite country. He was longing to solve the puzzle. Not wanting to read in the dingy office, he got himself a sandwich from the Belgravia Café and took himself out to the dairy farm, found a quiet spot and opened the box. The logbooks were clearly of a later date than the ones he had already seen. But like the others, these also were carefully and neatly kept. All the logging was done in blue ink – in fountain pen, which must have been extraordinarily difficult to keep going in the desert with the fine sand getting into everything after a day in the field. The sketches and graphs were done in pencil. Later it was no longer simple core logging, but commentary on trenches and some real estimates of the size of the ore body.

But in the margins, scribbled in vivid green ink were comments of an entirely un-geological nature, which gradually took over the page. There were too many comments on the beauty of the place, the whimsy of its people, and sporadic bursts of poetry. '*I love it when it rains here, the silence, the peace is deepened by that insistent, rapid sound. The smell of the earth answers the rain – a union of the gods, Hendrik calls it. A union, which lifts the parched spirit.*' "Solid geophysical information, that!" Joshua thought wryly. It went on over the page, '*Then one's own merely human thoughts are free to roam, too, free to dream oneself into the mystery of things.*' Joshua cringed and felt like a trespasser, but read on nonetheless. And so he began to get to know a careful and thoughtful scientist as well as a man both generous and tormented with self-doubt. Once again he felt not at all sure that he wanted to delve thus into the being of another.

The last page: *What should I write about Pniel and what would it mean? The grey river, the black Kimberlites, the iron-rich sand, the koppies, which do not rise like Sheba's breasts from the land pointing the way to Solomon's treasure. Only an elusive dead river's deposit twinkling like the mistaken stars in a sky I could not read. Only a woman I held long enough to love and be loved and then discarded, afraid...* Joshua turned from them, thinking they were not much use. He reached into the box and his hand closed on a bundle tied with red string. They were letters, addressed to Miriam. Surprised and curious, despite himself he opened one, and here the tortured solipsism was relieved. The words, in being directed to Miriam, found a clarity, a joyful weight, which flew true and certain, released from the relentless circling angst of a rather over-educated and self-conscious sensibility.

I try now to remember the first day I saw her, realised her beauty and find it is impossible. Somehow she emerged from this tangle of desert and myth and treasure-seeking, from the quartz and the red sand. And then it was as if she had always been there – those dark eyes finding mine, those bare feet, planted before me: challenge or invitation? I did not know. And still I can hear her laughter.

It had been a long and dusty road. John Shackleton had driven all the way from Johannesburg where he had given a report on the value of further exploration of the Kimberlites in the Northern Cape, not only for diamonds but base metals, too. It had been a good report he knew, and things were going well for him. He was missing his family, his wife and young daughter, a little – but life was an adventure, too. He had arrived in the afternoon and made his way immediately to the farmer's house, wishing to thank the man for his hospitality as courtesy required, and wanting to get the first introduction done.

In the beautiful garden of the farmhouse, he had heard laughter and splashing of water – a shocking wastefulness he thought in such a dry area. In the garden was a woman in shorts and t-shirt holding a hose and she was splashing two giggling children with the sparkling, precious water. One a toddler, naked and gurgling with delight, the other a boy of about twelve in boxer shorts, now glowering at the younger child over some imagined preference in his mother. John stopped a moment caught by the simple, intimate scene, before the woman saw him and laughingly turned the water off, scooped the slippery toddler in her arms and came towards him. He rocked a little on his feet as he always did when feeling uncertain, and fluttered his hands restlessly behind his back.

'You must be Mr Shackleton?'

'Yes,' pause, 'Mrs Vermeulen?'

She smiled assent, 'this is Nella and here' – an imperious and conciliatory hand to the boy, 'is Abraham.'

The scowling boy held out his hand. John shook it solemnly.

'Hallo Abraham. How nice to meet you.'

He straightened up and looked at her. 'Mrs Vermeulen, I am sorry to intrude, but I wished to introduce myself to your husband and thank him for the beautiful campsite as soon as I arrived. Is he in?'

Miriam smiled at the tall formally dressed man, at his rather ceremonious courtesy, the like of which she had not heard since she left her parents' care many years ago.

'Yes. He is in his study. If you would follow me, I will show you.' And they walked around the house to another door facing the back garden, where Adam was sitting at his desk, trying to make sense of the chaos of papers on his desk and the uncertain finances of his large farm during a drought.

Miriam had left them there to take the children to the kitchen for a drink and cookies, out of the heat. She settled them on the couch and read to them, from the *Mantis and the Moon*. Nella soon fell asleep and Abraham slipped off to play with the dogs outside. Miriam was left thinking about Hendrik's stories so like the ones she had just read – and then her thoughts turned to the man who had just arrived.

Adam invited him to dinner that evening, to which he returned still in his suit and with a bottle of wine.

'Mrs Vermeulen,' he said, 'I'm so sorry I do not have flowers for my hostess. You should have had carnations, I think. But,' an ironic half smile, 'in the circumstances the thought of them will have to be enough.'

Miriam laughed and nodded, nonplussed by such easy charm. 'Please call me Miriam.'

'In that case you shall call me John,' he beamed at her.

They shook hands again, as Adam joined them distractedly from his study.

'Please,' Miriam said, 'Adam will you open the wine? I must see to things in the kitchen.'

It had been a pleasant evening, though Adam had remained far away in his thoughts about his land, hunters' meetings and the effect of the repeated states of emergency on his labourers.

John, despite being a geologist preferred to talk about books or concerts he had been to in England, and about which he told wonderful anecdotes most of the evening to entertain Miriam. He had about him an assurance as he spoke of these things, a natural arrogance almost, which was tempered by his slightly diffident charm. He seemed to Miriam a creature from a different world. One she had sensed in her mother's stories about Germany. And she felt again her mother's homesickness – her longing for the ceremonious grace of that European cultural life, of which she had only been able to dream in the desert.

So the months had passed, and finally in November the rain had come and relieved everyone a little. And then the Christmas season was upon them. It was John's first Christmas in the Southern hemisphere. He was amused by the fake, tatty snow in the shop window, and the tinsel which faded quickly in the relentless sun; but then also moved by the devotion with which Miriam passed on to her children her parents' traditions, which were made almost impossible by the searing heat of December.

He came upon her one afternoon, baking the fragrant breads, biscuits of their home country here in the ridiculous heat: cinnamon, almonds and honey. But she looked charming in a frazzled kind of way: hair curling about that high forehead and as always coming undone in the nape, cheeks red and eyes bright with joy as well as impatience. She had given him a long cool drink and sent him out onto the shady stoep until she finished. And then she had come out to join him, her arms up embracing the freedom of all the baking done for the day.

She'd smiled at him and asked, shyly, 'Will you excuse me for about ten minutes.'

'Of course.'

She ran to the dam, he discovered afterwards, and simply flung herself into the water full of mud and chlorophyll. He would have loved to have seen her, emerging from the almost solid water, streaming with weeds and her wet clothes tangling about her legs. By the time she returned to the house, the clothes were only slightly damp, but she felt able now to curl up on the bench near him and talk to him about whatever he wished. He always had something to discuss with her when he came over, a book he had read, or a poem. And she was glad to talk, being lonely with Adam so preoccupied and often away at meetings in Kimberley or even Johannesburg.

They would take long walks along the river to discuss them, or simply to watch the bright dart of the malachite kingfisher, to listen for the sudden splash of the leguan disturbed by the dogs, or to play with the echo like children.

On this occasion he had brought her Neruda's *Hundred Sonnets* and with his usual mixture of charm and diffidence said, 'I think his Matilda must have been something like you.'

She had not known them, accepted them cheerfully and promised to read them while he jetted home for the week between Christmas and New Year. And when she had read them, she was filled both with joy that he had given them and with fear as she realised for the first time what it might mean. Alone with these thoughts, she turned to Hendrik and said to him, 'Hendrik tell me again the story of the white kudu.'

John endured the festive season with a restless impatience on the other side of the world and thought only of her reading those sonnets. When he returned he was determined to speak to her.

On the evening he made his declaration, she wore a white dress which shone luminous as the quartz on Witkopje in the moonlight. They had sat, Adam, Miriam and John, long into the night over the snoek braai Adam had prepared and drank the impossibly light wine of the desert vineyards along the great river. Miriam and John had talked again about this place, the meeting point of Karoo and Kalahari, its many mysteries, the poetry of Adam Small, while Adam wondered about the likelihood of a mine saving Abelshoop from its slow and painful demise amid the threats of land claims as the violent end of Apartheid escalated around the town.

Then Adam had decided to go to bed. It would be cattle dipping in the morning, always a tiring and long day and then he had to head for Johannesburg for a week to meet lawyers and the mining stockholders. So he left his lovely wife to walk John to the gate across the dark rose garden and the open veld. And John had chosen that moment to speak, though he did not understand exactly what had come over him, there in that strange place, which, he was half afraid, half hopeful was changing forever with his discoveries. Gold and diamonds anomalously together, a rare alchemy of the earth . . .

They were both even then, afraid of that moment, which opened the door to such pain, such joy: all that lay within another human being, revealed by love. It had been unimaginable – to a scientist, searching vainly for gold in the far distant inhuman past of the earth – and to a woman who had turned her back on her own world for the sake of the quiet desert and a humble farmer.

They were intensely aware of each other as they walked. Miriam led the way, laughing at his tall, urban uncertainty in the dark veld. He followed close behind, their easy friendship now almost unbearable. When they got to the gate, which lead to his encampment, they stopped. She leaned on the gate, stepped up onto it, and was swinging gently to and fro in the darkness, as she looked up at the stars and pointed out the Southern Cross to him and its nightly march across this more deeply and widely starred heaven than he had ever seen.

'Look,' she whispered, 'it is the sky caught in Hendrik's net of stars,' glad for once to be the one instructing. On an impulse, John put his hands upon her shoulders, which stilled her movement abruptly. She froze as he said without thought, 'That's better' meaning his own longing, the ache, which had been stilled by that touch. She leapt off the gate and turned, eyes blazing on him, 'What do you mean?'

'I, I just wanted, I needed to touch you.'

'Why?' her persistence. 'You can't just do that.'

'Do what?'

'Touch people, really touch them and think the world can stay the same,' fierce, hopeful too. She turned and left him to find his own way home, to the small camp beneath the peppercorn trees.

The next morning Miriam found John and said, her eyes serious: 'We must talk about this – walk with me,' imperious again.

Then she said, 'There is no decent way to do this.'

'No,' he said, 'there probably isn't.'

'Then we shouldn't. We have friendship – that must be enough. And our families.'

He agreed. But they found themselves constantly drawn together, walking again along the river or meeting suddenly at Witkopje, while the children played their wild games about it. All the while Adam hoped only for gold, for diamonds to save the farm from a ruin he now thought inevitable.

'What is happening?' John asked one day, filled with tenderness at her struggle to hide her joy at seeing him.

'Come with me to Hendrik,' she responded, 'I think he knows.'

And as John listened with chilled spine to the story of the white kudu, he knew he would not step back from it now. As they walked back, he took her hand and asked, 'what choice do we have?'

She agreed.

Who can describe the joy of their meetings? Amongst all the agony of betrayal, of deceit, of the lack of freedom, there was undeniably the simple joy of being impossibly together. John was enchanted by the discovery of that joyous body and overwhelmed with wonder and gratitude for its shy generosity. Every day was celebration and the bleak desert was radiant and perfect. He felt invulnerable, unconquerable and thought not a moment about how this gift would change both their lives.

And when Adam did discover it, like them he felt helpless and thought of his brother Gideon, who had first brought Miriam to Pniel. Gideon had met her at Stellenbosch University where he was a junior lecturer in the German department and she had arrived from her missionary home to study the literature of her parents' tongue. Adam had never been able to understand why she had in the end chosen him, the quiet farmer instead.

But she had fallen in love with the land, with the vast possibilities of it and with Hendrik's tales, which had been Adam's only chance to offer her anything like the erudition of his brother.

'I never did think she was mine,' he realised, 'only wanted her to love this place, this home. So I focused on that. And now I will not fight the inevitable. Like Gideon I will simply step back.'

While John wrote in his diary: *How does one atone? After the sordid discoveries, shame and fear drove me back, drove me away, and I could not face Abelshoop or the desert again. I awoke in hospital with my wife, Elaine sitting beside me. She had flown me to Johannesburg, away from the desert and back to the comprehensible urban world of medical routine, where I was being treated for a severe concussion. Elaine seemed glad to have me back, but also afraid of what had happened to me. When I told her, she claimed I had been lost in another country, bewildered by its savagery, lonely and despairing without the usual comforts of a structured work environment. Blinded she called me and seduced too, by a woman gone native and shameless, no doubt.*

I knew it was not true. But Miriam was so far away and all our wonder lost in the domestic horrors of trust betrayed. And before me stood my daughter, eyes wide and alive with curiosity as she held a shimmering quartz out to me and asked me its name, while my wife used all our insurance to get me moved and taken care of in a hospital 'at home'.

So I chose to live in that reality, because I lacked the courage for the other one, the shimmering at heaven's gate, but also because I knew that here were small fidelities, bonds I could not break. I drifted back into my old place, I did not choose but simply let the current take me. I failed to act and could even pass myself off as honourable, as having done 'the right thing'...

And the language he used in his explanatory letter to Miriam now denied all the beauty of what had been. She was wounded deeply by it, more than by anything else. He had taken something which had seemed sacred, and turned it through the language of convention into something sordid.

The diaries continue: *My life now will be penance for the life I destroyed in three swift months. But where does one begin? This child of a desert farm had taught me to love with abundance unheard of in my world. The inklings she had given me enriched infinitely my life, my loving and my family. The world was transformed by her generous vision and I felt I owed her everything . . . I try to share that joy with Elaine, but she is too frightened, too hurt and of course rightly mistrusting now, to accept it. And my joy is tainted for her with the unbearable pangs of jealousy.*

And then it seems to me that I have used the gift Miriam offered merely to add decorative colour to my life; stored the precious memory of her in the recesses of my mind to be taken out and contemplated with nostalgia and ever-fainter stirrings of a pale heart. That remains unforgivable.

Relentless, merciless and self-indulgent was the notebook's self-berating: *I left her, feeling unworthy of her, of her generosity in giving herself so wholeheartedly to me, who could not stand so bravely in the glaring brightness of the day. This wonderful gift seemed wasted on me, so I tiptoed away and hoped to return with what little honour was still intact to the life which had been determined for me – a family, a sensible, good job – by gods less generous in their proportions than Hendrik's Ou Groote. To live a life reduced in joy but dutiful and good, nonetheless. Is that what I have done? I do not know.*

Joshua looked up and stared unseeing into the blue kopjes of Kimberley's dolomites. Everything he knew about Pniel had changed. This entirely unremarkable story of a failed romance had nevertheless transformed his project. It could no longer be purely geological, although geology was undoubtedly caught up in it. He leaned his head back against the rough, warm bark of the tree behind him and closed his eyes, wondering what story he had got caught in and whether he would be glad to be so.

'Hey, Joshua,' a voice recalled him. Paul had come to find him out at the dairy farm. 'Anything useful?'

'What?' Joshua joked, looking down to hide the other world still reeling in his thoughts, 'in Shakespeare quotes and comments on the joys of the wildlife?'

'Is that all?'

'No not all, there are some interesting surmises about the nature of the deposit that do not fit with his later decision.'

'Yes, we know. He left under rather a cloud as you know.'

'A cloud!' Joshua said, irritated with the ridiculousness of it all: the clichéd affair, the secrecy, the land claims, even the white kudu. 'I haven't read them all yet. So just have patience.'

'Well,' Paul said lifting the box for him, 'that will be some bedtime reading for you then, won't it?'

'Yes.'

'Paul, what exactly was that cloud, according to the company?'

'He had an affair with a woman out there, no one knows whether it was one of the farmers' wives, or a native of some description. Rumour has it he went a bit native, I suppose, and somehow his wife got wind of it and it all went rather pear shaped for him. Went home with his tail between his legs and has been the dutiful husband ever since.' Paul tried to dismiss it in the usual way: a witty comment, a bit of banter.

Joshua knew this humour was not cruel, but a way of preserving distance. So he laughed, letting the sound, the lightness of it, bring his mind back a little from the pain he had glimpsed in a story, which he sensed would catch them all, as it strove to an end, which might contain no laughter at all.

That night, Joshua found himself sitting in his bed, a cup of coffee at his side, opening the box once more. He thought about what he knew now: there had been an affair, somehow John had pulled back from it and Miriam had died – in childbirth, afterwards? He did not know, and knew he would never ask. Was it as simple as that? What did it mean?

Another thought struck him – what does the white kudu have to do with all this? All that promise Hendrik and Klaas talked about? He could see only pain in this story. Frustration took hold: why should any of this matter to him – a foreigner, a scientist, who had blundered into all of it by an accident of fate? He searched through the box and found at the very bottom a strange parcel addressed to John in Adam's hand, but shaky. He opened it and found another parcel, a little smaller, and a note:

John, she has left, I am not sure where. She gave this to you. You have no business trying to give it back. You must live with it as must we all. Adam

And with a profound sense of trespassing, Joshua undid the strings of the smaller parcel, addressed to Miriam, in John's unhappy hand. Inside were the torn and haphazardly piled pages of a notebook. Without a cover, they seemed exposed and forlorn.

Glued onto them were photographs, some old and faded, others fresh and full of life. They were a small chronology of Miriam's life on the Mission station in the deepest Kalahari, pictures of children posing, restrained for annual gifts to far away grandparents, but also of games in worlds unimaginably lost as one grows up: amid the golden veld and occasionally in the green luxury of another dam and another river. Each picture came with a brief and tender explanation and tracked a woman's life – school, awkward adolescence and finally her own children. Only the last one stood alone on its page – a portrait Joshua recognised from Adam's desk. She looked directly into the camera, with eyes serious and questioning yet also smiling, radiant with joy. On the back of this a note:

Dearest, there is so little you could possibly want on a birthday from this world I live in. I can only give you this: myself and an inkling of who I am – this person you so wondrously love.
Yours always, Miriam

There followed on other paper a later addition to the collection, pages of what seemed to be half diary, half notes and the odd snatches of poetry, surrounded by doodles – small flowing figures, whose delicate fluttery lines were highly expressive. Initially there were quotes from Rumi: *'deep within me moves the ocean of his splendour'* and then her own rather more inept fragments:

Thinking of you, I feel
Radiant with grateful wonder
– unexpected grace.

But gradually despair seeped in: *I am an animal now, seeking a place in which to go to ground, hopelessly licking at wounds I do not understand.*

A fragile prayer from the missionary compline:

As shadows lengthen into night
Mother of all, we pray to you
Show us still your tender care
Far from us drive all evil dreams
That prowl at night, and keep us free from stain

And the bleak daily round:

I wake up very early, while the day has as yet hardly begun and is still untouched by the noise of its inevitable business. Only the birds sing, half-sleepily, into the grey world of dawn. I creep softly to the kitchen, where the stone floor is breath-catchingly cold and real, to put the kettle on. The cats are the only ones to hear me and they weave in and out of my legs in greeting and pleading their hunger or pride at some poor feathered gift they have left for me under the table. I feed them and then tiptoe softly back to the bathroom to have a shower. Then with the birds more certain of their note, as the horizon pales and slowly the morning star begins its long farewell, I make tea, light a candle, play Bach's 'Schmücke dich, o liebe Seele', music to break with longing and then to heal with longing the human heart exiled from God. Is a landscape transformed by having Bach played in it? There is a book says so – and would the transformation last I wonder? It does not matter now. I try to read my dear Rilke, but it is too painful.

Joshua pictured the dark-haired despairing woman curled on the same bench in the photo, on Adam's wide stoep, with the window to the living room open so that she can hear the music without disturbing the family as the world comes awake around her. He imagined all the usual business of morning beginning. Hendrik going out to milk the cows, the dogs lying expectantly on the grass, cars alert, waiting for Adam. And he began to understand a little of such a quiet moment, of the stillness, which lies in such fragments of time from which one can quarry the strength to face the blazing days of love betrayed, and duty not enough.

Joshua struggled again to see where he would fit into this story. How he, not John, was to become the stranger of Hendrik's prophecy. He did not see what he could do to heal the wounds of such a story. So he searched on through the letters and journals, fragmented attempts to contain the pain and limit the damage which held Abelshoop enthralled still.

It was not new, this age-old tangle of love and betrayal and wonder and pain. And Joshua wondered then: How does one find responsible action in such a quagmire? It was a question Adam had asked his brother, too, when Miriam had left.

Gideon had answered, 'You lead the life in which you find yourself.'

'But it heals nothing and leaves despair entirely untamed. This will live, her name will echo always in the empty places of my skull.'

'What else will you do? Every morning you will lead this life, after the cats have quieted down and the music has reached its beautiful conclusion. You will make the breakfast, find school shoes, sign homework.'

'And what will they do – John and Miriam?'

'They will lead their lives, too.'

'And you – what did you do, when she chose me?'

'I am here now.'

'Yes.'

'Let that be your answer.'

Joshua felt their despair creep over his own as yet untouched heart as he read the final entries of Miriam's diaries: *I have let John into all the corners of my soul and there is no escape. Wherever I turn I see his face and it is no longer consolation.*

I have no name left, I am no longer the blessed beloved of John, nor Adam's Miriam, I am no longer my father's daughter, nor

Adam's wife nor yet myself. I am no one and I feel myself begin to fade.

She had risked much: scandal, gossip, her family's disapproval, and had hated her own betrayal, but had not thought she was alone in her doings. Then she found herself treading air above a terrible and lonely abyss.

When Miriam found that her despair neither blossomed into suicide, nor faded and healed, she made a different choice entirely. She made a gift of her life to others having no more use for it herself. She gave her son to Adam and gave herself to the work of missionaries deeper in the Kalahari where the river's song and the dance of the white kudu could not disturb her memories with longing.

In local legend of course she had been swallowed by the gaping holes of the trenches where she and John had been discovered, trapped by the fall of the excavator perched on the side of a trench made unstable by rain.

Yet Joshua sensed that there was something she did not see. He peered into her world, trying to see what it was. She did not see Ou Groote, the white kudu, who often stood just beyond her vision, waiting for her to look up to see him. What had Hendrik called him? An odd sound, harsh but ending plaintively. Joshua could not remember but saw again the animal in his mind's eye beneath the waving willow trees. !Kia, Hendrik had said, !Kia was the moment of union of the embodied soul with the great world soul.

And that was the best one could hope for, Joshua read late into the night in the English translation of the *Duino Elegies*, borrowed from Cecilia. It seemed strange to him that a somewhat effete and pampered, self-indulgent German poet, and a Bushman farmhand, could nonetheless share the same wisdom: that in that moment of longing for the divine lay the radical dignity of all souls, no matter how imperfectly they long for an impossible perfection.

And then Joshua could see what Ou Groote had seemed to know all along: that the longing itself is a glorious gift, not only its achievement. How had Miriam and John not seen it too? He dreamed of them that night and many others – until their voices and faces, their hope and despair, became as familiar to him as his own.

5
Kara/tuma

When Joshua prepared to head back to Abelshoop, he left with many injunctions from various senior geologists and management types to find enough gold and diamonds to make him, and all of them rich. But his thoughts would not be drawn from the box, which sat next to him on the passenger seat, all the way back to Pniel. The excavators had arrived just an hour before him and Adam was entertaining them on his stoep with cold beer and hunting stories.

'. . . and the great kudu bull had been wounded by the shot. He fell at first and I thought, good it's OK after all. But it was not. He got up again and galloped off. I had to chase him, the bloody American would not come, but only sat down right there and waited. I was furious, he should have let me re-site his gun on arrival. I never allowed another hunting guest to refuse.'

'Anyway so began the longest hunt of my life. I followed the track, Hendrik, here, helped me, though he was bleeding so it was not hard. He must have been wounded quite badly, there was much blood. But he ran far all the same – a great battle. His hind legs were weakening, we could tell by the way they sank deeper and deeper in the sand – he was in pain. Finally none of us could run any more. The kudu had stopped beneath a camel thorn. He was brave – he turned and faced me, waited for me to catch up. I stood stock-still and we looked at each other for a long time. 'I am sorry,' I said to him, 'I am sorry.'

He stood completely still, presenting his side but head turned towards me, only his skin shivered because the flies were bothering his wound. I lifted the gun, our eyes locked. He and I were one in that moment. I pulled the trigger and the shot rang louder than ever I have heard a shot ring. He crumpled. I went over to him, knew I had to, knelt and put my hand on his neck as the light died out of his eyes. I bloody wept over that animal as I have rarely wept. I killed some part of myself that day, but also felt myself a part of something so much bigger than just the two of us. It was the animal's gift, much more than his life to me...

'Ah,' he interrupted himself when he saw Joshua standing listening just below the steps, 'here is Mr Hunter now, gentlemen.'

'Adam,' Joshua said, 'I didn't know you hunted.'

'I don't anymore.'

The afternoon was taken up with poring over maps and placing the excavators. Then Joshua took the manager of the excavation company out to dinner at the Hotel in Abelshoop, where they ate wonderfully succulent kudu steaks with the inevitable pumpkin and peas. The managers spent the night there and would go back north in the morning. Joshua went back to camp well past midnight. As he turned off the tarred road into the newly bulldozed turn-off for Wonderfontein and Pniel, he stopped suddenly, arrested by a movement on the road ahead of him. He switched off his headlamps and waited, staying in the car. And there he was: a kudu – tall, graceful, the large ears playing softly in the wind, the sounds of the world made beautiful by that listening. The proud head held high and looking forward with that charming mixture of curiosity and intentness. Slowly Joshua got out of his car, the kudu watched quietly, ears still and forward now, the face gentle. They stood opposite each other: the wild animal and the man, who prided himself on being nothing if not a realist, yet here he stood, hoping that he was seeing again the white kudu, which belonged to the stars. He did not get a chance to speak, he took a deep breath and the kudu was gone, the road empty and silent. Joshua walked to the place where he had stood but in the dim starlight, he could not be sure there were any tracks. As he turned to leave, his eye was caught by a soft shimmering on the ground. Just off the road lay a rock freshly exposed: quartz and mica glinting in the pale light amidst the dark, still steaming pellets which the animal had left behind. He picked the rock up, smiling at his skittishness and put it into his pocket as a reminder of who he was and what he was doing here.

In the morning the excavation began. Ben and Josef vied with each other to be allowed to drive the monstrous machines which they immediately named Kgokgo – monsters with which to frighten children at night. Joshua thought nostalgically of Rommel, who in comparison with these huge efficient monsters seemed quite friendly and harmless, leaving only her own tiny bite, not these gaping wounds across the pans. Still, soon the joy of discovery overcame these feelings and he hurled himself with enthusiasm into the trenches left by the greedy mouths of the machines to see exposed at last the pure white quartz vein, unstained by the iron of the earth, which marked the fracture-edge of the mineral rich deposit. It was beautifully, unbelievably, white. He searched eagerly for the telltale streaks of black tourmaline, which indicated the passing at least of his ore body. The impurities in the quartz were the clues he needed.

As soon as school was out Thomas joined him in the trenches, handling with delight with the sharp and sparkling white pieces of quartz which were tumbled on the ground by the machines.

Nella too could not keep away, but watched it all with wide-eyed wonder. 'Where is the gold, Joshua,' she kept calling, 'Where is the gold?'

Joshua laughed, 'You can't see it Nella.' He was glad of their company, because Adam now kept away, asking only that Joshua come by and tell him how things were going. Joshua knew only too well now the reason for this hesitation and the knowledge, unspoken, lay heavily between them. It must have been a dreadful day, Joshua thought: the public nature of the revelation of his betrayal and hurt because others had found them, half buried in the trench. And then the waiting for the verdict at the hospital while fear for her safety battled with anger and pain; the phone call to John's wife to tell her of his injury must have been extraordinarily painful. So Adam kept away, trying to find a new source of water, to build a new dam for his sheep.

And then one day at midday on Wonderfontein, just as Esther – who was spending more and more time at the excavations, terrified but fascinated, too – was coming up with a bottle of ice cold water for them all, Ben refused to go on trenching. One minute he was carefully aiming the head of the excavator in order to pull it back towards himself and the body of the machine along the line the first layer had already made, and the next he halted wide-eyed, listening for something in the wind, above the roar of the engine. Then he switched the machine off, climbed down and ran back to camp, refusing to come out. Josef too refused to go on with the trenching and when Joshua, in irritation, tried to climb up and damn well do it himself, he pulled him down, saying, 'No, no there is a powerful ghost there and angry already.'

'Ghosts? Ghosts!' Joshua stormed in fury that the work was being held up, unsettled by too clear memories of a dead woman's despairing voice and a shimmering white creature on the road before him. His rational self went on, 'In the middle of the day?'

'Ja,' Josef would not budge.

Joshua turned hopefully to a labourer on loan from Pniel for the day.

'No, baas, it's the miesies come back to tell us not to dig here,' Solomon agreed with the conviction of the truly superstitious and held with Ben and Josef that they should not go on. 'You see she died in these trenches, they ate her soul and she has come to warn us all,' was the only explanation he would give.

Hendrik came up at that point and turned first to Esther, pale and anxious with the water still in her hands. 'Don't be afraid,' he said. Gently he took the bottle from her and led her back to her house, then returned to find Joshua still raging at the men, who would not say anything, but would not go on trenching. Quietly Hendrik took Joshua by the arm and led him away, telling all the others to go and have a lunch break. 'Baas Joshua,' he said, recalling him to his dignity, 'did you not know that the ghosts of Africa walk at noon? Now, you stay here in the shade and I will go and see what ghost this is. It is not the miesies; that much I know.'

He walked cautiously over to the excavator, climbed under its enormous predatory limb and stood there in silence a while. Then he got down on his hands and knees and began searching for something intently on the ground, passing his hands lightly over the hot sand in slow sweeping motions. Despite himself, Joshua drew closer. 'Well,' he said eventually when the small form stopped and sat back on his haunches, 'did you find anything?'

He looked up, 'Aai Baas Joshua, this is serious. There is one of my ancestors buried here. It is not Mevrou, of course, but it is a spirit disturbed now.'

'What?' Despite the increasing noonday heat of late September, Joshua felt a strange shiver and goose bumps rise on his arms.

'Ja, look here,' he said and his finger gently stroked what Joshua had taken to be a piece of quartz but on closer inspection saw that it was too smooth, too round – it was the curve of a forehead, the beginning of a skull.

'Oh bloody hell, what do we do now?'

Hendrik quietly got up and drove the machine away. He used branches of wit-doring to cordon off the burial site and then took Joshua to Adam, 'We must tell him,' he said. 'And also,' heavily, 'what the men are saying about the miesies.' He turned fiercely to the men sitting in the shade eating their lunch half fearfully. 'It is not the miesies,' he said, 'you know that. She went away, into Botswana.'

'So who is it then?' Solomon again, also Ben, who had crept back, not wanting to be alone.

Hendrik cast about for an answer and finally said, 'Let us call him Kara/tuma – that is the name of the first born of my people. This skeleton is the first of my people whom I have found again here on this land where I knew we belonged.' And Kara/tuma he remained after that, alone and half-exposed on the desolate veld.

As Hendrik and Joshua headed back to Adam's home, Hendrik said, 'I don't know what they will do. But I would rather tell baas Adam than baas Abraham.' Joshua agreed. Also he wanted to get in touch with Paul. There was bound to be some company policy for such a situation.

Paul listened. 'This is just what we need,' he sighed, 'a bloody buried ancestor. I'll speak to head office and let you know. Probably best not to do anything, these things can get so sensitive and if the media get hold of it, we will have hell to pay – again! Stay near the phone.' Joshua remembered just in time the number of the young archaeologist who had given the talk on the paintings. Perhaps she could help? He gave the number to Paul.

'What's her name?'

'Sharon Shackleton her card says,' Joshua said.

'What? It can't be,' and then after a pause, 'Now I am seeing ghosts,' he laughed at himself. The line went dead. Joshua went out onto the stoep where Adam was eating a sandwich and drinking a glass of Janine's wonderful lemon juice.

'Well?' Adam asked.

'I'm to wait, what else do I ever do?'

'Have a drink so long.' His resignation made Joshua sorry instantly for his petulance.

Adam went on, 'Hendrik has been clearing the sand gently around the skull – it looks like we might have a complete skeleton there. A bushman, from the way he is sitting and the fact that he has his bow and arrow with him and an ostrich egg for water. It is difficult to tell how old, though Hendrik says the bow and the arrows are the same as they make them now. But then the Bushmen themselves have not changed. They do not move with the times, do they? Only with the seasons.'

Adam went back to town. 'No sense in both of us waiting here and I need to find Johannes, the water diviner,' he said. 'He lives on the outskirts of town on the other side, near the river. You geologist might like to come along when he comes. You won't be able to do much for a while.'

Then Paul. rang. 'Don't do anything,' he said, 'head office has gone to Wits university with this woman's name. They hope she'll work quickly and Lefika will be able to keep the whole thing under wraps, but will also not offend anyone. We will have to do some sort of ceremony, probably.' A pause. 'Be prepared for anything.' Despite his concerns over company procedure, Paul had quite a strong bent for the dramatic, Joshua decided.

Then followed a period of aimless waiting, though Joshua reinstalled Rommel and Strooi, this time on Vergelegen on the other side of the river, to track the extent of the deposit, to see what effect the river had on it. Life resumed that uncanny desert silence and slowing down, in which chaos and stagnation threaten, disturbingly. The grass, the trees grew brittle, everyone was restless, waiting for the relief of the rain. Thunder was beginning to rumble far away and occasionally the forked bright lightning would tear the evening sky, but no rain followed.

One evening as they were talking quietly on the veranda of Cecilia and Rosalie's house, enjoying the green shade after the bright glare of the veld, Adam sat up, alert. He sniffed the air and got up to scan the horizon. Rosalie stood up and headed for the shed behind the kitchen.

'Come Joshua,' she said, 'help me.'

They drove her bakkie up to the shed, piled sacks on its back and then drove over to her dam, where Rosalie began soaking the sacks in water. 'Help me.'

Joshua did.

'What is it?'

'Fire,' also scanning the horizon anxiously, 'I think perhaps over on Waldecksplant.'

'How did Adam know?'

'He has a sense for it.'

By the time they drove back round to the front gate, loaded now with the wet sacks under a large tarpaulin to keep the moisture in, and a large petrol drum filled with water, Adam had located the smoke spiralling in the air and Cecilia had begun the string of phone calls. Everyone else got in and drove towards it. On the way they met several of the other farmers similarly equipped as they drove in purposeful silence towards that dark smoke. All the gates had been left unlocked.

Ted Sharpe was already at the fire with several of his "boys", herding as calmly as possible the livestock out of the camp. The animal eyes were wild, and they were ready to stampede any minute, but the four men kept talking to them, "Come my beauties, let us go this way, here through this gate yes," and "come away from the fire, come walk by the still waters, kom Ouma," to a cow that had taken the lead. Some stopped to help there, others drove straight on towards the fire.

Three of the neighbours had begun, with their men, to clear a swathe of the veld setting a strip across the kamp alight with fire too, which they watched and guided like a skittish herd, keeping a close eye on the wind.

The fire was taller than Joshua could have imagined but each man took a wet sack and began to slap out the flames. It was backbreaking, hot work. The wet sacks soon became unbelievably heavy, the progress of the line painfully slow and a gust of wind would turn the fire in new and unexpected directions. The men remained cheerful, through joking and laughing, talking to and about the fire as if it were alive. Cheerful cries of "Hey you foul thing, let me at you," or, "come on then, my friend, what do you want, come and get it." "Haai wena" punctuated it all. Their entirely blackened clothes and faces made farmers and their labourers all but indistinguishable from each other. Someone had had the foresight to bring cold beer as well as wet sacks so occasionally the burning throats could be relieved. The silence increased as the night wore on and the fire would not give in. All now worked with a fierce and silent will, which was matched in implacability only by the fire itself. At some point a black cat was spotted and then seemed to be everywhere, walking calmly through the flames.

'She is there every time there is a fire,' Adam told Joshua, who could no longer recognise him in the flickering smoky light and beneath the soot. Despite the thunder rumbling still on the horizon, the sky remained bright with stars beyond the smoke, and no clouds offered their assistance in the battle.

Finally towards dawn it began to seem like they were winning, the fire sulked and smouldered now in isolated places as the men walked the line beating at it with diminished strength, the swing coming from rather lower than the shoulder height of the start. But the men grinned at each other, triumphant, exhausted. It had been a good one they decided: grudging admiration for a worthy enemy. They trudged back to the cars, which stood over a mile away, not talking much for it hurt to take the acrid air into singed throat and mouth. They all drove together to the Radcliffe place where they knew that Cecilia would have made huge pots of soothing tea for them. Joshua noted that Rosalie had stayed to the end, though she had mostly taken on soaking the sacks rather than beating out flames.

'What causes these fires?' Joshua asked once the first couple of gulps of tea had made speaking possible again.

'Dry lightning mostly – at this time of year. In the winter it is the blacks – they burn the veld to make ashes so that next season's grass will be sweet after the rain.'

'When will it rain?' Joshua asked, 'Why does the storm remain dry?'

'It will not rain until the vlei loerie sings,' Esther told him. She had come over to help Cecilia make tea and sandwiches, unable to sleep with the knowledge of the fire. Joshua moved closer to her, 'And when will I know that the vlei loerie has sung?'

'You will hear her song – it sounds like water bubbling and soon after you will smell the rain. I waited and waited for it last October, but it only came in November and the rain was poor, for all she sang so hopefully.'

That day everyone did only the most necessary things; milking, fixing, and resting, though sleep was made difficult with backache and burning eyes and lungs. Then back to waiting for skeletons to be rescued, for the ancient past to make way for an uncertain future.

Joshua was grateful that Adam had the problem of finding water. Together they pored over maps and tried to track the passage of the water underground. At nights, Joshua crossed the river to watch again as Rommel and Strooi began and ended their strange sand dust dance. He was glad of these distractions, for his mind dwelled too much on the journals of John on the one hand, and the strange story he only half knew but was afraid to ask, of the white kudu. The clear piece of quartz lay always in his pocket, though he himself could not have said why. Adam failed to contact the roving water diviner and seemed anxious about this, too. Esther would often come out to the site of the skeleton, which they had all been instructed not to touch. She would crouch down beside the little foetal form and stare at it for hours. Joshua watched her but did not dare ask what it was that moved her to do this. Everything had ground to a halt, the endless world arrested by this small skeleton as all business waited for his release.

When release came, it came as a surprise. Joshua bumped into her on his way back across the river from the wearisome noise and incompetence of Rommel and Strooi early one morning. He was dog tired and frustrated, having spent the night squinting into a spotlight-illuminated dust cloud from which emerged no core, but only the continuously broken mouth of the huge mantis. The desert was not letting go of its treasure easily. And the sand, which in the daylight was as undulating and indolent as a lake in the heat haze, became at night implacable, forbidding in a stubborn and unyielding way, which left the two men and their ailing technology utterly helpless. Rommel and Strooi's casual attitude of "we will try again tomorrow" (and tomorrow and tomorrow and tomorrow, thought Joshua) did not help as he trudged back to his 4x4 to face yet another day of inaction in the unbearable heat, which yielded now neither water nor gold.

Dawn was just breaking and he could not help but be brought to a standstill by its beauty. It is a very short moment, dawn in the Sandveld, as the flat and wide horizon does not long keep the secret of the rising sun. Every morning, it was a pale-blue, light-grey sort of moment, the mood undefined, while every detail of the waking world was surrounded with a crystal clarity it would lose all too soon in the haze of the heat as the day progressed. So against the pale blue-grey of the sky recently bereft of the stars, the pepper trees and the camel thorns stood quiet, watchful sentinels of the passing of time: every thorn was briefly itself, every silvery fluid-hugging leaf trembled its own rhythm, before the world would lick into flame as the sun slid free of the horizon. In that clear brief moment, the bird calls too sounded with perfect clarity, undistorted by the buzzing, glaring heat and drone of mosquitoes. The insistent call of the diederick cuckoo sounded hopeful of what the day might bring; the sparrows chirruped softly as they flitted busily about, knowing that later the day would be too hot to move, and from the river came the high anguished cry of the fish eagle rising from the water with its glittering catch.

He caught himself thinking of Miriam's description of her early mornings, in which she took up again the battle with despair. Without thinking, his hand slipped into his pocket to close about the small piece of quartz. He drove on with one hand, looking out at the clear morning, in which he could still hear the soft song of dawn.

As he was driving along the kloof at the riverside, he saw a woman, crouching over a rock looking at it with an intense delight. She was squatting like a bushman (San, he corrected himself, guiltily, he really was going native now), bare feet firmly planted on the red, still cool sand, legs bent at an impossible angle, arms folded over the knees. Joshua stopped the car and walked over. As he approached her she tentatively, reverently, reached out one hand and traced something on the rock. Then he realised what she was looking at: a rock painting. She only looked up from her entirely absorbed tracing of the drawing when his shadow fell across the rock. She looked up, but did not seem to register his presence at all and said so softly that he had to bend down to catch her words:

'This painting definitely shows that a great shaman passed this way.' Her hand now was flat against the rock, and from behind her fingers Joshua glimpsed a white antelope figure. He felt again the familiar stabbing thought of the white kudu Hendrik had told him about, and remembered from confused and overwhelming dreams Miriam calling John 'kudu' in a voice of aching tenderness, as Klaas' wife had done after the dance. He felt the world closing in on him again and sought refuge in studying the woman before him.

Ms Shackleton was different in daylight. Like Strooi or even the Radcliffe sisters, she fitted into this world: Khaki combats, a sleeveless men's black vest, reversed baseball cap from which spilled a tangle of dark hair, and at her side a much more delicate hammer than his geopick.

Joshua held out his hand and introduced himself again.

'Yes, I remember. Hi,' she said. 'Please call me Sharon, I'll be here for a while. You excavated the skeleton?' She did not wait for an answer but continued with the fervour of an enthusiast. 'It is a wonderful find, really, though I understand it may have been a bit of a shock. The San are . . . were, the lost, but possibly the first, people of Africa. In discovering them we can begin to discover who we truly are. Look,' pointing at the delicate painting on the rock. 'Look at this figure here emerging from the rock, stepping through a doorway between realities, the world of the people, the day lit world and the world of the stars and of dreams. See how he comes out of it, part person, and part kudu.'

Joshua crouched down next to her and indeed, with one leg still in the crack was clearly emerging the torso of man, with the head, the wide ears, sensitive and red on the inside and the wide white outline, the two spiralling, graceful horns, each a full three curves, of a kudu. Behind him was a kudu cow, her head gently lowered but her ears forward and attentive, bidding him farewell? Before this man was a group of people, who seemed to Joshua to be doing a Conga or line dance, and further away were more antelope, not clearly defined, but also turned attentively towards the man emerging. Sharon's fingers traced the figures.

'They're doing the rain dance,' she said, 'and he is the rain animal/shaman, who has been to the kudu here in the other world, driven by his longing for love, by his longing to be known again in the world. And his longing stilled will bring the rain again. So the people dance, they celebrate how brave he was in asking for love.'

She looked up at him seeing him properly for the first time. 'My apologies, I do go off on one sometimes, please forgive me. But the tracks of the world they lived in are so light, so delicate it is a wonder every time to find them. Would you like some coffee?'

'Sure. Can I give you a lift – where have you set yourself up?'

She had parked her ancient and rickety caravan near the deserted farmhouse on Vergelegen. She had a wonderful view from up there across the Vaal River and onto the oddly incongruous wine farms on the opposite banks. They had walked the last few miles amid the verdure of the riverbank, which never ceased to amaze after the yellow red silence of the Kalahari. She set about making coffee over an open fire she had already banked in front of her caravan. She placed a rusty, blackened kettle onto three stones within the fire, and soon it began to hiss. She found two cups in a tin cabin trunk and spooned out a boeretroos kind of coffee. Finding also an enamel plate, she tipped out some Ouma beskuit. Finally she sat down on a log opposite Joshua's rock and gazed with him into the fire. 'Oh! There is something about these early mornings in the veld, isn't there? The world seems so complete still, so perfect. My father always said it could restore one's faith in almost anything – this clarity.'

'Your father?' her clipped British accent made Joshua's spine shiver.

In answer to his question she began a long and rambling response. It made it clear to him, who had been 'in the field' for several years now, that she had probably been alone for about two months, when the company of any other human being is transformed into instant and profound friendship by one's loneliness. And as he had been with Adam, he was again too shy, too inept with words to stave off the confidences he did not want.

'He came out here to Africa when I was a child. He was a geologist, like you. He didn't speak much about it, but I could tell he loved it; though my mother never wanted to hear the stories.' She paused, uncertain of the interest of her childhood for a stranger. But Joshua, with a brief flash in his mind's eye of a small girl holding out a rock to her father and asking its name, nodded encouragingly. It was this or having to face the frustration of his project's failure to yield results.

'All through my adolescence, after my father came back from Africa, when he did speak of this land, he spoke of it, the Kalahari with such longing that I soon came to think of it as paradise, never having seen it. But the fascination was strong enough to lead me to read Van der Post's *The Lost World of the Kalahari* when I came across it in our town library. It painted a picture of a world far away, which was the first good thing about it, as far as I was concerned. Home, school, everyday life was a world of restrained fury, you see. I didn't know why, but it was there. Both my parents were angry and this simmered its way into my life. I didn't know what it was – only that my father seemed to have lost something and my mother's spirit was broken, exhausted from holding on to things she was no longer sure had any value.'

'Not in the usual way an unhappy childhood, is it? In fact it was an unspoken rule – always the hardest to break, aren't they? – that we were a happy family. I sensed, as children do, that this wasn't true but knew no alternative except the ones I found in games and books. I escaped with relief into Middle Earth, learned Quenya with infinitely greater enthusiasm than I learned French or Latin, and took up archery. Van der Post makes this lovely imaginary link between the little people of Britain and the San, though he called them Bushmen still. Undoubtedly factually this is nonsense, but imaginatively it holds some truth.'

'Anyway,' Sharon shook herself, 'that was how I came to study anthropology and archaeology, with a specific focus on the Khoisan of Southern Africa. That's why I'm here.' A pause, a wry smile. 'Also because the mining company asked the university to send someone to look at this skeleton and make a decision about it for them. And I needed money. The mining company pays well, doesn't it?'

'Yes, they usually do.'

And then establishing again her academic credentials, 'As the Khoisan and their religious beliefs are the topic of my research, I was the obvious choice for the university, though it took them a while to find me – I was out in the field in the Drakensberg.'

'Of course,' This polite agreement and a desire to withdraw were thrown by the simplicity of the next comment.

'I'm glad to be here.' And she poured the coffee.

So they found each other in the pale light of the day's beginning and in shared stories; these two strangers who had come as the past and the future into this remote world, which always seemed on the brink of something, a silence, which never was merely quiet, but brewing a storm, which did not come to bring relief.

'Come and I will show you Kara/tuma.'

'Kara/tuma?'

'Yes, it's what Hendrik calls the skeleton.'

'And who is Hendrik, that he knows the names of San mythology?'

'An old Bushman,' irritated by her political correctness, 'he has the most wonderful stories. You should meet him.'

'I sincerely hope I will.'

He drove with her to the site of the trenching while he told her a little of the project, its unusual values, and the problems which beset it in terms of the land claims disputes raging about the land.

'But don't you think the people who are native to a place should own it?' she asked.

'I'm not sure,' he replied, 'How does one decide who the land belongs to? How does one earn the right to call a place home?'

But she was already scrambling out of the car in her eagerness to see and Joshua found it impossible to stay irritated in the face of her enthusiasm. She knelt beside the curled up form, reverently brushing the sand, brought by the wind, from the skull.

'Hello,' she said softly. 'It is terrible for you, but we need to move you from this, your last resting place. I am sorry. I have found a good place for you, though. It is warm and good and not too far from here.'

'Where?' Joshua asked, feeling like an intruder on this conversation.

'The McGregor Museum in Kimberley is enlarging what they call their hall of religions and they want to include a piece on the San. They thought he could be part of the display.' She paused, as if she now doubted the wisdom of her choice after all.

'I've been talking to them, that's why I was so long coming here. But it seemed better to do it that way round than to have him waiting in a box in my boot or something while I organised a place. Now I'll be able to move him straight there. It seems awful, though. He looks so peaceful here.'

At that moment Adam drove up and came over to greet the new arrival. He came towards them with his hand extended. Joshua introduced them.

'Sharon,' he said, avoiding the surname, 'meet Adam. And Adam meet Sharon.'

They shook hands. 'You have a beautiful place here,' she said warmly.

'Yes,' Adam was short, Joshua alert.

Sharon turned to her car and took out a box of tools – fine brushes, soft cloths and delicate-looking tongs lay neatly side by side with an enormous camera. She took out the camera. 'It will take a while to actually move him,' she said. 'We need to record exactly how he lies so that it can be replicated.' She set to work, taking photographs from all angles, then crouched down to clear a little more sand from the shoulder and skull, which were all that were properly exposed so far, apart from the weapons, which Hendrik had found.

Adam and Joshua left her there.

'You all right?' Joshua asked Adam who was not usually short with guests, least of all such as praised the beauty of Pniel.

'There's something about her face, I don't know what it is.' Adam confessed.

Then they talked of other things.

Late that afternoon, Sharon found Joshua in his tent poring over John's journals and logbooks.

'Hi, what are you reading?' she was already looking over his shoulder. Joshua tried vainly to hide them. 'Joshua, please,' a sudden fierce intensity, 'let me see, I think I know what they are.'

He showed her, knowing it was inevitable. She looked at them a long while, and then up, her eyes desolate. 'They're my father's journals, aren't they?'

Joshua didn't know what to say. He stood up and hovered over her anxiously as she paged about in them.

Finally, 'May I take the personal journals?'

'Of course. I only need the logbooks.'

A long silence. Then she asked to be taken to see Hendrik.

'Well, come on then,' Joshua said.

As they walked, she asked awkwardly, 'Do you think Adam knows who I am?'

'He will guess soon, or he'll hear your name. Your face has already jolted his memory.'

'What should I do?'

'Just do what you came to do. What else can you do?'

They walked on, silent but companionable.

At the farmhouse it had been one of those mornings, leaving Janine in despair. The child had run away from school, walked the ten miles and come finally to the kitchen door, where Janine found him with bleeding, bare feet. She opened her arms to him, saying nothing, and he flung himself into her embrace in a storm of silent tears. He wouldn't stay in the kitchen but ran to his room, left his school bag there and out again. Janine found him minutes later, sitting in ball on the stoep bench, curled so tight that even she could not unwind him, nor Nella when she came.

'What is it Nella?' asked Janine, 'What is it that upsets him so much?' She had never been to school and so could not imagine the cruelty it brought out in children trapped and belittled and made to sit still too much.

'Ag, they tease him at school,' Nella replied, 'they call him Boesman's god and tell him to make the rain, to dance with his beloved until the rain comes, like our mother did.' Nella too was close to tears now. 'Janine, what did our mother do? Why do they say that?' Janine did not want to answer these questions, knowing that the answers held only more pain. Pain everyone should have long forgotten.

At that point Joshua and Sharon walked up the red stoep steps and Janine shuddered a little, for suddenly in his hat and veldskoene he looked so much like John that she felt she was years back in time. There was also something about that university woman's face which disturbed her.

'Janine,' Joshua said, 'this is Sharon Shackleton, the archaeologist, come to sort out the skeleton and she wants to talk to Hendrik about the rock paintings here. Would that be all right?'

And then Janine knew there would be no escape from these stories, too much was falling into place now. 'Meneer,' she said, 'will you help me? I must take this child to Hendrik, too. He needs to hear also the whole story of the white Kudu, who somehow or other is his ancestor.'

Joshua, no longer surprised by anything, obliged and picked up the small, hard bundle and carried him, walking alongside Janine and Nella to the familiar hut behind the Vermeulen house, halfway to the river.

'Hendrik,' Janine called long before they had arrived, 'Hendrik!'

He came out. Janine put her hand on the child's head.

'Tell him. Tell him what you know so that he can begin to understand who he is. I thought he at least could be free of the dream, which dreams us all here. But he is as caught in it as are we all. I wish it were not so, but you were right – he needs to know.'

'Put him down here,' said Hendrik, indicating a hollow near his fireplace. Joshua put the child down, and Nella sat down behind him and wrapped her arms around her little brother. He did not stir. Janine sat opposite the two children and Joshua perched once again on the hollowed, shiny rock, leaving the other corner for Sharon, while Hendrik settled himself in storyteller pose, squatting on the floor, playing softly on his thumb piano.

He looked briefly at Sharon and at Joshua, 'Yes,' he said, 'you are part of the story too, you too are being dreamed here.'

He paused then, giving them time to change gear mentally. He took a deep breath and drew upon himself in that moment the mantle of the storyteller and intoned dramatically: 'Gather about me, oh you children of the rain,' he intoned, 'and listen to this ancient tale:

One early summer a young kudu was born, just here on the edge of the pan under the camel thorn trees. He was pale and beautiful, strong, but he struggled to be born. His mother sensed it was because he was afraid. And because she had always drawn strength from looking up, she sang a song to the stars, begging them to take his little bit of a fearful heart and give him a strong star heart.

'A star maiden who heard her song leaned out of heaven so far, being moved by the song, that she tumbled right out, losing her heart to the young kudu. She fell to the earth, right here on Witkopje.

Nella and Janine, clearly well-versed in the conventions of San storytelling acted surprise: raised eyebrows and clicked tongues disbelievingly. Hendrik smiled, pleased at their participation.

'Ja there by the quartz wall on Witkopje. And there she lay all night stunned by her fall and from the loss of her heart; dimly only she felt beating in her breast a stranger's heart.

'This happened at the time we call N'osimasi, when the gods walked on the earth and the animals were still people.

The introduction and exposition done, Hendrik sat down cross-legged now and the little piano was silent.

'The next morning the news went out amongst all the creatures of the pan that a strange girl had arrived here in the Kalahari. She dazzled, white as quartz and she was beautiful beyond almost what the eyes could bear. So the people called her the quartz maiden. Most of them were a little afraid of her: she was a stranger, with different ways; she sang

different songs and danced a different dance when the moon shone at night. But there was one calf of a kudu, who since first his gaze had fallen on her, could not forget her. He followed her everywhere – at a distance you understand, for he was very shy and did not understand his own heart, which was often a stranger to him. So he got to know her better than any of us and soon we all understood: The yearling kudu loved the quartz maiden. He loved how she sparkled in the sun, how the light danced off her bright hair and he loved how she glowed in the serene moonlight of the night.

All spring and summer they played together, running by the river, jumping over the rocks of the kopjes and chasing each other breathless across the sand and dunes. And when they were together their hearts were not strangers. But when winter came the maiden said she must return to the other sky, where her family prepared the spring rains. So on the last night of June she returned to her home in the sky. All through the winter the young kudu wandered disconsolate and alone in the desert, while the other young bulls played and began their first battles together. He would lie with his legs folded under him and lean his head sadly against the strong quartz outcrop on the hill where they had played. All night he would sit like that and beg his playfellow to come back and relieve his loneliness. The maiden in heaven wept for his loneliness but she could not leave her place in the sky till winter was over.

'*The young kudu, whose horns had just begun to sprout, leaned against the immovable quartz so much that his left horn, instead of spiralling upward as a kudu horn should, curled down beside his temple. The young kudu did not notice and the other youngsters soon lost the heart to tease him about it.*

'*When spring returned with the rain in October, the kudu began to look out for her. And one morning the quartz maiden was back and the joy of the young kudu knew no bounds. He leapt and bounded, he pranced for joy while the quartz maiden laughed in delight at his grace. All spring and summer they were again inseparable. But one evening as the maiden sat in the shade of the acacia and the kudu had placed his head in her lap and she was stroking his wounded horn and tickling his ears, he said, 'I could not bear to be parted from you again. Is there not anything we can do? Can you not marry me?' He begged.*

'She shook her head sadly, 'No darling kudu,' she said, 'I must go to my home in the sky when the year turns. If I do not go and come back, the antelope herds of the sky, the stars and the clouds will not know how to mark the time and the spring rains will not come and all the Kalahari will starve. Life is too fragile to risk that.' The kudu leaned his head harder against her breast and sighed sadly. 'There is more,' she said. 'I am growing too old now to be allowed to come and play here, this is my last summer in which I am allowed on earth. Soon we will have our last evening together,' she said.

'The kudu did not answer, his head became heavier and heavier on her lap. Suddenly the maiden's hands stilled. 'There is one possibility, dear, dear kudu,' she said.

'What is that?' he asked eagerly.

'That you come with me,' she said.

'Oh,' he said, 'that would be wonderful. How do I do that?'

'On the last night of June you must come with me to the quartz outcrop on the kopje and when the door opens for me we must both run through. You must not be afraid.'

'Yes,' he said, 'yes we will do that.'

'On the final night of June the two stood together at the entrance to the world of the stars. As the moon rose and its soft rays fell on the beautiful white quartz, a door appeared in the glittering rock. 'Come,' the maiden said, 'come to the world of the stars with me,' and stepped through the door.

'But the kudu was afraid again: afraid to leave the world he knew for one he did not.

'Kudu you must step through now, the door is closing,' the quartz maiden cried, but the young kudu stepped back. For suddenly he knew that when he stepped through that door he would never again belong to the earth, nor would he, being mortal, belong entirely to the stars though ever so beloved by one.

'Kudu!' he heard the quartz maiden cry. He turned too late. He saw with horror the shining quartz door shut as the moon rose higher and hung sadly in the branches of the big acacia tree. He ran at the quartz in despair, he called the maiden's name, but no answer came over the softly glittering sands but the hunting call of the owls and the farewell songs of the crickets as they bade summer goodbye. All night he stood again in silence at that wall of quartz, leaning his head once more against the cold stone, till his wounded horn hurt unbearably.

'Finally as dawn approached and there was only one star left in the sky, the young kudu turned to that star, for it made him think of his lovely maiden, this time he had lost forever. Softly he remembered a fragment of song, which he had heard a small bird sing once: 'take my heart, my heart small and famished without hope' and with that faint song in his heart he turned and left. Long he wandered and far away until one year in our time he came back to look once more on the land where he had found and lost his love. But his coat had turned entirely white.'

'How did you know it was the same kudu?' Nella asked, intrigued but also suspicious.

'Because he had only one horn and he sang only one song – the song of the famished small heart. *Long he looked at the land and saw its small beauties and stayed then to guard and to bless. For they say wherever the white kudu is seen and where he weeps the fruit grows plump and the grass is sweet. And the air smells of honey wherever he has been. So we mark those places with paintings – if we can.'*

Thomas had now fallen asleep, the tears dry on his face as he was peacefully rocked against his sister's softly rumbling chest. While Hendrik told the story, Nella had sat by and listened with shining eyes.

Clearly she loved the story. 'Janine,' she said softly, 'Janine, tell Joshua about what the bushmen say now, about the door and about the stranger who will come and open the door. Tell Joshua, I know that even in the town the people are talking about it, he should know.'

Janine looked at the excited young girl, 'Haai Nella, you cannot make fate in this way, you must wait for it.'

'Yes, Janine I know, but sometimes even fate needs a little help.' She stopped, but then plunged on:

'Janine the white kudu is Ou Groote, isn't he?" the young voice urgent now. 'Thomas and I we see him lots, he comes to Witkopje and he comes to the river. I know it is him, he has the horn curled down, it is almost killing him now, because it presses down on his neck and he is pale – almost see through. But it is him. He has talked to us, he loves Thomas, he loves Thomas so much it is like Thomas is his son.'

'Ag, kind,' Janine said, enfolding her, 'ag kind, laat dit so wees.'

'Janine,' Nella said, now shy and speaking so softly Joshua was not sure she had spoken at all. 'Janine, the kudu knows our mother, she lives in his land, he said. She too is waiting to go home.'

Hendrik said, 'Of course they live in the same land, they share the same sorrow.'

'Mother was very sad, wasn't she, Janine.'

'Yes my child, she was a sad person, I did not know a sadder one, except, of course, your father.'

'What was that song mother used to sing?' Nella was trying to remember a little sleepily.

Wenn ich ein Vöglein wär
Und auch zwei Flüglein hätt'
Flög ich zu dir

She stopped uncertain how to go on. 'Janine how did it go?'

'I do not know, I never understood the words, and they were in her own language.'

Sharon finished the song for her:

Weil's aber nicht kann sein
weil's aber nicht kann sein
Bleib ich all hier.

Nella turned wide-eyed on the stranger, 'How do you know it?'
'My father used to sing it.'
'Bedtime,' Janine said. 'This has been too much for everyone.'
Joshua carried the sleeping child, who was oddly light-boned, back to his bed.

Sharon drove back to her camp in the moonlight, humming softly that song her father had taught her, wondering at the small things which made her link to this family bearable. A barn owl swooped softly past as she climbed out of the car and walked towards her caravan. In the distance she heard the long slow howl of a jackal singing his praises to the sickle moon, magnificent in the glittering sky, and pointing a jewelled tip at the tiny star which Hendrik had said belonged to the quartz maiden, where she waited in silence for her kudu to come home.

One evening not long after that rather wonderful meeting around Hendrik's fire, Sharon cooked Joshua a bobotie, something she had just learned from Matilda in town. They talked about their projects; about the various claims to the land which put pressure on everything, and about the intractability of all of it if some sound economic base was not found for life in this desert.

After several glasses of wine the conversation turned to the rumours of the white kudu, which surrounded Joshua as they had her father.

'How does that make you feel?' Sharon asked, curious.
'Well, Hendrik's convinced that somehow my being here is a promise of salvation for Abelshoop and the surrounding area, and even Adam at times seems to go along with that idea.'

'Should we rename you JC?' she mocked gently.

He snorted: 'As if I don't get enough pressure from the Lefika guys. And I don't know how to make sense of it all.'

'Well,' she could not help the lecturer's tone, 'things are more than they seem. Your scientific facts and findings on the one hand, and on the other what they mean to the people here. The stories are their way of living with that.' She paused and went on, 'There is another possible reading of the story of the white kudu, you know.'

'Oh? And what's that?'

'It is this,' she said slowly, painfully 'that the kudu's refusal at the door is just that; a refusal – of love, a refusal of connection between the worlds, a bowing out – a retreat. Cowardice!'

It had taken a great deal to say that last word – but it was out at last and she found herself staring at it. Joshua recalled her to their conversation:

'And why would the story mean that?'

'Because,' Sharon said, 'there are people who have told themselves the story of their own loneliness for so long they are too attached to it to love, or to live. Oh they love, with passionate longing, yes, they hunger for love. But in the end the hunger seems better than the love itself, because it has been with them for so long, it is part of their treasured identity. So they cannot relinquish it, for fear of losing themselves. Because they believe their loneliness defines them, they won't reach out to end it for fear that it will kill them. They suffer terribly, but there is no helping them. You can love them but it's a very painful burden to take on. They remain locked into that dreadful silence which they think is their true self.'

'Why are you telling me this?' hurt by her pain.

'Because I think the only way to find out whether a discovery is a gift or a burden is to reach out. It's frightening, but not to do so is cowardice.'

She looked at his perplexed face. 'Because,' she added finally, 'I think it's better to risk the story than to refuse it.'

6
Calamity

Joshua, unable to sleep in the brittle and charged dry air and thinking too much of all the stories and of Hendrik's curious words, 'the dream dreaming us all', spent the night walking beneath the moon, that feather from the wings of the bird of truth, which lit the darkness, winking the glittering quartz into a life its whiteness had not known in daylight.

He found no real solution; found no way for his project to fit into the story, could not make the connection. The awareness of the past which lurked just beneath the surface of things, and the awareness of the power of a story he felt all about him, but could not fathom, lay like a blanket over his project and his own being alike.

So he was walking with the first stirring of dawn at his back towards Witkopje, deep in thoughts not entirely his own. There seemed to be a shadow on the quartz outcrop, which puzzled him for there was usually nothing to cast a shadow there. He walked slowly closer, idly interested. And there she was: a young woman, her dark hair in tangles about her shoulders. She had her back to him, one arm hanging at her side, the other was crooked up above her head against the white stone and her forehead leaning on her arm. Her shoulders were shaking. Clearly she was crying, though in the early sun-dazzled light of that bright quartz, that was all he could recognise about her. He was about to tiptoe away, feeling like a trespasser, when, as if sensing his presence she looked up and half turned. She wiped her face as best she could and gathered her dignity about her.

'Hallo, Meneer Hunter.'

'Hello Mrs Vermeulen, have you come to visit Nella and Thomas?' he pretended some normality in the encounter, not knowing what else to do.

'Nee, I just wanted a little quietness.' Moving between the two languages as she always did and tears again.

How does one respond to such a revelation of the soul's exhaustion? In the usual halting, imperfect human way.

'Do you want to talk?' a simple question, without a simple answer. And it became – what? A decisive moment, unspotted until it was too late.

She spoke again of her abbreviated course at university, how Abraham accepted that a basic degree was good for women because it made them educated conversationalists, but had not thought an honours degree worth pursuing in her case. And how, despite her good grades, the dominee responsible for her had agreed, all too clearly relieved at the thought of having her off his hands. How she had finally agreed for fear of losing Abraham, knowing she was not good at being alone.

She spoke of the dark green of the forests on the mountains, where she had been born, she spoke of how frightening this openness was, this endlessness, where there seemed no place to hide from Abraham's vengeful God. And in it all he heard again the daily small and relentless grind of ordinary married life. That cruel, domestic compromise, which is so small, so insignificant but which again and again can destroy lives, hopelessly and helplessly entangled in each other.

She was sitting on the ground now, her knees drawn up towards her body, arms crossed over them, hands dangling loose or gesturing in the vain hope of grasping what it was that was making her so unhappy. 'He is a good man. I know he is. He is just so angry at the politics, at the weather, at everything, at his father too, who he thinks is too weak with Nella and Thomas as he was with their mother. Most of all I think he is angry with his mother, but I do not know why. I think I may need to know before I can live here, before I can have children here. Oh, before I can have children.'

She put her head down and her restless hand travelled involuntarily to her belly, rested there anxiously as if to ward off disaster and wept again. Awkwardly, Joshua put his arm around her and patted her shoulder while digging for a handkerchief in his none too clean pocket. They sat in this way for a while, she sobbing about a pain she did not understand and he watching her long hair make patterns in the sand where they sat, beneath the picture of the white kudu. Gradually as her tears stilled, in exhaustion she leaned against him a little – like a child seeking comfort. Then she turned her face to him, a rueful smile now transfiguring the face and the still brimming eyes, till she seemed to be the most beautiful creature on the earth to him.

Unthinking, he leaned towards this face within the circle of his arm and unthinking, she responded. There was little enough passion in it at first, simply tenderness – an acknowledgement of the painfulness of life. And then when passion did stir, it was inevitably marred by the awkwardness of two bodies, which are strangers to each other and therefore misplace elbows or knees. But it did not seem to matter there on the sand still cool from the night, and the sky growing paler on the horizon, but the sun not yet slipping free of it.

They laughed at each other and the encounter seemed unrelated to who they were, not a conscious joining of bodies and souls, but simply a part of the movement of time; from morning through the fire of noon to the long silence of the afternoon, from silence to birdsong, from the blaze of colour to the quiet grey of evening, from the flight of bats to the darkness at last of the night, until the moon should rise softly over the river. And afterwards, when they could once again hear the birds and the insistence of the crickets in the midmorning heat, they were silent and parted that way, returning to their lives which Joshua at least, did not think would be changed by these moments.

He sat on the sand, naked and as she had sat only moments before, knees drawn up and hands dangling loose from their perch upon them. He watched her move swiftly towards the gate and her car.

She came back briefly, looking at him with bright intensity and said, 'I had not known it could be fun' and, laughing briefly, she ran to her car and was gone, trailing clouds of red dust, which circled the gate and then settled down again, leaving the world apparently untouched. He noticed that the patterns her hair had made in the sand were gone.

The day seemed unbearably beautiful and he thought of Miriam's letters in which so often that unspoilt moment lay at the heart of what she wished to say to John. It seemed to him, months later, strange to look back and think he sensed nothing then, that the morning, which had begun so intensely still seemed untouched, the crystal clarity of the Karoo as perfect, though less inscrutable, as always. He wondered what gift he had been given and what he had offered briefly here.

Finally he picked up his hat and dusting off his trousers and shirt, got dressed and headed back to camp and breakfast, ravenously hungry. The image of the tearful young woman and the clarity of that hour were already fading from his mind as he thought of the day ahead. Paul was coming out to camp this morning and he wanted everything in order to show him as clearly as he could the certainties of the ore body, the real possibilities as well as the careful hopes, which would be confirmed only by the results of the drilling on Vergelegen and the trenching, when it finally could go on. Joshua dreaded to think what he would say to Rommel and Strooi, to the strange late night rituals of ministering nightly to the monster, afraid of the heat and defeated by the sand.

He waited for Paul in his office, not wanting to speak to Adam this morning, unsure of what he had done. The hours dragged with anxiety. Paul arrived at about 10 o'clock. He was dressed as he always was at work, formally in a grey suit, a lilac shirt and a tie. Joshua was faintly amused – the formality seemed ludicrous for walking in the hot sand of the veld. But he was grateful that Paul was attentive and appreciative as they pored over the maps and grids of samples, the trays of core glistening promisingly in the dappled light of the peppercorn's shade. He was attentive to Sharon's concerns as she gently removed the skeleton, bone by fragile bone, from its eternal rest. It was slow and painstaking work: every step was recorded, every bone examined, then removed individually and safely bedded in the softly lined box she had brought with her for Kara/tuma's removal. Then they drove out to Rommel and Strooi together and to Joshua's relief he laughed at the monster and spoke briefly and amiably with Strooi.

Back in the car he said simply, 'Sometimes impatience is just not what it's about, but in the circumstances, I will try to send a new drill from head office. It should be here in a few days and the trenchers will soon be able to go on.'

And then Joshua, Paul and Sharon went out to dinner at the Vaalbos Safari park restaurant. It was beautiful: the sound of the water in the garden soothing after the searing silence of the desert, and the food was excellent. They spoke at length about the complexities, historical and geological, of the project and soon went on to the difficulties of the area in general, its economic problems.

Sharon said, 'It is entirely dependent on a non-existent tourist trade at the moment, the parks board has no money, so can offer no real jobs and the people are left stranded. They can no longer live but are unable to move away because they feel that they belong to this land.'

'The land claims commission rather makes things worse, too,' Paul said. 'That lawyer, Ruth – her idealism is driving it all forward, but it's quite misplaced.'

'Yes,' the young manager of the restaurant had come over to join them for a couple of drinks as the place emptied. 'The mood in the town is fearful, rather like the states of emergency I remember from my university days. You feel all the time that something dreadful could happen any minute.'

Paul nodded. 'I remember when I was at university there were constant states of emergency being declared. And the caspirs would patrol the streets and the spotlight shine down from the monument up on the hill sweeping over the township and the university. Looking for trouble, making trouble, what was the difference? It was all trouble then. The cops would burst into our digs and "find" dagga, and people would get taken off to be "questioned". Or they would set their dogs on us at demonstrations, beat us with their pangas. I saw a girl's breast split open once and we would sing to drown out the sound of the beating and taunt the dogs. We were mad. We believed so much in what we were doing. One day we were running from the cops and their dogs towards the university buildings and they shut the door on us. That was an odd moment.'

Joshua said, 'Status quo versus youthful idealism?'

'Yes and no. There was some of that. But the moral battle had already become political too and we soon found ourselves not fighting for freedom but for power and for the "right" policies.'

Sharon put in, 'The land claims feel rather like that. They should be about the people, about what would make life possible for them here where they belong. But it isn't at all is it? It's about profit and gaining votes. About being seen to do the right thing rather than actually doing it.' She paused a while, looking glum, then suddenly she looked up again. 'That's why I like working with the dead. They are peaceful. They have no more wars to fight; although someone should have fought for them. These small people, they fought well for themselves, but it was not enough. It's never enough is it, what the living can do?'

Joshua glanced at Paul, but he was listening to her intently.

'So I work with these, the long lost people, who were betrayed, and hunted by all of us who are left here. Everybody gets their hands dirty, don't they? In big ways or in small.'

She looked at Joshua. 'Here in this story of your predecessor (faltering only a little) is a little drama of a man who comes to strange country, a new continent and feels lost, does not know what to make of it all, is looking for gold in all sorts of ways. He thinks he has found it in a woman born on this land but not entirely native to it, though she loves it, too. Through her he learns to love this land and finds gold. It is difficult, neither woman nor the gold turn out to be his for the taking, so he abandons both, though it breaks his heart. Having ruined them, he abandons them and thereby ruins himself, too. Colonialism and post-colonialism in micro.' She was speaking almost through tears now. 'All are ruined by it in one way or another and are left exiles. Only the dead, apart from Kara/tuma of course, who is being disturbed even in death, get to go home.'

Silence. Then, with a lightness which was the only possible response, 'Right,' Paul said, 'last drinks everyone.' And they drank them in silence looking up at the bright stars of the southern sky, with their hunters' hearts and their wild inaudible song.

Esther went home from the encounter with Joshua knowing that nothing would ever be the same again. *She* would never be the same again. She walked into the blazing day, from the grey light of dawn fading in the Karoo to the pale gold of the Kalahari day. The world seemed more beautiful than it had been for a year. The soft carolling of the weaver birds in the willows near the dam, the much more insistent chatter of the sparrows disturbed by the arrival of a starling, large and shiny in their midst. And then the wild high cry of the fish eagle from the river tore through the bright sky and she stopped breathless, flinging her arms wide to embrace the wideness of the Kalahari, which in that moment offered her only its beauty and so was simply itself, not an openness waiting to engulf her. She held that peace for a day.

The next morning, she got up and made the porridge, boiled the eggs, kept the toast warm and set the coffee percolating. And these small domestic tasks and objects gradually diminished the morning's lightness. She thought back now more soberly on her life – it had been a little life, she always thought, little and troubled. Her mother had died in childbirth and she had only snippets of memory of the violence and anguish of her alcoholic father before she had been rescued by the parish and put into the care of a rigidly God-fearing but childless couple, who had done their duty until she had been ready to go to university at which point they declared her independent and left for Australia.

Abraham had seemed the only sensible step after her undergraduate's period of fear and aimless wandering: seeking solutions to her unpredictable heart in student action groups and in her studies of psychology. He was strong and safe and stable and had protected her fiercely whenever she had got herself in trouble, bailing her out of prison after a demonstration and had once almost certainly prevented rape.

She was grateful to him, she thought to herself: what matter that he was also rigid and controlling and often impatient with her now as he strove with the land, with his people and with his own past. He was kind and generous, too. And he had always taken care of her.

And then as the morning wore on, as the daylight ordinary world took shape around her, she became horrified at what she had done. It was a terrible betrayal – and on the morning when she was to tell him her happy news. Again she touched her belly softly, afraid of what it held: another bond she would not understand, and so would break. The only thing she could do was tell him, confess – that was the only way in which she, orphan and ignorant of family ties as she was, could be a wife still . . . and a mother.

When Abraham came in from his morning rounds, she said, eyes wide with fear and her breath nearly choking her: 'Abraham, can we talk?'

He looked up and sighed impatiently, his mind busy with urgent things such as sheep dipping, broken fences and the minutes of the hunter's association, 'Esther, what did you say?'

She stumbled over the words, and beneath his half impatient, half interrogative look, they came foolishly. Afraid to speak of both the love she felt for this large man and her fear of his huge sense of purpose, she simply retreated, thinking to negotiate later.

'Abraham, I have done a terrible thing. I have made love to someone else and I cannot be your wife any longer or a mother to your children.'

'Oh,' he said and paused, uncertain in his youth, wanting to seem strong, mature. 'Well, I am not an unreasonable man. You must do what you must do. I hope you find happiness.' Too stunned to say anything else, he got up from the table, though his food was not finished and said, 'I have to go now, have to see to the dipping on the Radcliffe place. We will talk more later, can it wait that long?'

She thought it impatience again; still overwhelmed by her guilt.

'Yes, sure Abraham,' she said, 'sure, whatever you want.'

He bent briefly to kiss her, his hand reaching for her shoulder but somehow her face may have told him something her words had not been able to. He paused, then turned, dropping his hand to his side, empty and walked out. He went into the kitchen, picked up the gun he had left there from his early morning walk, found the car keys on the counter next to the kettle and walked on out, whistling for the dogs. It all seemed so ordinary, dangerously ordinary.

Esther wondered bleakly what she had done. Had she just changed her world? Or would the grind of daily grey reality be clearly too strong and Abraham's certainty would simply out-silence her again – as the desert did?

She stared at their dishes. The cold porridge congealing now, small puddles of milk and crystal sugar at the bottom of the bowls, the spoon holding quietly the tide marks of the evaporating remainders. The butter was already beginning to melt, the coffee stale and bitter, the bread curling at its dry edges. How quickly the life she had lived was over. So simply all that remained was to clear the unwanted leftovers and clean up the traces of a shared meal. She paused out of habit. She heard Abraham's Toyota start and drive off, tyres struggling for purchase on the sand. In a trance she stacked the plates, the bowls, the sticky spoons and butter-smeared knives and carried them into the kitchen. Put the butter and the milk in the fridge, covered the bread and wiped the table before the flies should feast on it.

When all was clean again she felt lost, purposeless. She sat down at the table staring at the wooden grain, at the paths the living sap had traced. The lovely pattern, like agate, swung out about the knots, forming eyes, which stared unblinking up at her from the silent wood.

Mesmerised, her eyes locked on them and would not let go. Esther strained against the hold, pushing the edges of her palms hard against the edge of the table, pulling and pushing to break free of that wooden, dead gaze. She could not. The eyes of their table, accusing, would not let her go.

As from another world she heard the truck come back, heard the tyres squeal to a stop, heard the front door bang, the heavy tread coming down the corridor. Purposeful now, not the lost dragging steps of earlier. Somewhere she knew what that purpose was, but could not move, staring still into the blank unseeing eyes of the dead wood. Then he filled the doorframe, his shoulders seeming to hold the house up so big were they, so wide and brutally strong.

'Abraham,' she whispered unheard, 'what are you doing back so early?' In his hand was the gun, she realised without registering the fact.

But Abraham looked at Esther, registered everything about her with a terrible clarity, her dark hair, her swimming eyes, her delicate mouth. He looked at her as if he was seeing this woman for the first time in his life, in her life. This woman he loved so fiercely but did not know how to tell her except to marry her, to own her – as he owned and did not own the land he worked.

'What have you done?' he said. Then coming closer, desperate, afraid, angry and menacing; with an insistence she had never heard before: 'What have you done?'

'Abraham, I, I,' she found no answer. She did not, could not know what she had done, done to him, done to herself, done to the world they lived in. She had half-hoped it would start a conversation too long put off and so perhaps had needed to be done but what it had done she did not know. Nor did he, but he needed to react. And he did, in the only way his anger allowed.

He lifted the gun. Esther still could not move.

He said, 'If it is over, then let it be over, properly, once and for all. We were not meant for this world. It is all ruined now, all gone, everything our forefathers fought for. God has forgotten us. And you, who were supposed to be my helpmeet, supposed to fight at my side, you have turned against me, too. Then let us be together in death.'

He fired the gun.

Esther felt a wall of pain engulf her shoulder, fell to the floor with the impact and watched him blankly as he turned the gun around, closed his lips over the still hot mouth of the barrel and pulled the trigger a second time. A red sea closed over the world as his blood rained down on her, on what now felt like a stupidly clean kitchen. Esther heard the dog bark, and then sank down into the flood, hoping to drown in it; in her pain, in his.

Joshua and Sharon were having a mid-morning cup of coffee with Rosalie and her sister, when he discovered what he had done.

Adam drove up, pale and agitated calling, 'Rosalie, will you come with me?' before he was even through the gate and up the steps. 'I have to go to Abraham, who is dead. The police will be here soon.'

They drove in silence with him, as he told in a lifeless monotone how Rebekkah, Janine's sister, had arrived to help Esther as usual with the ironing and had found the kitchen drenched in blood. She had run screaming all the way to Adam's place. 'Abraham shot first Esther and then himself,' Adam said, 'like Petrus van der Walt last year. Abraham was always on the edge of it, but I thought he had learnt to hold his despair in at last, with Esther. He had seemed so much calmer recently with the end of the land battles in sight.'

He turned eyes dry beyond despair to all of them. 'I am sorry to burden you with this, but I could not go alone to another death, could not face him.'

Rosalie simply put her hand on his arm, 'Watch the road, Adam, we are here.'

Joshua, sitting in the back, felt an icy burning cord tighten about his heart. He thought, "What have I done, what have I done?" but said not a word. They arrived at the house, which seemed dark even in the blazing mid-morning sun. Each one was afraid to go in, thought Joshua, "because we are all afraid of death but I am more afraid of owning my part in this drama." So he schooled his face to its habitual careful neutrality and followed Adam in. Janine was there already and Rebekkah, cleaning up. When Adam arrived, they turned from the walls to the bodies.

'What about the police and not moving the evidence?' Sharon asked.

Adam turned to her and spoke with a quiet dignity, which silenced the questions of strangers, 'These family suicides are so common now amongst our people, no-one asks questions anymore.' So Sharon, with a questioning glance at Janine, tentatively picked up a cloth and helped, while Joshua stood awkwardly by, offering to carry the pails of water when they needed changing.

It was Janine who first discovered that Esther still lived. They had all assumed that covered in blood as she was; there was no possibility of life left in her. But Janine, beginning the terrible task of cleaning and preparing the bodies for what peace they might find in death, had felt the softest breath still over her hand, as she tenderly wiped the cheek. 'Adam,' she said, 'Baas, sy lewe nog.'

Adam turned, despair bleak in his eyes, 'Esther my kind,' he said bending gently over the body of the girl who had betrayed his son, driven him to this deed. To his shame Joshua's heart contracted with more fear at the thought of her living and being able to tell what had happened. As Adam spoke to her, her eyelids fluttered open, 'Pa,' she said, 'Pa, ek wou . . .'

'Toe maar, my kind,' Adam said. 'Don't talk now.' And he took her into his arms and wrapped her tenderly in a blanket, soaking his shirt in his son's blood. Esther's eyes wildly sweeping the room repeatedly found Joshua's face though he would not meet her eyes. When she had managed to still her eyes sufficiently to focus, she read his fear, for softly she shook her head. She would not say. He was pathetically grateful and then another fear washed over him. Would this mean that he would be burdened with this fragile girl? Would that one moment in the glorious morning, turn into a lifelong responsibility, fuelled by guilt? "Will I wake up every morning to this wounded woman?" he thought, ashamed, but unable to help himself. Almost he bolted right then, longing for the silence of stone, which made no demands on his heart and never moved or changed, but stayed still.

But disaster has its own rules and Adam picked her up, carried her out to the car and said simply to Joshua, 'Take her to Smitty, he will know what to do.'

Janine went with him, leaving Adam and Rebekkah to talk to the policemen, who had arrived just then. The police stopped Joshua briefly, but Janine shouldered past them, 'sy lewe nog, maar ons weet nie hoe lank, ons moet gaan, Meneer,' she said, polite, but unstoppable.

They let them go and turned to Adam, who shrugged, with that expansive all-inclusive movement which takes in all the incomprehensible brutality of life and said, 'I don't know what happened here.' He paused heavily.

Andries, the policeman, poured them both a drink from Abraham's cabinet, while Adam went on, heavily, doggedly. 'We know Abraham, though, we knew him. This was always a possibility for him, was it not?' Pleading for silence, for no more questions; knowing all the while that questions must be asked.

And that is the only answer to the riddle anyone ever officially got. The local newspaper held an article, sympathetic and gentle and the white farming population accepted the event as they accepted so much, as simply part of a destiny, part of the tide against them. Now and again there were those who expressed the despair they all felt. That was all. It was shocking, briefly, but not surprising.

Joshua thought he alone knew more, but in his cowardice he did not say a word. And Adam and his community, who had learnt patience in the wide unrelenting openness of the desert did not ask, accepted this disaster as they accepted so much else at the hands of a terrible and loving God, who had blessed them with an almost impossible life here on the edge of a great desert.

Smitty soon found the bullet, and removed it simply where he was in his small surgery. Bullet wounds, stab wounds he could always handle. Long familiarity with them made him efficient, able to take the edge off the horror of what they meant, of the violence they were, with quiet skill. So life could go on.

Janine watched Joshua's face intently as they waited. She had made tea in Smitty's kitchen while he had taken Esther into the surgery. They said nothing as they waited. The bullet was soon removed, but Esther, after that initial look of recognition with Joshua, remained shut away. Her eyes would not open, though Smitty said he could sense that she heard him, heard what was going on, that beneath the lids, the eyes followed his movements. He said it was the shock, and they had better take her to hospital.

So they did. Joshua took up that unwanted wounded burden only in the hope of finding somewhere else to leave it. Smitty telephoned Adam to let him know.

Janine, sitting in silence in the back of Joshua's car, holding Esther's lolling head thought: 'Ag I know you, stranger, I know what you have been doing, what Esther thought it was and how you thought it was something entirely different. And how Abraham could only think of one solution for all of it. A solution you, stranger, from your world, your strange world of dead stories, could not even imagine. Poor Esther did not know either. You two, like John and Miriam and Abraham and even Adam are helpless here, only the story has power.'

At the hospital, they saw Esther put into a bed and on a glucose drip for the shock. The white calm of the nurses settled Joshua's taut and jangling nerves a little. But he and Janine drove back to Pniel in the deathly silence of truths unspoken.

In the morning the world was silent and bleak once more. The dry and stabbing winds blew ceaseless, stinging dust, the air crackled with unrelieved static energy, while the arms of the camel thorns stretched into a pale and unrelenting sky. The people crept about, small and anxious and hopeless. The curator from the McGregor museum came to fetch Kara/tuma and was inevitably moved by the irony of removing such a strongly omened find in the face of the personal disaster which had befallen Pniel. He went about his business quietly with Sharon and left unmarked by anyone but Hendrik, who stood on Witkopje to bid Kara/tuma farewell.

Alone again Sharon walked disconsolately about, and finally wound her way to Witkopje, not knowing what she should do now, knowing she was not ready to leave this place where people wrestled with angels whether they believed in them or not.

Adam too was restless and walked out to Witkopje to speak to his memory of Miriam in his mind, about their son, about what had been between them, and about what he could do now.

There they found each other, Adam and Sharon, and talked of the past, which had hurt. They talked of the people they had loved though they had betrayed them. They talked of the story, which they did not understand but which had taken their lives and turned them into this.

It was a long and exhausting conversation of the kind that is only possible when disaster has left the heart unguarded. Painful as the memories were, there was relief in sharing them, in making them familiar and bearable, secret and shameful no more, overshadowed as they now were by this new horror.

'Maybe Hendrik is right,' Adam said at last, 'we must wait for the rain, when tears grow wings.'

Sharon looked quietly at this man, who was facing this renewed loss so courageously and trying to do it with dignity and generosity. 'There is nothing else we can do, is there?' she asked.

'No,' he answered heavily. 'Hendrik's story will have to bring an ending while we can only do what we must.'

When she had gone, Adam sat and thought for a long time – and made a decision. He walked determinedly home, where he picked up the telephone. 'Yes, Matilda,' he said, 'I need a Stellenbosch number,' and waited in strained silence as it rang.

When he heard the voice of his brother, which he had not heard in years, he only said: 'Gideon can you come here?'

'What is it?'

'The kudu is back, they are finding gold again on my land. Abraham is dead and John's daughter is here on Pniel.'

'I am on my way.'

Adam waited.

7
The funeral

Pniel became for the week which followed, both the busiest Joshua had ever seen it, and for him, the loneliest place on earth. A constant stream of visitors arrived and left with quiet, serious faces. The people of Abelshoop came to offer their condolences to Adam, this much-tried man. They said little, but brought him food their wives had made, drank a beer with him and left. Joshua was irrelevant in this and was consequently ignored. Pniel remained as it had been. The work of the farm must go on – and did.

Joshua watched Adam go about his work with the same quiet and purposeful movements as always. Perhaps his back was not as straight as it had been, his quiet eyes darker than before – but his voice remained deep and quiet and his instruction sure and clear.

This death on the farm was accepted as quietly as it had happened. Joshua waited for the proverbial large family to arrive – it did not and he wondered about that but dared not ask. He found out from the gossip of others that he hated to hear, that Miriam's family had returned to Germany from their missionary work shortly after she had left Pniel and that Adam's parents had died not long ago. So it was left to the dawn birds and the mournful gong of the windmill to comfort Adam and help him seek and find a reason in yet another calamity.

But in the middle of the night, Joshua heard a car drive up, as he lay sleepless. Vaguely he could make out a man climb heavily up the steps into the square of light as Adam opened the door. He saw the two men embrace, their shapes remarkably similar. Then the door shut and Joshua was alone again in a world he did not understand but where his actions had done irreparable damage. He was more afraid than he had ever been in his life and hovered anxiously about Janine when she left work in the evenings to hear news of Esther. Janine would only shake her head – she does not move, she said. And Joshua could not bear the contempt in those brown eyes as she said it. He could not bear to stay with his own work on hold and the tragedy of Pniel unfolding because of him, and yet without him. Nor could he leave – he felt trapped.

'Gideon,' Adam said when the door was shut, 'thank you for coming.'

'Brother,' Gideon replied. And then when Adam offered him a whiskey, 'tell me what happened.'

So Adam told him about the renewed exploration on the land, the promise of the findings, the land claims battles and of his choice to sell before they came to a head. And about Abraham's anger with him and Esther's pregnancy, discovered only in hospital when she lost the child and her unhappiness, which they had not known either.

'And John's daughter?' Gideon asked quietly.

Now Adam turned to the story of Kara/tuma – the skeleton that needed to find new resting ground, and the search for an archaeologist to do so carefully. And how Sharon had arrived to move the skeleton and awaken old ones.

'Poor girl,' Gideon said, 'Does she know what happened here?'

'Yes, she does.' overwhelmed. 'Is it not enough that he betrayed me, that Miriam is dead – must his daughter be here too to watch my pain – as my son is betrayed in the same way?'

'We have all been both betrayer and betrayed in this.' Gideon reminded him softly.

Quietly then: 'What do I do, Gideon?'

'There is nothing you can do, Adam. We must arrange a funeral and we must let this skeleton be moved. This new geologist must find what he is looking for and you must sell the land. Finish your drink and then we will go to bed.'

The week passed gradually then, the arrangements for the funeral took shape and brought what comfort they could. Joshua stayed in his office tent, where he was hopelessly sorting through data, pretending to work when really his mind could not budge from the hospital where Esther lay, or the morgue with the terribly mutilated body of Abraham. And no one in this week came to find him, except Thomas who came to play silently as always with the white quartz. Joshua found himself extraordinarily glad of his company.

On Thursday morning Adam and his brother were walking along the river that Miriam had loved so much. They walked in silence, the absence of urgent things to do making things awkward between them again. But finally Adam said, 'The funeral parlour has invited me to come and view Abraham. They've prepared him for burial and I have to do one, final identification. Will you come with me?'

'Yes of course.' Gideon replied, remembering the funeral eight years ago: the shock of seeing again the nearly transparent body – all that had been left of the woman they had both loved.

In silence they drove into town. Adam composed and still, his tanned and weather-beaten face seemed suddenly to have a marble smoothness about it, the skin taut over the bones, the brow clear, almost radiant. The suffering seemed to be leaching all the marks of his life from his face, leaving it a clarity, which surely, Gideon thought, only angels could usually command. They came to a stop at the red-curtained, large window of AVBOB and Mr Phoofolo greeted them at the door. He shook Adam's hand warmly and took them past the desk with the glossy catalogue of coffins and the pictures and the free-standing model of a headstone; past the coffee table with *Reader's Digests*, the plush sofa on which a black woman in a purple leopard skin dress suit was crying softly into a handkerchief, while a young man sat awkwardly by. Both had the haunted look of those who had spent many days at a bedside, where the ravages of AIDS took their terrible course. The young man too was emaciated.

At the back, the brothers found themselves in a small room, also draped in suffocating red velvet curtains. In the centre stood an open dark wooden coffin.

'Here he is,' Mr Phoofolo said softly, 'I will give you a few moments?'

Adam replied, 'Yes thank you,' but did not yet step forward. When he did, he was breathing slowly, deeply. For the first time, Gideon could see that he was clearly fighting for control. Seeing the body again, after all the abstract arrangements and carefully religious expressions of grief and sympathy, was hard. Quietly Gideon put a hand on his elbow, and Adam acknowledged this with a flicker of his eyes. No more. Gideon waited quietly for Adam to step forward, which he did as soon as he could. The apparition in the coffin was less dreadful to behold than Gideon had expected, the body had been beautifully dressed in Abraham's wedding suit, which still fitted. The face had been less destroyed than one would think, and it was clean now, reposing on the soft white cushion, its tanned handsomeness once again apparent. In death it had none of the brute strength, none of the looming presence Abraham had carried with him wherever he went when he was alive. Adam was shocked by his son's beauty and youth. He gasped softly, laying his hands on the edge of the coffin, where the white knuckles alone testified to his anxiety.

Gideon spoke first, 'Braam, seun,' he said, 'Braampie,' softly the old family name Adam had not used for his son in years. It was the name of childhood, when the world had still been whole.

Now Adam's other hand unafraid went out to his son, touched softly the composed face, did not move back too far to find the wound; did not explore the neat stitching over one eye; did not finger the broken cheekbone, but rested only on the high and clear brow. Adam's hands, not shaking now, not tight with tension, reached into the coffin and found his son's hand. It was cleaner than it had ever been in life and lay composed upon his quiet chest on top of the other hand. No sign, now, of the violence and the anguish they had known only minutes before death. Adam placed his hand over the hands of his son and said only, 'my boy, my boy speak to me, just one more time, speak to me.'

Silence.

Adam looked up. 'I knew,' he said, 'I knew how the world looked to him, but I did not know how to counsel such despair. I hoped only that the earth would teach him, as it taught me that our lives are only a small part of it all and that taken whole, they were beautiful, no matter how hard. But that was no consolation for him, he hated that littleness, I think. I should have contained his despair for him.'

'No Adam,' Gideon said, 'No one can contain another's despair. That, we each must do alone.'

Silence again as Adam looked tenderly on a son who had probably not tolerated a caress from him in years. As if remembering that suddenly, Adam took his hand off, half turned, but paused to look again.

'He looks beautiful, does he not?' Adam asked his brother after long silence.

'Yes he does, I did not know he had become so handsome,' Gideon replied.

'I want the children to see him, I want him to be remembered this way,' Adam said.

Abruptly he left the quiet room, in which the ghastly music, for all it was played so gently, choked the silence of death with too much familiarity and discreet, compassionate profit.

It was arranged that the body would be brought to Adam's house that evening, when things had cooled down a little and Adam would have had time to prepare his two remaining children. Satisfied he left the parlour and together they set out for the hospital, where Esther still lay in her wordless refusal. They spent a hopeless and helpless half hour at her bedside, with Adam softly taking those feverish, restless hands, which seemed to seek a hold in the air above her body, and speaking to her with gentle insistence. She quieted then, but did not turn her staring eyes or respond in any way.

That evening the coffin with Abraham arrived as quietly the hearse drew up at the front door of the white house. Hendrik, Klaas and Daniel were ready to help bear it inside where Janine had cleared the dining room table. She had taken the fruit off the sideboard and begged some arum lilies from Cecilia, and lit five tall white candles. The curtains were now drawn aside and the windows open to let in what cooling breezes might steal upon them in the night. The chairs had been pushed aside and placed neatly against the wall, while Adam's chair from his study had been placed near where the coffin would stand.

The men stepped calmly up to the car, ready to take up their burden. None of them had any nervousness about this. Quiet and serious and certain in their movements – death was no stranger here. There was only a brief flicker of uncertainty as they stepped into the house, when Klaas, from long habit of politeness, tried to stop to remove his hat. This nearly caused the coffin to drop and gave first Daniel the giggles, and eventually had everyone softly laughing as they manoeuvred the large, heavy box onto the stiffly starched white tablecloth of the family dining room.

Adam stood in the doorway to the rest of the house, unable to help, grateful for the normality of their presence, of their awkward giggling as Nella and Thomas arrived behind him to see what the commotion was about. Nella softly took her father's hand, Thomas stood with his ever-quiet eyes large and round, watching. The soft laughter was not offensive but made the moment bearable, restored a sense of ordinariness in the midst of nightmare.

Once the coffin was in place, Nella moved swiftly to the piano and began to play *Amazing Grace*. The men all stopped where they had stood awkwardly, and taking their hats in their hands, began to sing softly. Janine arrived from the kitchen and joined in as did Adam, holding tightly the silent Thomas' small hand. Gideon sang too with his warm baritone. As they sang the closing lines the men moved out, aware that Adam would find the thanks difficult, knew his gratitude anyway and left him to mourn his son in private.

Klaas turned to Hendrik, 'I am sorry, Oupa to have laughed.'

Hendrik said, 'Laughter distracts the wicked shades. You don't want them to feel there is anything of importance happening, they might come here to feed on the pain.'

They walked away in silence. In the flickering candlelight of the dining room, Adam walked over to his daughter who was now weeping quietly at the piano.

'Dankie, Nella,' he said softly as he put his hand on her shoulder, 'Come, greet your brother now,' and gave her his handkerchief. Thomas was instantly at her side and hand in hand the two young people approached the open coffin of their brother. Nella stood still for a moment looking at his face more peaceful, more handsome than she had ever known it. Thomas looked solemnly at the stranger who had been his half-brother and then swiftly he stretched out his small pale hand and placed it momentarily on the quiet forehead, but said as always not a word.

Nella bent over his face and whispered, 'Goodnight, may angels bear you home.' She turned and fled, followed by her little brother. Janine moved silently to be with them, to settle them, possibly to sing to them softly for while their father stayed sitting upright in the chair next to the body of his eldest. Gideon stood silent in the doorway.

Adam sat for a long time in silence, his head bowed, not looking at his son, not saying a word. He did not move until the house had quieted completely around him. He looked up and for the first time moving like an old man he stood and stepped over to his son. His hand found its place again on the rim of the box. And now his face crumpled, seemed to fall – broken as all his helplessness stood revealed.

'Abraham,' he said softly, 'Abraham, I did not know what to do. What should I have done that would have stopped your world from breaking? Everyone's world breaks, yours only did so early, so very early and none of us knew how to help you heal it, keep it inhabitable. All you could save was the tiny patch your anger saved from the pain, and when I sold that patch you saw no other way, did you? And Esther too could not soothe your unquiet heart, could not turn all your agony to splendour. She was a stranger to your exiled heart.'

'And was exiled herself,' Gideon joined him softly now.

Adam broke his eyes away from the terribly beautiful face. 'Miriam,' he whispered, 'Miriam, how I need you now.' He was a child again, overwhelmed by the incomprehensible; face to face with the old enemy. He thought back over the events, of their inexorable march, which had broken the intactness of his world. The months at the long border – not six months after finishing school, they had first come to this new and brutal version of their homeland, he and seventeen others from the High schools of Kimberley were dragged into the ignoble tactics of bush war – Caprivi strip, Angola, Zimbabwe. Lost and disoriented they had stormed villages in which lived only women and children: the insistent clatter of machine guns, the running feet, booted and bare, the wail of children and the terrified screams of women. And the crazed hungry bodies of his comrades taking and killing, taking then killing those wide-eyed women, who had not even time to feel the loss. Children shot in the back, sometimes two at a time when they ran with a baby on their backs, their mothers' backs having gone.

At nineteen he had returned quieter than before and of nothing so certain as that women were to be protected, were too vulnerable, fragile and died too easily, and that men were unworthy of them. It was their fragility which awed him. Their beauty only served to make it more apparent and it awoke in him the most chivalrous of impulses and the need to protect them.

He could not imagine allowing what they allowed: that intimate invasion, which left them wide open to both the worship and the hunger of men.

And when his older brother had brought Miriam home for his semester holidays one day, he saw only frailty in her dreams, and weakness in her generosity. He had been filled with an overwhelming urge to protect her. She had been moved by this and had loved him for it. But in protecting her from what he feared was the darkness of his own heart, drove her back into herself and then away: out into the wilderness. And there she found John and his articulate charm.

He turned abruptly from these memories and reached for his son. 'What were your demons, son? Why could we not fight them together?'

Gideon put a hand on his brother's shoulder, but Adam was oblivious.

'We could not. In the darkest night we each found ourselves alone: Miriam, I and John, too, and you. And you who had played no part, but were ruined by it anyway. But afterwards, afterwards, what words should I have found for you? Oh Abraham, forgive – what silences of mine gave death its victory over you?'

Gideon spoke softly now: 'Adam, your silence did not kill him.'

'But perhaps it did – perhaps if I had been less obsessed with my story, with avoiding my memories I could have seen it repeating for my son. It is my story, I should not have let it kill my son!'

'It is not your story alone, Adam. No story is. And this one is old, old as this land. And in the end, it belongs I think to the rocks.'

'But we are caught by it – and innocents are hurt by it.'

'Yes, that is true.'

'And it's cruel and unfair. What part did Abraham play – what part? And he lies dead. My son is dead.'

'He chose death,' Gideon said quietly.

'No,' Adam said fiercely. 'No, the story . . . Joshua's arrival trapped me so much in my past, I did not see the present.'

He stopped, his eyes full of the horror, remembering Rebekkah's cry and the bloody kitchen.

'Are we cursed Gideon? Are we cursed?' he asked.

'No,' his brother said, drawing back fastidiously.

'But we are trapped by this story – this terrible story of the Bushmen.'

'No, Adam, no – we have a choice.'

'What choice?'

'We choose how we respond to the story. We choose anger, or patience, we choose hatred, or love. We choose to leave or to stay.'

The morning of the funeral broke quietly on Pniel, where Adam sat exhausted next to his son, his head resting heavily on his hand, which lay helpless on the rim of the coffin. In Kimberley, Esther lay still on her bed with the wound healing quite well, but in her eyes remained a staring blankness and she did not respond to anyone or anything.

She had been put on a drip again as she refused food – and only now Joshua remembered that she was an orphan. Abraham's family was the only family she had. He was determined that they should never know what had caused Abraham to shoot her and then turn the gun on himself. He did not know they guessed.

Everybody on both Pniel and Wonderfontein stopped work by midday, so that all could be got ready for the funeral. Klaas and Hendrik, unasked, spent the morning cleaning the cars for the slow and solemn drive to the Church in Abelshoop. Clearly they would be dusty again long before they arrived there but just as clearly this was part of the ritual. Just before lunch Rosalie and her sister arrived. Janine had made a simple meal, knowing that no one felt much like eating, yet she needed to keep some level of life going, and they would all need sustenance.

In public Adam was quiet and composed through all the arrangements. He had lost his eldest in a shocking, brutal and potentially scandalous way, yet he never lost his dignity. He insisted on doing everything himself, from selecting the coffin, choosing the hymns and the printing of the orders of service. The dominee had of course come to him. Adam met him with a tired smile and asked Janine to bring tea.

'Adam, how are you?' the dominee asked. Like everyone else, he was lost for words before this quiet man who had suffered so much. He knew only the small conventionalities, which Adam knew for the helpless courtesy they were, but rejected as he rejected all help.

'What can we do to help? Would you like someone to take the children for a while, perhaps?'

Adam answered simply, 'No thank you, Dominee, my brother is here.' The dominee soon left, when the hymns, the prayers, pall bearers had been discussed and organised, knowing his place, and knowing the limits of his power, too.

And then Adam had turned to Gideon. 'I lost Abraham a long time ago. I think I lost him when I lost Miriam. He could never forgive either of us. He could not forgive anyone anything, because he could not live in a world which did not fit his sense of perfection. He could not bear its flawed nature.'

Gideon, with a brief and rare flash of irritation, said, 'Adam, you're right. You have not had this son in years, but it is because you have been trapped in your own loss. Your guilt about the war, your pain about Miriam has trapped your entire family – and you blamed it on Hendrik's story and allowed it to happen again.'

'I know. How do I break the cycle?'

Gideon put a hand on his shoulder, 'What about this Joshua?'

Adam's face closed.' What about him?'

'Well, he is here, should he not come to the funeral?'

'What?' Adam wanted to storm.

But Gideon's eyes held his, 'See it through this time.'

'Yes, yes. Will you ask him for me?'

'Yes I will – and John's daughter, too.'

So Gideon went over to Joshua's camp, paused awkwardly at the entrance to the office tent and cleared his throat.

Joshua stumbled from his desk. He looked awful – unshaven and grey about the eyes.

'Mr Hunter, would you help us out tomorrow?'

'I'd be glad to.' Joshua could have wept with eagerness.

'Would you chauffeur the Radcliffe sisters to the funeral? And Miss Shackleton? Then I could be with my brother.'

'Yes of course. When shall I pick them up?'

'At half past twelve.'

'Oh, I only have a pick-up . . .'

'Drive Abraham's car,' Gideon said after some thought.

At two o'clock the children and Janine climbed into Adam's car, while Joshua drove Sharon, Rosalie and Cecilia in Abraham's car. The children were dressed in sombre, smart and clearly uncomfortable clothes. Sharon had come back from Kimberley for the funeral and found a dress, and Joshua a jacket and tie. Janine looked regal and Rosalie and Cecilia looked silver and fragile in their dark blue dresses and the neat, obligatory hats. They drove slowly to the church in complete silence. Adam stopped the car, pocketed his keys, and climbed heavily out of the car. As he looked up at the church spire with the simple black cross on it, he thought, "Miriam, I needed you here for this." But no one heard this thought. They only saw a pale, still handsome man step composedly from the car; open the door for his children, take them both by the hand and walk towards the church with slow, measured steps.

Inside, the church glowed in the afternoon sun. The red aisle carpets and the wooden benches seemed to add to the warmth streaming in through the huge windows at the side of the enormous pulpit, which always dominated the reformed churches. They made their way quietly to the front row, where Adam settled Thomas and the sisters while Nella left softly to take her place in the choir. Adam then sat restlessly waiting for the sound of the hearse. It arrived all too soon and the coffin now sealed and loaded with the cosmos flowers Abraham had loved was wheeled softly, discreetly to the front. People began to arrive, neighbours, and the entire village. The choir was arranging itself with a soft bustle in the gallery, and the elders were gently and ever so aware of the gravity and dignity of the day, directing the congregation to their places with quiet whispers and graceful gestures. Finally all were settled, the ladies holding hymnbooks and handkerchiefs in white gloved hands, the men taller than usual, broader – aware of the need to be strong.

The service was long and dreary. Abraham had not been very well known amongst the people, and the manner of his death loomed so large before their eyes with horror, that God seemed very far away and of little comfort. So the words were often awkward and verging on empty, the doleful songs sung with protestant dreariness, only to be endured. Adam spoke briefly about the life of his son, but it revealed little to satisfy the curiosity of many who had come. Finally Adam indicated to Joshua – whose Afrikaans was not really up to the complexities of reformed theology and so had wandered in his mind – that it was time to step up to the coffin. With them stood one or two men who were clearly Abraham's contemporaries, possibly school friends and Paul from Wenendaal and Petrus from Vergelegen. The six of them carefully managed the wheels beneath the strange skeletal trolley on which the coffin stood, as far as the gate, where it was lifted back into the hearse. Then into their cars for the short, but slow and solemn drive to the dreary graveyard on the edge of town: a small piece of land poorly reclaimed from the desert struggling to hold sacred the memories in the scorching sun. At the gate all cars stopped and now the coffin had to be lifted onto shoulders and carried with care to the gaping hole, which would be Abraham's final resting place, "and also the first," thought Joshua, remembering the restlessness of that hulking frame, and the hands that could not keep still. The dominee spoke a few soft words and one of the choristers played a short piece on his trombone, then Petrus held a spadeful of dirt out to Adam.

As he reached for it the sound of singing suddenly filled the air:

Abide with me
fast falls the even tide,
the darkness deepens
Lord, with me abide . . .

The melody, filled with longing and foreboding, wound its way into the open sky of the early evening. The careful and predictable harmonies and cadences were transformed by that singing, which awakened instead of stilled for the first time, the sorrow of the human heart which must face darkness alone. The voices lifted the melody without accuracy and swooped between the notes, weaving them together into a cloth that might be placed around the shoulders of a mourner.

Adam looked up and standing beneath the blue gum trees rustling softly even in that still air, he saw the missionary choir from Bethanien, Miriam's last home. As they sang they looked at him, and he knew they were singing for him, not Abraham, who had no need now of an abiding God.

Gideon stood close behind him and put a hand on his shoulder.

'Adam,' he whispered, 'Miriam's favourite hymn. Do you remember how she sang it for Abraham when he was afraid at night?'

Adam half-smiled then, 'It was just about the only English hymn she knew.'

And at last on that long afternoon tears welled in his eyes, tears of loss yes, but also of gratitude and release withheld too long. The choir sang the song to its close, those at the graveside waited, humbled too, their hats removed to hear those voices. Joshua could take it no more. He turned and fled, fled from those voices mourning a death which should have been his, fled from Adam whose patience was beyond endurance and fled from a faith which allowed it all to happen. Only Hendrik, from his place in the choir under the blue gum trees, noted his going.

When the last note had sounded Adam took the handful of dirt and let it fall on his son's coffin, while the dominee said gently the prescribed words, which contain and comfort and make endurance possible. Then while Adam walked over to the choir to greet and thank Miriam's people who had come to sing for him, the others returned to the church hall for the tea ceremony and the long condolences Adam would no longer be able to put off. He grasped the hands of each singer with warmth in both his and said little. They knew what it had meant.

After the handshakes, cups of tea and dry cakes had finally lessened, Adam took his children home where they fell into bed, rigid with exhaustion.

'Pa,' Nella, said softly to him when he kissed her goodnight, 'will you be well now?'

'Well?' Adam answered softly, wonderingly, 'no, Nella, not well . . . but comforted . . . yes – comforted.' He answered finally.

"And that has to be enough," Gideon thought as he drove back through the endless Karoo the next day, glad to be leaving. Every time he came back, he struggled again with the choice he had made. He felt again the power of the magical story and of seeing Miriam in it. He had spent long hours, long years studying the enchantments of stories, and had become professor of Literature so that he could be free of it. He shook himself now.

'You chose,' he said to himself, 'or rather she chose and you did what you could to survive. It has been a good, a useful life. And someone needs to stand aside.' He began to whistle through his teeth unaware that he whistled the hymns Miriam had loved even as he drove away from it all.

But thoughts about this story of disaster and her father's part in it, kept Sharon restless all that quiet weekend, in which time seemed to have stopped. Even the river seemed to hold its breath as she walked disconsolately along its bank, reciting snippets from her father's journals. She hardly knew why she did this, only that she had to understand their shared longing for this land. But hers had always seemed simple to her: a longing for a different world, a world intact in a way that a Europe ravaged by two world wars and genocide could not be. His longing seemed unbearably tainted to her, swamped by her mother's fierce hatred for the land that had borne his betrayal – and yet from the journals shone a love so clear and true, she could hardly bear it.

She searched unaccountably among the paintings she loved for an answer, not knowing that Miriam had searched too in the poetry and music of her own homeland – trying to make sense in a human way of the story, which Hendrik said was dreaming them all. Were they all merely its victims? To what end would the story drive? What good could possibly come of it all? How could a white kudu save them from such a mess?

And what should she do with her kinship with Abraham's pain? Had not her childhood been marred by the story as his had? She had come too late to the story she knew, and yet it would not let her be. She walked restlessly in the moonlight.

And early on Monday morning, just as dawn was beginning to outline the dark horizons, Sharon saw – or thought she saw – Hendrik's white kudu. She had walked much of the night and was heading across Joshua's campsite and out towards Witkopje.

And there beneath the quiet reaching branches of the Witdoring boom where, unknown to her, her father and Miriam had met so often, he stood. Graceful, tall and utterly still. His coat white, the mane and single magnificent three turn horn silver grey, his eyes dark. The markings of the usual kudu coat were almost invisible, half imagined as they flitted across that lovely coat, as a watermark does across paper. She stood still, silenced as she had not been all night by the sight.

The kudu simply stood, looking at her with quiet animal eyes. The large ears quivered, turning on the wind as if to catch every possible sound, adding to that so-distinctive look of surprise and curiosity of the kudu. She did not know how long they stood like that, a moment beyond time and yet not frozen but pulsing with life. As the sun began to clear the horizon, he turned and calmly walked away into the veld.

She knew then that the consolation of the funeral was not enough and she knew also that here was a gift. But she did not yet know how any of them would live with that.

8
Time of the Hyena

When Joshua ran away from the funeral he had no idea where he was going. He was lightheaded and faint, not having eaten or slept for several days. He only knew he could not face any more of that funeral for which he felt responsible, but lacked the courage to say so, and he could not bear the thought of the young woman lying unseeing in the hospital bed, replaying heaven alone knows what horrors in her mind. Horrors he was afraid she had thought he could redeem. He did not know what to do, so he ran, his mind's thoughts as noisy and overwhelming and lacking in direction as a busy flock of communal weaver birds, chattering, squabbling, and flying about their large and messy nests in agitated confusion.

And then the clamouring voices beset him: Paul asking where the ore body had gone, Esther calling for her baby, her dead baby, Abraham demanding why he sought treasure on land he did not love. Even Adam asked sorrowfully if he had come to betray him, too?

No of course not, he cried out. I did not know what would happen – I did not mean to do any harm. I didn't know the kind of people they were. It cannot be my fault!

Finally the pounding of his blood became so strong the voices faded, and Joshua almost felt relieved, but the pictures came now with that same insistent intensity. And they were all of Miriam.

Of the days she struggled to keep order for her children, to rise in time, find books for homework, food at the right times: but food burnt unheeded on the stove, the flowers wilted, sketches sought and failed to find the only form she loved, the one she could still bear to shape and not bear any longer to think of, as she stared unseeing into the emptiness within her, which became Esther's terrible white absence on the hospital bed.

Joshua tried to prise his eyes away from the figure finally sitting as Esther had sat, but swelling pregnant, large with child, her hair unkempt and matted, her clothes dirty, her face lifeless, and all its loveliness gone. He felt his bile rising and then, as it rose, her face suddenly looked up at him and said,

"Yes Joshua, it is the self-disgust which is the final push, which brings us to the very edge of doom, where we must know whether we can relinquish the paltry treasure of a beating heart or will cravenly hang on to it for all its pitiable worthlessness."

In his head her voice was cracked and hideous, with the frightening cackle of madness he feared above all else. She was weaving now with her clawed hands, then plucking beads off strings and laughing as she popped the beads in her mouth, red juice running from her mouth, which grew and grew until it loomed over him and he saw now that the beads were heads: the heads of all he had got to know at Abelshoop, and finally he saw dangling on a string on the strange web she was weaving, his own head. In horror and screaming now, he scrambled up.

Hendrik could have told him: 'The time of the hyena has come upon you.'

But he was alone. He ran again, his hollow skull throbbing with emptiness and he felt it begin to crack, and was glad. He knew it was too small to contain the vastness, the endless agony of the desert so he wanted it to break, to break open and let all that space in – that wide, wide endlessness of nothing, which was all there is, or ever would be. And as night began to settle on the Kalahari, the weaver birds flew chattering in and out of his skull, their words meaningless, even as he recognised them now: "core" and "minerals" and "samples" and "God" and "God" and "God", the least: smaller than "tourmaline" or "pyrites", the indicators of his ore body, which he now knew he would never find, and like the woman it was laughing at him, the deep and terrifying laughter of the earth, which knows it has defeated man, laughter like the haunted cry of the hyena on a moonless night.

And he ran again from the laughter, calling out to the unheeding presences, 'But I am not John, I am Joshua. I am Joshua.' Yet everywhere he went the emptiness went with him and the memory of Esther. So his steps slowed and he wandered across the endless world that did not know him, and did not know his name and so could not speak to him. And he had lost all words for it too, knew not the names by which it might be spoken to.

He knew life would always be a waking up to the wrong birdsong and going to sleep beneath the wrong stars and the cry of despair this wrung from him would always be mistaken for laughter. He knew himself hyena, though he hung on to his name. He walked until the earth beneath him disappeared.

He felt a boiling in his spine and he felt himself falling into a tunnel which pulsed and roared and propelled him forward, then squeezed him until he gasped for breath. A blinding light fringed in red beckoned from the end and he saw that he was not alone. Tiny figures ran in the pulsating, constricting wall, their faces distorted as if screaming as they came tearing towards him, their eyes filled with horror, their gaping mouths growing greater as they approached till they seemed to swallow him and he found himself in another, smaller louder tunnel. The roaring now became discernible as a million voices called to him as he ran in the impossible tunnel.

And he recognised the figures now, though they were bizarre. There was a tiny wounded bird-like woman, limping with dragging wings, whom he knew to be Esther. She held out her strange winged hands to him as she went by, but he covered his face and the voices became unbearably loud – mocking now, asking what he ran from – the voices or himself?

So he lifted his face and forced himself to look at the moving creatures, kneeling to see them better as the voices gradually subsided. He saw John running from the graceful figure of the white kudu frantic with fear, his hands reaching out to Joshua as Esther's had done. Miriam was on the other side also watching John's running, laughing but weeping too as she said over and over again one word: coward. And in a sudden fury Joshua hunted John, knowing now with a terrible certainty that he had come here to kill his predecessor. But the pursuit was difficult as the sound of Miriam's voice – now mocking, now pleading – became more insistent and Joshua found himself drawn to it, crouching nearer in the constricting tunnel, leaning closer to Miriam's tiny form with the huge mouth until he fell right into its words and found himself on a desolate plain in a sudden and bleak silence, knowing he had lost his quarry. He sank to the ground, defeated and blind.

Then the voices were back calling his name, enticing and threatening at once, beguiling and wheedling, then laughing at his poor hunting.

'Look brother,' they said, 'look up and see what has been done.'

And he looked up. He saw on the far plain the corpse of a white kudu with meerkat swarming over it. 'No,' he called, and then the weaver birds were back, flitting in and out of his head with meaningless persistent chatter, which would not leave his empty, echoing skull. With his last strength he ran, waving his arms and calling in despair to see the beautiful creature dead. He found he had a fly swat in his hand which he waved angrily at the meerkats as they swarmed greedily over the still white form.

They had torn open his abdomen and his organs lay exposed on the ground, staining it a deeper red even as it seeped up into the beautiful white ruined coat. 'No,' Joshua called again. 'No! How could you?' and flailed helplessly at the chattering creatures who turned to him with mocking smiles, their small paws clutching greedily at the bleeding fragments.

Joshua pounced then and felt beneath his foot the sickening slip and wet pop of the gall bladder. He froze in horror as he felt the bile pour from it. It poured in profusion and would not stop until the black liquid had swallowed that plain. And all was lost to the darkness – the kudu, the meerkats and Joshua, too. And as the black liquid closed over his head, despair closed over his mind. Now too exhausted he let himself and it sink to the ground, curling into the warm cave of the kudu's exposed ribs. In his dreams, he saw over again images of Esther: her smile, her animation as they had talked, her anxious look as he dropped her home, her shy and then utterly free and generous behaviour at Witkopje and then the terrible blankness on the hospital bed. And at last he felt pity for her, not fear.

When he opened his eyes he found a small meerkat lay curled next to him. 'Why did you kill the kudu?' he asked, without anger now.

'You wanted us to, and we were hungry,' the little creature replied and snuggled closer to Joshua's form for the black liquid was icy cold.

'So was I,' said Joshua, 'but not for meat. And now we're both cold.' He held the small animal in his arms.

"Here,' it said, 'take this.'

In the darkness Joshua groped a little helplessly before he found what was being held out to him. How he knew what it was he did not know. It was an ostrich feather.

'What do I do?' he asked.

'Wipe the darkness from your eyes,' a sleepy reply.

He did so and those soft strands had power to move the darkness. Joshua saw himself standing on a hill beside the dead kudu, holding a small and fragrant creature sleeping softly in his arms. In wonder he tossed the feather away and it floated into the sky to become a moon in this new world beyond the darkness, which in its light shone silvery and soft. Joshua walked about in wonder, carrying the sleeping meerkat.

He walked till he could walk no more, and he fell onto the earth which knew him not, but held him nonetheless. He curled upon the shifting sand and became at last the silence of the rocks he studied.

And because he was a rock all night, Joshua did not know that at last the promise of rain came. He did not hear the thunder, nor saw the lightning dancing in the east; he did not hear the gallop of the rain bulls as they followed the lightning and heeded the thunder calling them from their peaceful grazing. Despite his unconsciousness, the rain came softly and hesitantly, despite the wild rejoicing of the thunder and soaked the anguished loneliness from the earth.

When Joshua awoke in the still darkness just before dawn, the rain had gone but left a deep quietness, in which Joshua could just hear the wild soft song of the stars, the flowers of the sky pastures. And when he turned he saw before him a small fire and beside it sat Hendrik, hunched and singing softly with the stars. Joshua leaned up on his elbow and drew breath to speak when Hendrik turned to him. 'Sjjt sjjt sjjt' he said again as he had that first time and smiled and shook his head. Joshua lay back down, not understanding how these things had come about, but not minding now as the world gradually took shape in the grey light of dawn.

When the sun slid free of the horizon and the grey world leapt into colour, Hendrik brought Joshua bitter herb drink sweetened with wild honey. Joshua looked quietly at his steaming clothes beside the fire and with a sudden impulse of joy he had not known before said, 'Hendrik did the rain come?'

'Yes,' Hendrik said, 'it has begun. Sit up now and drink this.' Joshua found that he was only in his boxer shorts. Hendrik draped a kaross about his shoulders as he sat and drank the bitter-sweet tea.

'Hendrik,' Joshua asked. 'I don't know where I have been or what I have done. I did not understand. I wanted to kill, that I know and I think I was hunting – both John and the kudu, but I found a meerkat instead. And I dreamed of Miriam and Esther – I think.'

'Do you know the story of the rain animal?' Hendrik asked. Joshua looked up at his honey-gold eyes enquiringly. 'Come,' Hendrik said, 'come closer to this fire and listen. This is the other side of our story.

The rain animal, restless with his own longing to create, to give shape to the things which stirred in his heart, which made him lonely, was flying amongst the stars searching for something with which to shape his imagined longings. From amongst the stars he heard, faintly at first a song:

Under the sun
The earth is dry
By the fire
Alone I cry
All day long
The earth cries
For the rain to come
All night my heart cries
For my hunter to come
And take me away

And in that song he knew himself and thought to find an end to loneliness. I am the rain and so he followed the lingering call of that song; followed it all the way to earth and as he flew he shaped an answer to that song:

Oh listen to the wind
You woman there
The time is coming
The rain is near
Listen to your heart
Your hunter is here

And he landed here, where the Kalahari almost begins, and found the woman and they were one and in their union the world was renewed.'

Pause. Joshua was not too sure why he'd been told this story.

Hendrik continued, 'All stories are about the dream of consciousness, the dream of becoming ourselves, discovering in that moment our loneliness and the search for companionship. They are about the gulfs of loneliness we live in and the bridges on which we dance to reach across them – because all love is love for a stranger, is it not?'

Joshua was silent.

'That is why we greet strangers in the desert with, "I have been dead, but now that you have come, I am alive again."'

Hendrik paused and stood up to bring him a tsama melon, 'Talking to strangers is always a risk – but it need not always be a failure – that is the dream dreaming us all. Miriam and John . . .'

At that point Joshua stood up, not wishing to hear again the name of his predecessor, which had haunted him all through his time here and of which he wished to shake himself free. He stood in the morning light, with the sun rising behind him and looked in silence at his shadow and, in that shadow, saw himself, distinct from all that was around him.

'I am Joshua,' he said and turned to the man behind him, looked into his eyes honey gold and deepest brown, full of his own isolation, and knew himself again, but this time not alone, 'and I have come here to this desert to find gold and the desert has come into me and set my dreamless heart dreaming again. It was a gift, which destroyed the giver, but this time it will not be refused.' And then Joshua knew what the kudu said at the dance: I want to go home.

And he could answer: 'Yes, we all want to go home and I must find the place where that can be.'

'That is a great task Joshua,' Hendrik said, when he fell down again, weak still from his long night of wandering, 'but you will not be alone.' And they spoke then all day of simple things, of childhood: Miriam's born into her mother's exile, but filled soon with the hopeful names the missionaries gave to their homes, to their places: names of hope and revelation: Bethanien, Lobetal, Pniel, and Emmaus. Names one can use to make the world a home, to bring the exiled heart back to itself. Names to recall stories. Hendrik gave him other names too, the names for little things and big, names from a different time and different language, but names, which wove stories unknown and yet recognised because they brought the world alive and let it speak to the lonely heart.

'And you,' Hendrik said, 'what should your name be, here in the desert?'

At noon they slept and when the heat of the afternoon abated a little, Hendrik said, 'It is time to go back Joshua. Soon they will miss you.'

Joshua dressed in his own clothes and stood looking quietly at the ashes of their fire, knowing that he stood between worlds and, knowing that the crossing from one to the other was difficult, knowing the fearful power of the other world to kill the knowledge of this one, knowing the lifeless names it would have for what he had seen here: going native, heat stroke and madness. Nevertheless, he turned and headed back to Adam's house, where he found Sharon and Adam, talking softly.

'Adam,' he whispered. 'I have abused your hospitality. I have destroyed your son . . . I took something from him that I had no right to take.'

'Yes.'

Joshua did not know what more to say. Adam struggled, too.

'We are all held by the compulsion of this story and yet how to respond to it – with anger, or with mercy, with fear or courage – that remains our choice.'

On Sunday evening Sharon and Joshua were walking along the river, where the cry of the fish eagle had ceased and the soft chirping of the night jars had begun and the bats had taken up their dance in the light of the moon, which they both knew now as a feather of the bird of truth and understood the longing of mantis to hold its great light in his tiny hands.

'It's been a strange week, has it not?' Joshua asked.

Sharon remained silent, listening.

'You know that Hendrik says we all come to the desert to find healing?' Joshua asked.

'Yes,' Sharon said, 'I know he says that.'

'I don't know how to explain where I have been . . .' Joshua began.

'No need,' Sharon said, 'my supervisor, a very wise woman, would tell us now: you have both come here to take upon you the mystery of things.'

Monday came, bringing with it all the un-mysterious, small tasks by which people gather up the threads of their daily lives, by which the body must be fed and clothed and taken care of, no matter where the spirit may roam. So Sharon went out with her sketch book, digital camera and marking dowel sticks to record, trace and protect what was left of a long ago culture, which lived still in the rocks and the stories Hendrik told.

Hendrik milked cows, checked fences and repaired a windmill, the children went back to school and Eve began the long hot process of making jam from the fallen plums at Wonderfontein. Adam returned from taking his children to school to find a wandering figure on his doorstep.

'Johannes,' he said, 'I am glad you have been able to come. You are a sight for sore eyes.'

'Adam,' the apparition replied, 'I am sorry for your trouble, your loss.'

'Thank you. Have you eaten?'

'No, not yet and will not eat this morning. But I would like a cup of Janine's wonderful tea.'

'Come in, then, come in, and we will drink tea before we go to find water.'

'Do you still want to do that?'

'Yes.'

'Why?'

'Because life must go on.'

'Shall we sit outside, then? It is a beautiful morning.'

So Adam called for tea into the kitchen and the two old men sat peacefully on the deep red stone of the veranda and watched the birds flit through the garden. Just then Joshua came through the gate.

'Good morning, Adam,' he called. 'Ben and Josef are trenching again this morning and Rommel is drilling at Bloukrans.'

'Fine,' Adam called back, swallowing strain, 'come and meet Johannes. Do you have time this morning? This is something a geologist should see.'

'What is it then?'

They shook hands, the young geologist, neat in his khaki shirt and his sensible hat, and the old water diviner, ragged and dirty with a drooping hat, which half covered his deep set eyes as blue as the invisible sip wells of the bushmen.

'Johannes has come to help me find water for Gannakamp,' Adam explained.

'Oh,' Joshua said, 'I'm very glad to meet you. This will not after all be an ordinary Monday. I have always wanted to meet a water diviner, in many ways you are the geologist's ancestors.' He was a little anxious that this could be misunderstood.

But after an initial crinkle in his thoughtful eyes, Johannes smiled.

'Dag, kind,' he said in Afrikaans, 'ja come and see how it is done.' A generous offer, Joshua knew. It was not work that easily allowed an uninitiated audience. He had also learned by now not to thank profusely, but to sit quietly and accept a cup of tea and follow the flight of the birds with the two older men.

Eventually Johannes stood up. 'Right, are we gone?'

In silence the other two got up, shook out their hats and set off for Adam's land rover. As the youngest, Joshua knew his place and swung himself up onto the back, while the other two climbed into the front seats. Willingly he leapt down at every gate and came patiently to Adam's window to wait for the right key to be found and handed to him with brief instructions about the idiosyncrasies of a particular gate. He noticed that Johannes sat in absolute silence, his head back and his eyes closed. He held his sharply angled divining rod, a gnarled and ancient twig from a tree Joshua did not recognise.

When they came to Gannakamp, Klaas and Hendrik had just finished offloading several half drums of water from a trailer for the parched sheep from the wind pump at the home kamp. The sheep crowded eagerly round them as the engine shuddered into silence. 'Well, here we are,' Adam said. 'You know the lie of the land, Johannes.' And he gestured invitingly to the entire kamp.

'Sjjt,' was Johannes' only peremptory remark. Adam accepted the rebuke, climbed out and indicated to Joshua to keep silent. Joshua climbed down over the tailgate of the land rover and looked down at the swirling red sand at his feet. Even after a night's rain, it was dry as dust. He looked up questioningly at Adam, kicking the dust meaningfully.

Adam only said, 'Wait and see, wait and see.' And for the first time Joshua saw again a glimmer of light in his eyes. And so in silence they waited for the water diviner to begin his work.

He did not keep them waiting long, but got quietly out of the car and walked a few steps in each direction, indicating to them to stay where they were. He walked east twice, nodded and then beckoned them to walk with him, but to keep behind. They walked aimlessly for hours it seemed, and yet always Johannes held his rod before him. The intensity of the focus was palpable and the pointed sharp bend of the stick was always in front. This much Joshua could see.

Then almost at noon, there was a cry from Johannes and an echo from Adam. Joshua ran forward and saw the rod in Johannes' hands spinning wildly, circling within his hands while his feet circled, finding the place where the spinning was most intense and the stick seemed to want to leap from his hands and bury itself in the sand to find the water. Johannes' eyes were glazed with effort, his mouth slack, until suddenly he planted his heel firmly in the ground before him.

He looked up from his rod. 'Here Adam,' he said, 'here!' and marked the place. 'Not there, not there,' pointing with his toe, 'but here!' Adam took from his pocket an iron rod and dug it firmly into the spot Johannes had indicated.

'Yes, Johannes,' he said meekly, 'I know, I know. Here, exactly here.' And then he knelt up to catch the frail old man as he collapsed. 'There's a bottle of water in the door of the car. Will you fetch it?'

Joshua fetched and between them they revived the old man, but still Joshua walked again to get the car. They lifted him into the seat, where he slumped. 'Right. We need to get him to a bed, and then I need to ask you whether we can borrow Rommel and do some drilling.'

'Of course,' Joshua said as he balanced precariously on the running guard, so the safety belt could keep Johannes from banging his head during the drive back to Adam's. Adam drove carefully and between them they managed to get the old man onto a bed, which Rebekkah had placed on the stoep in preparation for them. He always collapsed after.

Adam said, 'It takes his whole being to do this. You'll see he won't take payment for it. It is a gift to be shared and it takes everything you've got. Our job now is to take care of its container.'

They left the old man lying on the bed covered lightly by a blanket, with a bowl of fruit nearby and a jug of cool lemon juice. Rebekkah promised to watch over him, while Adam and Joshua headed out to Vergelegen with sandwiches to get Rommel and Strooi.

Strooi was still asleep when they arrived but he was soon infected by the excitement when he heard the news of a new borehole and clearly proud to be asked to be a part of it. Most of the afternoon was taken up with moving Rommel to Gannakamp, which Adam and Strooi managed between them while Joshua went to see how the trenching was getting on. He walked carefully up and down each trench, mapping what he found, mentally matching it to what the sand sampling grids had revealed of the surface and what the diamond drilling had shown lay many feet below. It was a long and slow process, especially as his mind kept flashing to the spinning rod in Johannes' hand and wondering how they had got from such devices to these, looking ruefully at pencil stub and notebook, at the huge monsters and his cheerfully destructive crew. They were calling encouragement to Kgokgo, of whom they had clearly grown fond, "this way, yes, drag your ugly head so, Kgokgo, that is a good trench," patting the sides of the machine. It was reassuringly ordinary after the strange morning.

They had made good progress and he hoped that when they collated all the data, not much more trenching would be needed. Finally it got too dark and he felt he could head back to camp. Josef, who had gone ahead to prepare supper, already greeted him with the news that they were invited to the borehole party. Two sheep had already been slaughtered and were being spit braaied at Gannakamp. Adam had sent him a message, would he please bring Johannes and a barrel of ice from the house. All the gates had been left unlocked for today. Joshua agreed and was now himself hardly able to contain his excitement. When he went over to Adam's house, he found Johannes deep in conversation with Sharon.

'It is like and not like,' he was saying, 'the sip wells are the secrets of the Bushmen and my rod will not reveal them. My water, the water I find is deeper than the sip wells. I would not dream of revealing their secrets, for we must all live, nê?'

Sharon turned to Joshua as he came up the steps, 'There you have it in a nutshell,' she said. 'The very simple rules of a working ecology: we must all live!'

'Ja and now let's party,' Johannes said. Sharon helped Joshua with the barrel, the ice and the drinks, folding chairs, and the large trestle table. The phone rang as they worked and they were asked to pick up the Radcliffe sisters who had made salads. Finally they managed to get the petrol drum onto to the back of the bakkie and all the drinks. With Sharon and Johannes sitting on the back, keeping an eye and a hand, even a foot on things as they bumped their way back to Gannakamp via Wonderfontein, where Rosalie and Cecilia waited in joyful expectation. Along the way they stopped several times for those of Adam's men who had not yet got to the drilling site, and had been finishing off the day's chores before the celebration. Soon the mood on the back of the bakkie was jubilant. Joshua looked in his rear-view mirror and saw several imitations of the divining rod's spinning and that half hidden laughter with the brief glance upward, which became freer and freer as they approached the site. They were greeted with shouts of welcome and approval. As soon as Joshua stopped the bakkie people poured over its side, leaping into the sand and began to undo the tailgate and shift the petrol drum. The table was set up and Cecilia took out a white tablecloth and spread it over the wood, while Sharon and Rosalie found rocks to weigh it down. Soon there was even an arrangement of Swart-tak twigs and bright carnations from her garden in the centre. No one laughed at this, no one helped either, each person busy with their own preparations for the feast.

Adam was basting and preparing the ram on the spit braai, Strooi was thumping Rommel encouragingly with an admiring audience of children clambering all over the machine. Joshua looked out for Ben and Josef and found them at the fire, which was being watched by several men, who would occasionally extend a foot to shift a log further in or hunch down to stare into the flames, almost invisible in the bright heat of the fading day.

Joshua did not dare ask the question: 'what if there was no water there?' Why were they all so certain? He wished he could share such faith. Slowly the happy business of the preparation stilled and all gradually came to crowd around Rommel as Strooi climbed into the seat and the loud engine sputtered into action. The appalling noise itself was unable to disturb the intense silence of the watchers, as the drill mouth sought delicately and found the spot marked earlier by the diviner. It began to bite into the shifting sand, and for a miracle it went on doing so, delving smoothly deeper into the ground. The yellow shaft sank away from sight, while the machine above kept shuddering and wailing with willingness that Joshua had not seen in it before. He pursed his lips in exasperation but then was lost again in the anticipation of all those around him. Mesmerised, they watched the ungainly monster work its head into the ground. The whine of the machine changed, rock had been hit and the delving became slower, meeting resistance and the diamond bit had to work harder.

In silence they watched. Strooi, aware of the importance of his mission held the controls steady and kept his eye unwaveringly on the disappearing head. He seemed to be muttering endearments, thought Joshua, not the usual curses. There was a light in his eyes as they followed the descending head of his monster And in the evening light of the swiftly setting sun, the scene seemed astonishingly beautiful, thought Joshua.

The moments seemed to last forever, and Joshua scanned the horizon for signs of dusk. Birds were wheeling overhead, and his heart was ready for gloom when the noise changed again.

Joshua's attention instantly returned to Strooi and his movements, but there was no panic on his face and the silence in the group did not break up into consternation. Rommel kept biting into the ground and did not stop her descent.

A gurgling sound emerged from those unseen depths, but all went on unperturbed and the watchers only leaned forward breathless with expectation. The ground around the hole into which Rommel's ungainly head had disappeared darkened and a dirty trickle oozed about it. Before Joshua could even remark on this, the ooze snaked off and was lost in the powerful jet of water, which now fountained up around Rommel's neck.

Red at first and brown and muddy, but as Strooi kept Rommel on course, it soon became clear and beautiful and strong. Around him laughter bubbled up, and the stillness and the expectation were over. Hands reached forward into the water cupping it, bringing it to thirsty mouths, or the faces leaning into the precious fluid and then released to cup again, spilling it now and splashing into it, bare feet dancing joyfully in the mud. Joshua looked up and caught Adam's eye. He searched for Rosalie and Cecilia, and found only Cecilia, Rosalie being amongst the dancers who had begun a stamping, gurgling circle around Rommel and Strooi.

Johannes called out: 'Enough! Enough!'

Instantly Strooi silenced his monster and the dancers too stilled, not chastened but stilled by wonder as the water alone leapt into the indigo light. The moment held – sacred as the miracle of it sank softly into each soul present. Adam stepped forward, removing his hat. All followed suit, bowed their heads and sent their thankfulness to the creator, to the dream, which sent them such gifts.

And then began the laying of the pipes, securing the feet of the wind pump, for which the patient Rommel was needed again, joining her voice to the human throng. And then there grew next to the fountain, which stilled not one bit, the delicate, shining frame of the wind pump, with long, graceful limbs and a new fan head, which turned with the wind as it took its place on this renewed skyline. At its feet was placed the length of a water trough, secured against tipping over by piles of stone eagerly carried there by the children. And so the water, which bubbled so generously from the earth, was covered from the rays of the sun, and the elegant length of the wind pump guarded for a long time after, the place of its emergence.

Now the party began in earnest, the meat dripping sizzling fat onto the coals beneath it, the salads beginning to wilt and the pap was getting a lovely thick crust – time to eat. And then time to laugh and time to dance and time to sing. Slowly the stars rose over the scene as the children giggled at the strangeness of toasted marshmallows Cecilia was showing them, and the adults nursed a final drink. It had been a long and tiring day, full of labour, wonder and the unexpected loveliness of the desert. And so, quiet descended easily as each looked peaceably into the flames of the fire and the only voice still to be heard was that of Johannes, naming the southern stars for Joshua, who traced the path of the Southern Cross, and gradually realised that these stars were no longer strangers to him.

In the morning Adam found two faxes from the Company head office, one for himself and one for Joshua. He took Joshua's out to him and waited awkwardly as Joshua read it. Joshua looked up. 'They say I must go ahead. Results about the size of the ore-body are urgently needed now, because a big land claims meeting is scheduled within a week and the company wishes to attend with all the facts at their finger tips.'

'Good,' said Adam, 'good. Something must come of this, for I am about to sell my land.'

'I will do my best, Adam.' They shook hands across the maps, which represented all the acres that both separated and bound them.

Joshua set to work. He felt like Judas and could not bear to look into the eyes of Hendrik, or even Josef and Ben. He did not know how Adam could do it.

Adam only smiled sadly. 'It is no piece of paper that can determine whether the land is yours or not. These agreements will only make the difference between continued poverty and welfare, the land will always belong to those who love it, who dance on it. You heard Hendrik, didn't you?'

Joshua remained unconvinced, but continued to earn his keep by searching daily for the extent of the ore body, which had become a race against time. He faced daily phone calls and was repeatedly tempted to dig in his heels and do nothing. Finally a fax arrived to say the company would buy the land regardless of the size of the ore body. They were confident they could dress up a small scale operation and have a presentable rainbow nation mine, integrated into the community, to make them look good. So, Joshua thought, they will come and the earth will be hollowed even if it is only a sham, but the people do not need a sham, they need the real thing. He awaited the morning with dread.

9
Changes

The morning of both the proposed selling of Pniel, and the big land claims meeting in Abelshoop, dawned in the usual quiet Vaalbos way – the sky turning gradually from the indigo of night through various shades of grey to palest blue until the sun rising from the dark line of the horizon blazed the world into colour: blue, blue sky, red, glittering earth and multitudes of yellow and smatterings of dark green about the white glinting spears of the Witdoring trees. The bright jewels of birds flitted between them all, as Hendrik stretched and greeted the sun. He looked up at the sky, scanning its clarity for signs of life. He saw nothing, but then from the river came the bubbling, low melodious call of the Vlei Loerie.

'Oh, little sister,' Hendrik murmured, 'your song is very welcome today.'

In Abelshoop the open empty field, which claimed to be the town park, was once again abuzz with people and excitement. The trestle table was being set up but this time the people were not as one waiting to hear, but were divided into factions and glared at each other aggressively and many a bruised face testified to a rough night preceding this meeting. The lawyer from Cape Town was there again and another one, representing the white farmers, who were anxiously waiting in the lounge bar of the Royal Hotel for the meeting to begin. They had no intention of waiting outside, and did not plan to give an inch on the compensation they expected.

Then the government car arrived and the Northern Cape MP was riotously greeted and accepted this graciously, but went only to the podium and took his place in solemn silence.

A white Mercedes drove up and out of it stepped a man in light grey suit, wearing a pink shirt with a silvery tie. Here was an unexpected guest! He ignored the crowd, and had eyes only for the Cape Townian, whose hand he grasped firmly. 'Leon Goldman is the name. I represent Lefika Mining Company.'

Ruth de Jaeger of the land claims had expected him and feared his arrival, knowing what he represented and what they in turn wanted from all of this, and her heart was anxious at the thought of it all.

Soon Sharon arrived. She had become a familiar figure among the local people and moved calmly from group to group smiling and asking after families. 'Will you speak?' she was asked eagerly time and again.

'I don't know yet. I will see whether I have something to say.' She sat down finally on the grass with Dawid, Hendrik's son, and all those who still thought of themselves as San – the smallest of the groups and sitting a little away from the others, reviled for centuries; equality did not come easily in a land so long divided.

On Pniel, Joshua and Adam stood on Adam's stoep now in companionable silence – there was nothing more to be said between them. They watched the dust clouds move closer and closer – too quick for sensible driving on the sand. The clouds slowed, as if in response to the two shaken heads. It was morning still, but only just when they finally arrived in their white company Toyotas at the gate and parked in the shade of the willows. Head office of Lefika Mining and Exploration had arrived.

Paul was the first to get out of the car. Hot and sticky, he nervously straightened his crumpled trousers and damp shirt back, and pulled tight the tie he had loosened for the drive. Then he reached back into the car for his jacket. Despite the heat, this was clearly a transaction to be done properly. Joshua no longer saw this as foolishness but approved of the discomfort it would cause. After all, Adam stood next to him to in his suit, uncomfortable but strangely beautiful as he was about to sell his land so that his wife's child by another man could speak, could learn, and their daughter eventually go on to university.

Even Joshua had donned a suit and now he walked forward as he must, to greet not only Paul but also Mr de Wet, Mr Horne and Mr Redding – all senior managers of the gold mining division of Lefika Company. They seemed grey and lifeless vultures to him as they walked hesitantly towards the beautiful house of Pniel through the dappled shade of the trees, straightening ties and brushing down heat-crumpled suits. Janine arrived on cue with long cold drinks in frosted glasses. She smiled briefly at Adam and Joshua but the shutters of subservience closed down as she served the new arrivals, only Paul thanked her. They sat down on the stoep, talking as one does about the weather, about politics in a non-offensive, non-committed sort of way and asked about crops. This was followed by a brief and awkward silence, after which Paul reached into his briefcase.

The various lawyers and the one lonely government dignitary began to take their seats on the podium. Ruth handled the introductions. They were the leaders of the groups: Jakobus Pienaar and his lawyer Hendrik Venter; Leon Goldman in splendid isolation; Dawid, likewise on his own; Ruth de Jaeger with Petrus de Kock and Solomon Bloem of the 150 year old community of Koranna; Baster and Batswana who lived half on Pniel and half on Wonderfontein and whose field of life was a barren wasteland of overgrazing and litter. Also Andries Richter of the parks board. Finally the MP stood up briefly and reseated himself when all the others had ascended and found their places.

A breathless hush fell on the entire crowd, and even babies were silenced. Ruth opened the meeting in her clear and lilting Cape Town accent. She explained why they had gathered and what would be decided. She introduced each of the people on the podium and explained that each would speak in turn stating his case and what they were hoping to gain today.

The first speaker was Jakobus Pienaar who had been a pallbearer at Abraham's funeral, Sharon realised as he stood up. He spoke in Afrikaans, but Hendrik translated as much as possible and Jakobus spoke movingly of the hardships of farming in this district, of the struggles and triumphs of pioneering families, of their love for their land, of the people they had buried there. Not least Abraham Vermeulen, who had been driven to despair by this personal struggle, which had become entangled in the political and economic battles of a hopelessly divided nation.

The crowd was not unsympathetic and there was no booing or hissing, only gentle listening to the voice of loss. What the farmers wanted was an amount they felt would be adequate recompense, at least financially, to begin a new life elsewhere. They knew their claim to the land stood no chance in the current political climate; that having ploughed one's sweat into an unforgiving soil all one's life meant nothing now; that loving the land, knowing it well – its difficulties, its sudden beauties and its birdsong, was not enough. The only question which remained was who the money would come from – the government in support of the ancestral land claims; the parks board or the mining company – perhaps a mixture. He only hoped they could all be fair in their agreements. He sat down and received warm applause and a brotherly handshake from his lawyer.

'Mr Vermeulen,' Paul said to Adam, 'we are grateful that even at this time you have agreed to meet with us. This is the contract of sale. It is neither subject to the outcome of the meeting in Abelshoop, nor dependent on the size of the ore-body, if Joshua could only find out.' The little joke was lost in the tense silence.

Adam stood up: 'Thank you gentleman. If you will excuse me, I should like to read this in private please.'

'Of course, Mr Vermeulen,' and on a sign from Paul, everyone stood up. Adam's hands shook slightly as he walked into his house, with his head up until the door closed behind him. The others were left clearing throats and looking out over the garden, where N'tsa was half-heartedly chasing doves.

'Shall we walk, Joshua? I'll show you the plans,' said Paul.

Joshua accepted only too gratefully, for he felt that he had nothing to say to these men who had answered all his ambitions and would make him a powerful geologist in this mammoth company that ruined the world and gave it life at the same time.

Still he remained puzzled. 'What the hell was all that about?' he asked Paul. 'How can it not depend on those factors? Why is the company buying this land then?'

Paul cleared his throat uncomfortably: 'Well, it's like this. Lefika has made a deal with the parks board, they will not push their claim against us if we promise to mine underground and conserve above ground – a public game reserve, not only for employees but open also to tourists – and more local jobs, you see. So even if the mine operation is only small or temporary, we will gain something and especially credit with liberal overseas investors and with the government: the headlines will read "mines give back to the communities" and other restitution-like stuff. Basically still worth doing, though of course not as productive to the community as a decent mine would be. The mine would ensure we could pump more money in: the school, the library . . .' his voice trailed off, knowing how inadequate it all sounded.

Joshua stopped, amazed at the speed with which things happened in the world where internet connections worked and sand did not determine the speed of travel. "So fast," he thought, "so fast a fate can be decided and ours remains only not to wonder why, lest it drive us mad." He was filled with a terrible sense of loss, foreboding and betrayal.

Paul took out a rolled map and they walked away from the house towards Witkopje, the whiteness of the quartz dazzling in the midday sun. It was almost unbearable: that white smudge in this red world had come to mean so much. Fortunately, Paul was talking, opening the map and showing Joshua enthusiastically what would be what. Only much later did Joshua learn that this enthusiasm had been feigned for his benefit. 'This is going to form the centre of the recreation club and leisure park. I thought it would be nice to have this as the play park for the children. Because you said Adam's kids played here a lot.'

Joshua smiled grimly still half dazed by what he had heard and yet moved by this attempt to honour what had been, to honour what was being destroyed in the name of progress and economic success and political expediency, the still exploitative functioning of post-colonial Africa. 'Yes they did.'

'And over here, what you now call Doringaar will become the first shaft, called /huma. And here we will have rock mechanics and here the metallurgists will perform their alchemy – at Bara plant. I have tried to keep some of the names but Head Office people are rather insisting on African, in fact San names (thanks to Sharon's help) for everything – politically expedient and it looks good to the liberal overseas shareholders.' He smiled apologetically.

Joshua barely saw, and thought only of how lost Adam and Nella and Thomas would now be on this land, which had been theirs for so long. How the names of their places would no longer sing their story to them and so let them know who they are. It would no longer tell them how Nella fell at Doringaar and was nearly pierced through the eye with one of those long white thorns; tell them Thomasie found a snake at Queen's Prize and played with it for hours before anyone realised, and was not hurt once; tell them how they fitted into this great puzzle of a place, of a life, part of the pattern no longer. They would need to leave these stories behind to find new stories with unfamiliar names in the unfamiliar country of a city, where the red earth quivered beneath the constantly melting tarmac.

Their land here would become hollow as the tunnels of mining began to extend further and further into the bowels of the earth. Tunnels that would make the tentative trenches look like child's play.

He stared at this world, which he had never quite felt he knew and yet knew that he had become inordinately fond of it.

Paul watched for a while and said, 'You'll see it's not all destruction. Change is as inevitable as tomorrow's sunrise. And the area is in a dead end life now and the mine will revive it, the money generated will be pumped back into the town and the people will have a better life, we are expanding the school, and we've already begun extending the library. The mine will provide training, too. In fact people are already calling the mine N'osimasi – the time of the gods, I believe.'

'Yes, but don't get big-headed about it will you?' Joshua did know all this, he really did, but at that moment it was hard to weigh up the loss and the gain in that way. Fickle the people and fickle the gods too, who cared little for human love and loss but went on generating forever the cycle of life and death. Those who refused it were simply discarded.

Paul, watching his face, continued, 'You've got too close to it all. It's good you're being taken off this project.'

'Yes, I take it I have you to thank for that?'

'Mate, you are being sent into the deepest recesses of Bophuthatswana, well beyond Zeerust, into uncharted territory – here be dragons – just as you like it.'

Joshua smiled, glad to look forward to a landscape empty of human entanglements, un-storied, unnamed in any tongue that he could understand, or that could ring in his ears with burning memories of expectations unfulfilled.

The second speaker was Solomon Bloem, who gave eloquent expression to the plight of the pastoralists of Pniel and Wonderfontein township, and of their need for more land to be able to sustain their way of life. He spoke of their hopes of becoming a tourist-attracting area of game and traditional lifestyles, and so to generate enough money to build schools for their children and to live as they have always lived on their ancestral land. The humility of their desires and needs, and the clarity with which they saw their organic relation to the land, without which they would not survive, was convincing in its simplicity. Even though it revealed with devastating cruelty, their hopeless isolation from the world of the impending 21st century in which the decisions that affected their lives irreversibly would be made. Still, they got the greatest applause, having the largest number of supporters at the meeting. Ruth got up to hug him after his speech and Andries shook his hand as they crossed paths between one plea and another.

Andries spoke briefly about the unique ecological system of the area, how important it was to preserve it unspoilt, and how it would benefit the people locally, providing employment. Their indigenous knowledge of the veld would be useful to all the world and could help develop homoeopathic African medicines, which would definitely put Abelshoop on the world map. The crowd listened to him politely, but there was now no warmth in it. The experience so far of the Parks Board at Vaalbos Game Reserve was not great: it was chronically short of money, mismanaged and unpopular as an employer.

Dawid spoke after him. He had no arguments for or against land ownership but spoke simply of the need for healing, of how long this land had been the site of vendetta and distrust, of drunkenness and violence. He told of how they had danced the dance of the white kudu and how the time for healing was at hand. 'Look around you he said, look how many strangers have now come and at Pniel are many more and we have seen Ou Groote again.' Finally, he said, the important thing was not who owned the land but how they all lived on it, grateful for the rain.

Leon was delighted with this speech, feeling it set the scene wonderfully for his own. He leapt up with alacrity as the crowd began clapping and chanting, stamping their feet for Dawid. Dawid stood smiling dazedly at the applause. So truly unaccustomed was he to public speaking that he finally simply turned round and walked off the podium to join his father on the grass, no holding up of hands, no slogans called out, simply a smiling thanks and a dazed return.

Leon waited for silence and then began to paint a picture of a prosperous Abelshoop with a school, a library, a well-run beautiful safari park, a mine, which employed nearly the entire town and with tourists coming to admire both the land and its people. All this would be done properly because it would be adequately funded and so also sustainable. No vague dreams he said, no vague dreams but a reality based on genuine discoveries in the soil of the area. No more mismanagement of funds; no more muddling through; no more empty promises but real prosperity at last, is what Lefika Mining Company has to offer this town.

Sharon raised her hand. 'What about the Rock paintings – this is a national heritage site, there are things to be preserved here. Will you take care of those?'

Leon smiled, she could not have asked the question at a better moment, he thought. 'Yes, Miss Shackleton,' he said, 'we will preserve the story of Ou Groote, we will commission architects to design and build a museum of San Art right here in the grounds and near Witkopje where Ou Groote, um, 'lives'?' This earned him an appreciative laugh for he played the role of the ignorant white man, full of respect for African tradition to perfection. 'It will all be preserved, studied, and be made known to the world. Miss Shackleton, would you like to be curator of such a museum?' This got another laugh from the audience, while Sharon seethed.

Ruth rose to speak again. 'There will be a brief break for lunch in which you can all discuss what you have heard. Food has been kindly prepared for all by the mining company and will be served at the tables behind you. After lunch we will meet again and you will each be given a chance to vote at the voting booth beneath the eucalyptus trees.'

All eyes turned to the strangely curtained little box standing oddly out of place and alone beneath the rustling trees.

A hand was raised. 'Is our esteemed MP not going to speak to us?' The man had to be wakened, he was all but snoring. He looked up confused and soporific still. No, he did not want to speak, but yes he would like some lunch; and he heaved up his mass to go with the others into Abelshoop's Royal Hotel to discuss, wheel and deal and see how the government could manage to look good without actually doing anything. The people of Abelshoop looked at each other, disappointed but not surprised.

They shrugged and fell to eating with a will. The future had never been something to lose a free meal over. They sat in groups on the grass and talked. And ate and talked. But there was no great sense of a decision being made. They knew that the real players of this game were eating inside and that they would probably do what they had always done: wait, work when work was available, eat, sleep, love and die. They only hoped that things might be changed for their children and they knew the only way that would happen was through school. The best school proposal seemed to be that of the mining company – they had the money.

Sharon did not wish to stay for lunch, but Leon cornered her before she could get away.

'What did you think?' he asked, 'will we get it?'

Wearily, she looked up at him. 'I have no doubt you will. It's expedient, the most realistic option. Above all it leaves the government with a sense of virtue without having to lift a finger. Ruth will not give in easily. She has genuine missionary zeal about the land itself belonging to the people.'

'Come and have some lunch with us, then you can hear the discussion too.'

'No thanks, Leon,' she replied, 'I want to get on back to Pniel and see how things are going there. It will be a hard day all round.' And she went off in search of Hendrik, to whom she had promised a lift home. He was quite happy to relinquish his lunch to Dawid, whose eyes sparkled with the excitement of the meeting. He was clearly enjoying himself, partly because he had so few expectations of this meeting, simply grateful to have been heard. Both turned to Sharon as she arrived and smiled at her drawn face.

'The important thing, remember,' Hendrik said to her, 'is that old ways are not entirely lost, and that the people get to live. We agreed, yes?'

'I know Hendrik, I know, but it feels so much like betrayal.'

'Betrayal and blessing can come in one package . . . Come on, let's get home.' Dawid merrily waved them away and turned back to the gathering. There were people there he had not spoken to in too long and it was good to see them again.

Joshua walked away from Paul and headed for the willows around the dam. He sat in their shade, the map with the new old names still rolled up in his hand. The names, he thought, were both return and destruction: a home restored and an exile made. It still seemed so full of questions to him. "What gives one ownership of a patch of the earth? Being born there? Serving it? Coaxing life from its hard soil? Finding its riches and having the means to exploit them, to find them, to take them and to give life with them?"

The questions circled unanswered in his mind, "the earth belongs to herself, we belong to her, but to what spot, where do we belong?" he wondered. "In that spot where the bones would finally rest? Perhaps only then will we be finally home." A shadow fell across him.

'Hi,' Sharon's voice. 'A tough day?'

'Not for me,' he answered.

Then he remembered where she had been all morning and rounded on her. 'Why didn't you tell me what you were up to? What negotiations have you taken up with the living? What the hell were you doing at the meeting, sitting with Hendrik, with Dawid, when you know . . .?'

'Joshua,' she said, her hands pleading at first, then angry on her hips. 'I sat with them so that they were not alone and they knew that. They need a reality now, not dreams alone. Above all they don't need government and Parks Board crap any more They need something to happen, jobs with money, not tracking in a park without either resources or tourists, which is only paid sporadically because no tourists or rich hunters venture this far into the land. They need to be able to feel safe in both worlds: their own and the one history has forced on them. Only the mine has that kind of money. You know that.' And he did.

She sat down next to him. 'What's this?'

They became companionable again with that question, outsiders together in this drama of loss. 'It's a map of the plans, the mine . . .' he trailed off, helplessly.

She took it, reading the names. She dropped the map as if it had burned her.

'What?' he said, 'What?'

'These names,' her voice shaking, 'these names they are !kung names, the seasons, the gods, their stories.'

'Really? What do they mean?'

She translated. '/Huma is the spring rain and Bara is the warmer summer rain and Tobe is autumn, you know in march, and !Gum is winter, the dry season – the five seasons and N'osimasi is what Hendrik calls Eden, in this case perhaps all of mortal time in one place?'

The enormity of this future struck home. She covered her face, 'Oh Hendrik, Dawid and all your long lost people, I wanted you to be remembered, but like this? Like this? Your names for the land will be heard again, though their meaning will have changed. They will be names now for the gaping wounds of the earth.' And after a pause and a long stare at the map, 'And what will happen to the story of Adam, of Miriam and of Thomas and Nella, even of Abraham?'

She was weeping now. 'Where's my father in all this?'

Joshua sat quietly next to this woman who had tackled so much here, who had not wept when she discovered her father's past, who had not wept as she moved the fragile skeleton. She wept now for a family which had cast a long shadow over her childhood on the other side of the world.

'Sharon,' Joshua begged, 'we remember them, what else can we do?'

'What difference does that make – the land will swallow us all alike, won't it? The land itself does not care, we love it and care about it, we give our sweat and blood to it, like Adam did, and then time and the sand just roll on over it and all becomes meaningless. We forge a little meaning for ourselves and those we love, while memory serves and while there is enough light to see by, but darkness awaits us all. That is the only certainty.'

She turned to him, fiercely through her tears. 'What good these names now? What good these memories of a people long dead, their stories, their way of life long swallowed by the sand and the hideous history of this country? What good these names now?'

Joshua had never thought to see Sharon so despairing. She'd been Sharon the hopeful with the delight of discovery constantly on her face, and her unfailing search for the traces of an almost lost people.

He turned to her, searching for words of comfort and saw out of the corner of his eye a flash of white beneath the Witdoring boom. He held still to look at the tree and the world around it; and beneath the tree stood the old kudu, white, majestic. One back leg taking the weight off, the head with the wonderfully spiralled single horn held level and steady. He stood there, utterly still, his dark eyes watching the two people.

Softly, filled with wonder, Joshua put his hand on her arm. 'Sharon,' he whispered, 'look who is here.' She looked up and for a moment creature and woman looked at each other in silence.

Neither of them remembered how long the moment lasted, before he turned and walked silently back into the desert he had come from. They sat in long silence as the sun shifted from the searing bright darkness of noon onto the gentler afternoon, which promised the eye some relief.

Much later after the contract had been signed and the flurry of white Toyotas had left, Joshua sat on the stoep nursing a whiskey. Adam came on soft tread out of the house behind him and stood before him with the map.

'Joshua,' he said, 'I can't work out what they are doing where. Where is this?' He pointed to Gannakamp – on the map, Bara.

'Adam,' Joshua glanced at the old man in concern, 'that is Gannakamp. You're holding the map the wrong way round. Look, if we stand here and turn it this way, you will see this spot here is Doringaar and here, this is Queens Prize and this here is Ouma se Hek.' Joshua pointed to the places with strange names on the map, but Adam stared at the map, in perplexity.

Finally he shook his head. 'I would be lost,' he said, 'I would be lost here when they change the names, I would not find my way home.'

He dropped the map onto the low wall surrounding the stoep, his hand suddenly shaking again. 'What will happen to Miriam's grave?' He covered his face with his hands, overwhelmed by the extent of the loss.

'Oh Miriam . . .' – the name was agony. It rang out into the evening, disappearing into the great sky, becoming part of this world as her bones had already begun to do.

The next day the packing began. Joshua worked with enormous intensity, determined, now that all was lost in terms of land ownership, to find at least enough gold to sustain life here where different deserts met, and the people had agreed to sell their land for their lives. He willed the ore body to reveal itself to him and to be large enough to give a little life here. It was a rather odd begging, he thought, begging the earth to give so much of herself, so much to be ripped from her womb. No matter how you turn this, he thought, we are destroying something. Destruction has become inevitable.

Just after dawn the large vans' arrival stirred the dust and when they stopped beneath the willows once again, Thomasie ran away. He simply went missing and everyone was so busy that day, packing and marking and remembering where everything went, finding and sorting, deciding which bits of their old life to keep and stopping occasionally to dream of the life caught up in these objects. The child could not bear it, and left, taking only his lovely white stones. Probably they were glad he was out of the way, probably it left everyone free to get on with the work, without the child underfoot.

By evening of that long and heart-sore day, Joshua came to the house. The removal vans were just closing up for the night and everyone was sitting down for a drink on the stoep. He had brought some quartz for Thomas, which he held out to Adam. Gleefully Nella took it and turned into the house to take it to her brother. She came back quickly, her face suddenly pale, realising she had not really seen him all day.

'He is not there,' and ran to his hiding places in the garden only to return with the same answer. Now everyone was back on their feet. No use calling for a child who will not answer, though call they did as well as finding others, everyone else only asking, 'Have you seen Thomas?'

Calmly at first, the child after all was always off playing in places no one else knew, and then with increasing urgency. When the removals people left, everyone searched. They searched the garden, and they searched at Witkopje. No sign of him. Adam searched methodically, trying not to think of the depths of the concrete bore-hole, the slippery sides of the dam, the river, especially not the river, where Miriam had always run when things had got too much. They did not find him in the garden, so began to move beyond the gate.

'Witkopje first,' Adam ordered, 'and perhaps Hendrik's house.'

Janine said gently, 'I'll take this path.' It led to the river.

Finally N'tsa barking called to them from a long way off. They followed the sound and converged gradually in the half-dark. She was standing at the edge of one of the trenches. Feeling a weight crushing his heart, Joshua ran forward and there, in a crumpled heap at the bottom, lay the small body of the white-haired child. Without a thought or even a moment's breath he swung himself into the trench, and in the torchlight of Klaas, saw the lurid pool of blood which had soaked the sand beneath his head.

'Thomas,' Adam moaned softly, 'Klein Thomasie.' Cautiously Joshua crouched down by that crumpled, still form.

The child was breathing faintly. Gently, Joshua tried to examine the rest of his body. It seemed unhurt. Only then did he look as the others caught up, looked up into bright torches beyond which he could barely make out their anxious faces.

'He is alive.'

Janine threw down a blanket and swung herself in, too.

'His head is hurt,' Joshua said as he wrapped the blanket carefully around that frail body. The child did not stir, his quietness made more intense than usual: a stillness of the body as well as the voice now as the injury had taken hold of him. Ben and Josef carefully let down a ladder and held it as Janine carefully placed the child in Joshua's arms. He took the child up cradling his head carefully against his shoulder, where Janine's hand supported it. He was a featherweight as Joshua took the ladder step by careful step, his eyes, everyone's eyes, always on the child, their hearts straining, listening for that faint breath. Adam could not watch, could not bear the possibility of further disaster and had gone for the car already. Nella waited impatiently till her hands could touch the little brother. The car came back, too fast over the sand in the darkness and stopped in a swirl of dust.

Adam stood up, leaving the engine running. 'Janine, you stay here with Nella. We are going to the hospital.'

'No,' Nella said with great conviction and simplicity and climbed into the back of the car. Janine, barely glancing at Adam, followed suit, every move expressing her contempt for such a notion. Adam shrugged and helped Joshua slide carefully into the passenger seat. He was already heading for the gate as Joshua closed the door.

Abelshoop had no hospital so they had to go to Kimberley itself. It seemed terribly long, that drive, despite the speed. Nella's little hand reached over now and again and shyly patted her little brother's shoulder, carefully avoiding the wounded head. She whispered softly to him incessantly, whispered to him stories of who knows what comfort, though the words Ou Groote could occasionally be made out. Janine in turn kept her hand on the child's back as she whispered to her brother.

In the night the familiar bushes on the side of the road looked dark and monstrous with reaching, alien arms that loomed out of the darkness and reached in Joshua's imagination for this child, which had lived in the shadow of death and pain all his life. Adam drove, his face fiercely forward, eyes locked on the road – not once did he look at the child, did not, like Janine, surreptitiously try to examine the wound just behind his temple. Eventually the lights of Kimberley twinkled in the dark. Faint and few they seemed, too little for what they hoped from them. Adam now jumped a red light and then turned gently into the Outpatients drive of the small hospital where all was dark. He went on ahead to bang on the door, banged and banged, leaving Janine to help Joshua manoeuvre the boy out of the car. Finally a sleepy nurse opened the door.

'Yes, what is it?'

Joshua stepped forward into the pale yellow square of light. She took one look at his blood soaked shirt and stepped back, all sleepiness gone. The room, the corridors, the lights, the people all leapt into action behind her as a trolley was brought forward, forms rapidly found and doctors were phoned. Joshua was loath to lay the child down. Somehow he could not bear to relinquish this burden now.

But the nurse gently led him to that strange bearer of human injury, the hospital trolley bed and said firmly, 'Put him down, Meneer.'

Joshua laid him on his side as he had lain in the trench, but on the other side with the terrible wound now showing a gash, which laid bare a fragile skull as white as the quartz he loved. With quick and careful fingers, the nurse cleaned the wound, while her assistant filled in the form with Adam. She cut his lovely pale curls, dark with blood and they fell to the floor in terrible matted little heaps.

Her face looked grim as she worked but she kept talking, asking what had happened. She sensed that Adam needed to talk, afraid of that absolute stillness in the body of the quiet child. She asked about the child, his name, his likes, what he had done that day, calmly as if enrolling him on a course. This soothed Adam and, looking at the wound for the first time he told the story of the day, breathlessly fast at first, but slowing gradually, as the little body seemed to ease under her fingers, the small hands unclenched as she put in the glucose drip for the shock. Already the unreality was receding, and felt a little less overwhelming as they waited for the doctor to arrive. When he did, the child was taken off to theatre without any further preliminaries. The nurse was left offering tea. Janine insisted that everyone accept the offer.

They sat anxiously sipping sweet tea. Nella became restless and unhappy until she was taken out to the car to sit wrapped in the blanket Janine had brought for Thomasie. She curled up on the back seat and seemed happier there than in the chill corridors of the hospital. Joshua waited with Adam as Janine sat with Nella in the familiar smell of the car.

Slowly, Adam began to talk in a soft frightened monotone, terrible to hear. 'Little Thomas, wounded child of the wonder of quartz.'

He looked at Joshua with helpless, questioning eyes. 'What have I done with my children? Abraham I lost a long time ago, long before he ate your bullet. This one I am not sure I ever had, he was part of Miriam, part of the dream she always spoke of, all that was left – of her or of her dream?'

A pause and then, 'Do you think we are doomed to unzip our children merely to leave them blinking in the fires of hell?'

Joshua, not knowing how to answer such a question, reached forward to press gently on the older man's arm.

Adam continued, 'Thomas is what I could not give her,' he said, 'my hands could work the land she loved, could maintain a home, a life, children and what love my clumsy heart was capable of. But my tongue could not form those words she loved, though I loved her, love her still, but it was not enough.'

'This child does not know who he is, this child who is silent always, who does not know any words, hers or mine.' And with the sudden, frightening intensity of a heart pushed almost to the edge, 'I cannot lose him too. I cannot.' And he broke free of Joshua's grip and walked jaggedly towards the door behind which the child had disappeared, hands raised. But as he reached the door, reason, dignity and a curious mixture of hope and despair held him, stopped the fists from beating on that door, and he whispered, 'Oh, what is it that you do? You geologists who come searching for gold in our desert, what is it that you do to our lives?'

Joshua, no longer simply a listener, but a part of this story, could once more think of no answer beyond, 'I am sorry, Adam, so sorry.'

'No,' Adam said, 'don't be sorry. What you have done will bring life to our town, twelve years overdue. John brought life only to me, when I lost everything I thought I held dear and discovered my children and my land and my heart again.'

'How so?' Joshua asked.

Adam returned to his seat. His voice its old self now, though softer, seeking carefully amongst the words for the truth.

'You know what happened here. After the scandal, he was placed at head office, and taken off the project. As far as I know his wife came out to patch up the marriage and they finally decided the best thing to do for this would be to return to England. He went into management then, I think.'

'In the meantime Miriam had gone to Kimberley. She was waiting for him to come for her as he had promised. She waited in increasing despair as the gaps between phone calls got longer and longer and finally dwindled into silence. He lacked even the courage to tell her a final decision. Perhaps he did not make one, drifted into one, dazed by pain himself? It is not for me to say. Of course I only learnt all this much later.

'Miriam finally came back She could not bear the exposure of waiting so vulnerably in public, so powerless, unable even to communicate and so dependent on decisions that were not hers. She lived with Cecilia and Rosalie for a while, and Nella and Abraham would visit her. I did, too.

'There were letters for a while. It was hard to see her read those letters of ever-diminishing ardour. Very hard. To watch love die is a terrible thing, even a love that breaks your heart, perhaps especially so. Perhaps it validates our own brokenness, I don't know, I know only that I could not bear to see her diminish, broken by this misplaced love.

'But she would not live any other way – her despair as complete as her joy had been. Watching her become grey I knew suddenly what colour was and radiance had been and in losing her, loved her truly. I was no longer afraid of the brief transience of beauty and of joy, but knowing it as part of the whole. I saw her again as I first had without fear, just when I had reason to fear for her. She was finally almost transparent, a shadow of her former self despite her swelling womb.'

There was a commotion at the door and then Cecilia and Rosalie stood in the room.

'Oh, Adam,' Rosalie said, 'we came as soon as we heard.'

Adam stood up and went to her, taking both her hands in his, 'Thank you old friend,' he said, 'but there is not much we can do. We must wait.'

Cecilia placed a basket on a chair. 'Then we will wait with you. We have done that before.'

'I was just telling Joshua how Thomas was born.'

'A good time to be telling it,' Rosalie said and they settled themselves down, passing sandwiches from their basket.

'Miriam spent much time in your garden, didn't she?'

'Yes,' Cecilia said. 'She would sit by the willow near the fountain for hours weaving flower crowns for Nella, or any other child who happened by, or she would walk in the apple orchard, singing softly to herself, picking carnations and lilies with holly to bring into the house. Also of course the rose garden, where we all go when we hurt.'

Adam resumed the thread of his story, 'Thomas was born at Wonderfontein. He was beautiful. He did not look like any baby I had seen before, so pale. We thought he was albino at first, but he wasn't, his eyes were as dark grey then as they are now and his hair as white. When Thomas was born, she felt that she had atoned. She seemed relieved and had come to some kind of a decision.' Adam was still frustrated by the things he did not know.

'May I?' Cecilia asked gently.

Adam nodded mutely.

'She had decided to find out the truth. So she took baby Thomas to England, wanting to give him to John. He refused to see her.'

Joshua could hear that despairing voice, how should one manage the leap from "you mean the world to me" to "I will not compromise my family by seeing you" ringing out in the wilderness.

Rosalie spoke now. 'He was really a diffident man, and though his language was so pompous, he was quite self-effacing around Miriam whom he thought an angel. I think sometimes diffidence of that kind, which denies the glory called forth by love in oneself, is the cruellest response.'

Adam continued, 'She returned. She brought me Thomas. She would not look at him and said only that he was mine, all mine, as she could never be, and left. Though it broke her heart to leave, she did not think she could be a mother then.'

Adam poured himself another tea and stared in silence for a while out of the dark window into the silent night. 'Well, geoloog,' he said, using the old word for Joshua, 'you did not think to find such stories here, did you? Here in the quiet desert, where people become unbearably small.'

Cecilia went on again, completing the story. 'She went to Bethanien, where her father had been a missionary and taught at the school there. She lived a truth she thought she had found and she thought it meant she should live alone, a life of sacrifice. It was not a bad choice, I think. Like her father she was loved there and did much good, but she pined nonetheless and faded eventually. Hendrik, whose daughter lived at Bethanien, says she left one day to live in the land of the white kudu. Her ashes were brought back to be buried in the garden at Pniel, where you see the small quartz angel beneath the willow tree.'

They were all silent for a while, caught by this story of loss. The silence was relieved by the arrival of the nurse who came to tell Adam that Thomas had been concussed and would need to spend the night at least in the hospital. The wound had been stitched, and they would not know what damage had been done until the swelling of the brain subsided. He was now stabilised and Adam could go and see him briefly.

Adam insisted on staying the night, so Joshua drove home with Janine and Nella, who had fallen asleep in the car. They drove slowly through the quiet night, the trees now more like sad wraiths reaching longingly for them, the living, as they moved rather than monsters threatening the littleness of their lives.

Nella was furious next morning when she woke up, that she had not been left at the hospital with her father and brother. 'He needs me,' she cried, 'he needs me. I want to go to him.'

Sharon, who had come over, and Janine and Joshua decided that she would probably be no good at school in any case, and would be less use with the packing of everyone's things. Therefore Sharon would take her to see her father and brother. She packed a bag of things for Thomasie.

'Where are his stones?' she asked.

No one could find them. They searched his room. Finally she said, 'They must be in the trench where he fell, perhaps they fell out of his pocket.'

They went to look. The ladder was still there, a forlorn reminder of the previous night's accident. Joshua climbed down, with Nella right behind him. She could not resist. She found them, too, still clear of sand as down there no wind could blow and cover them as it did all other tracks in the desert. As she crouched down to pick them up with a small joyful cry, she looked at the walls of quartz on either side and fell silent.

Then, 'Joshua,' she said, 'what is this?'

Joshua came towards her. 'What is what?'

'This here. In the quartz, right at the bottom of the trench against the floor, these dark specks in the quartz.'

She had noticed tourmaline and pyrites in the quartz. Joshua knelt and looked carefully, then began to clear the sand from the spot to try and trace the dark specks along.

'What is it?' Nella asked. 'What is it, Joshua?' aware of his excitement, but not knowing what it might mean in a quiet world suddenly filled with extremes of disaster and joy.

'Is it something good, or something bad? What are they? What are they doing in the quartz, those black things? Shall I help you find them?' And she began searching the other wall all along the floor of the trench.

Sharon swung herself down too. They found more and discovered a pattern. They could not repress their excitement any longer, though two of them hardly knew what they had found. But Joshua had found his ore body again. He whooped with joy, with finding, as he crawled along the bottom of the trench, scrabbling in the dirt and sand. All else was forgotten for the moment. All disaster faded in the face of this discovery, which meant he knew that the betrayal had not been complete and would not be in vain.

'Hey, what's taking you so long?' Janine's voice above the trench. 'What are you doing in there? Some kind of war dance?'

'Look. It's back, I haven't lost the ore body after all,' Joshua said as he stood up at last and looked radiantly up at Janine, and twirled Sharon and Nella alternately in the trench. 'I must get to my maps and grids and see where this goes. I must get the excavators to change direction. They have to look along here. Here where I thought it ended, it only really begins.' He clambered out of the trench ignoring the ladder and went off to his tent.

Sharon said, 'Nellatjie, I think we may be going to hospital without him. I wanted to go into Kimberley anyway.'

Joshua distractedly yelled an apology, which they ignored. He traced the possible directions of the ore bodies, checked with samples of sand and core and finally, miraculously, the structure of it all made sense, how could he have missed it before? Of course the ore body did this, it went deeper, much deeper than any of them had thought. Joshua went back to the core boxes he had given up on and there near the bottom, on the last pieces were the indicators. It was simply a fault, a huge fault in the earth, which drove the gold to unimaginable depths. Joshua ran to Adam's house and phoned the Kimberley office.

'Paul, you have to come out here. I've found it, I've found it. It is huge, I think, but very deep.' Paul agreed to come out the next morning. All day Joshua spent poring over the maps, while the excavators exposed more and more of the fault lines and confirmed the direction of things in Doringaar and through to Queen's Prize.

By lunch he was exhausted and sat down to muse over the accidents of fate. If that child had not fallen into the trench he would probably not have found the ore body again. He did not like to think he could have been so careless, but the possibility remained that this silent pale child of his predecessor had shown him what was what. In the afternoon he decided to drive into Kimberley to get some supplies for the next day as Paul was coming out for a couple of days and possibly not alone. Also he wanted to share this news with Adam. Joshua wondered how he would feel now that it had happened. Would he be as happy as he thought he would? Was he truly ready to see mining happen to his land? Or would the thought of his earth hollowed out beneath the feet of those who lived on it, finally fill him with horror?

As he drove towards Kimberley the air seemed charged to explosion, lightning licked at the ragged horizon and dark clouds came roiling in behind the dust, which whirled itself across the parched earth, a frantic death dance or a welcome for the rain?

At the hospital there had also been developments. Thomasie's left lobe had been quite damaged and would need some time to recover. He was still on the drip and was almost transparent. His sister and father looked anxious.

Adam responded to the news with resigned gladness. It was all over for him and he was only glad it would be more than a sham operation. The jobs would be real, the money too, and the development of the fickle tourist trade would be backed by a solid mine. There was almost a kind of shy pride that his land should have yielded such riches, which would provide the impetus for recovery.

Thomas, despite his paleness, was recovering with the speed usual in children. He had begun to draw with the things Nella had brought him and the quartz crystals were back in a little pile by his bedside. He glanced over at them occasionally, smiling at their familiar presence. He indicated to Sharon that she should come nearer and look at his pictures. They were all of Ou Groote, Sharon was delighted to see. Ou Groote beneath the Witdoring tree, Ou Groote on his own, staring softly at the viewer from the picture on which Thomas had carefully traced also the cracks in the rocks from which Ou Groote emerged into this world. And finally the last one, which he held out to her with shaking hands, his eyes wide and luminous with joy. It depicted Ou Groote leaping across the page towards a star that glowed like a jewel in the night sky, and Ou Groote was bigger and more beautiful than ever in this: he was a light himself in the dark veld he leapt across, and up into the night sky.

Then Thomas beckoned Sharon closer. She bent down to him and he whispered, 'I have been to the land of Ou Groote and seen my mother at last. She was weeping still so I took her hand and told her we had met. So Ou Groote can go now, he can go home at last where the quartz maiden is waiting for him.' Through tears, Sharon looked carefully at this last picture of Ou Groote and the star maiden, while in the room around them the silence grew into wonder: Thomas had spoken.

He spoke again. 'Will you take this picture? Will you take it to our father?' Sharon took it gently from his slim hand. 'Yes I will.'

And with eyes as blue grey as his own, she smiled at her little brother.

On the asphalt in the hospital car park the first heavy rain drops hissed and steamed. Even in the sanitised rooms of the hospital the smell of rain could be sensed creeping about the corridors, whispering a secret joy of relief.

By next morning Janine was passing the news out to everyone as they went about their chores listlessly, sensing that they might soon be meaningless with the coming changes, but not knowing what else to do: Kleinbaas Thomas had spoken.

Hendrik's eyes shone with delight as he saw her running towards him at the milking. 'I know,' he said, 'I know – but tell me anyway such news.'

'He spoke,' Janine said with tears in her eyes, 'he spoke of his father and the white kudu.'

At evening, Ben and Josef, Hendrik, Klaas and Joshua all found themselves sitting about a fire at Joshua's caravan. They had teased him about his Englishman's braai – with jacket potatoes instead of pap – but had eaten the blackened and buttered spuds with obvious relish anyway. They were aware that this too was ending, and talked about Ou Groote and about prophecies and how oddly they worked out.

'So in the voice of a child, his mother's spirit is released at last,' Hendrik said. 'Ja, Joshua – you see what you have done?' Ben added.

But Joshua remained dubious, 'I did nothing.'

'Ja, that's true,' Josef said, 'you only dug the trench that the child needed to fall into to let his mother go and find his voice.'

'But that makes no sense.'

'You cannot put it on a grid, geoloog,' Hendrik said, smiling at the old name now, 'but it does make sense. Here it does. Here where so many worlds are meeting.'

'Hey, geoloog,' Josef laughed, 'I have a new name for you: Mvundla.'

Joshua bridled a little, expecting mockery: 'And what does that mean?'

'Where I come from Mvundla is a hare.'

'Is that because I dug a warren of trenches across the land?'

'Ja, that and ...' Josef hesitated.

Hendrik smiled. 'Tell us a story. It is about time for another story.'

So Josef told the story of the lovely maiden Tembe, who lost her voice to a terrible curse.

'A woman was walking home from a feast when she stumbled over a pitcher, which someone had carelessly left on the path. She fell and cut herself. In her anger she cursed whoever had been foolish enough to leave the pitcher on the path.

'Now not far away lived an old couple, to whom life had not given much, only their small daughter Tembe, whom they loved above all things. The angry curse of the woman found Tembe and stole her voice.

'The unhappy parents sought throughout the land for a cure — medicine men and witchdoctors could not help. No one could help. The girl grew beautiful and clever, but she had no voice.

'Then one day a young man fell in love with her and he wished to hear her voice. So he spoke to the spirit of the trees — he begged them to help him find her voice.

'Mvundla, the hare, happened to be sleeping in the roots of the tree and, skelm that he is, he saw an opportunity for his own profit.'

Joshua became restless, anxious about where the story would go. But he had learned enough about fireside manners by now and did not interrupt. The others enjoyed his discomfort, he could see — it was part of the story for them.

'Mvundla told the young man that he would cure the girl if the young man brought him a fresh supply of berries and green grass.

'The young man, thinking it was the spirit of the tree speaking, obeyed and brought fresh food every day to the tree. He himself became thin in

the process. So finally Mvundla's conscience was stirred (he was not really a bad creature – winking at Joshua). *And he set off to find the girl, who was working in her father's field, planting Sorghum. She did not see or hear Mvundla and he got angry. He grabbed some of the little plants and planted a whole row upside down, with their roots looking strange in the air, to get her attention.*

Finally she saw what he had done and spoke in irritation.

'What have you done, you idiot? Now I will have to replant them!'

Then she realised that she had spoken and ran home to tell her parents. Mvundla turned away in disgust. She did not even thank me, he thought. But then he remembered the piles of fresh food and all was well between him and the young man and Tembe, who got married after all and lived happily till they died.'

Hendrik said, 'So the desert has named you – Joshua Mvundla.'

'Ja, you helped here by mistake,' Ben laughed, but he put his hand on Joshua's arm to show how it was meant.

Josef looked at him, 'Never mind,' he said, 'Mvundla, it was good mistake, nê?'

Gratitude almost overwhelmed Joshua/Mvundla. He knew that, however mistakenly, he had become a part of something, of a story – an event. Here for a moment he belonged to the world and savoured the passing minutes, not sure that they would be enough to contain the fragmentation that lay ahead.

10
The chattering of weaver birds

Sharon had expected to leave the confusion of Abelshoop behind gratefully. She would be glad to go back to Johannesburg, hectic, but not disturbing one's equilibrium in the way one's father's unresolved past did, she thought. So after the Vermeulens had driven off behind their removals vans, she went soberly back to her caravan and began sorting through her papers, sadly neglected for a while with the land claims meeting and the departure of so many people who had become dear to her. The very air felt different, and though she knew that summer would go on till well into March, it felt as if it were waning already and the reckless generosity of the stormy rain season was over. It still rained occasionally, but it was simple rain, no blessing in it, just weather.

She put off leaving without knowing why. Several of her copies of rock paintings were unsatisfactory and she decided to re-do but found herself only staring at them trying to see the meaning in them and in the story of her father. She wanted and struggled to understand why she should have somehow become a part of it, though it stretched far into the past before her.

She sensed that she was only procrastinating, putting off the moment when she would have to face her long anger at her father's ineptness and her mother's creeping despair, which had thrown such a long shadow over her childhood. But it felt so quiet here now, before the storm of industry's arrival – and for the moment all she wished to do was to sit before the painting of the white kudu and sense a threshold there: into another world, into herself and into her father's heart, without the disturbing presence of Adam's pain or Thomas, whom she tried to think of as a brother. Yet a part of her shied from such thoughts and feelings, because of the overwhelming presence of her mother's loss in them. She knew dimly that it was her father's ghostly presence that kept her on Pniel. The puzzle of his life which she had stumbled on now blocked her way back home. She did not know what to do with this knowledge about him; this view of him as human, vulnerable not simply father.

Down a long, clean corridor of Kimberley's hospital, lay Esther Vermeulen, her body recovered from the wound. The bullet had lodged itself in her collarbone and had presumably hurt a great deal but had not done any permanent damage. No organs were hurt, the lungs not even clipped. The verdict was that the body would recover almost entirely, apart from a small scar. Physically, nothing vital had been touched. Despite this, the doctors were puzzled – it was exactly that: the vital spark seemed to have gone. Nella, in her generosity, decided to pay her a visit too while her brother had so many other visitors, and Joshua went along.

She lay in bed, seemingly in a trance: silent and still, hands tensely restless at her side, eyes staring at the ceiling, unmoving, almost unblinking. Adam and the Radcliffe sisters visited regularly, brought flowers, such cruel bright, breathing tulips that brightened the room unbearably, but nothing happened. The simple bullet wound case had of course been complicated by the presence and loss of a twelve week old foetus, so the doctors in their wisdom surmised that this, along with the terrible death of her husband right before her, may have caused the shock which had turned her away from life.

'The nurses say we must talk to her. She can hear us, they say, even if she does not respond. We must tell her that Thomasie is better, and of the beautiful pictures he has drawn. Also that he speaks. Perhaps that will encourage her to speak again too,' Nella told Joshua.

And she hurried on those light feet through the corridor to tell her sister-in-law the good news. Joshua walked a little behind and marvelled at the girl's seeming resilience, her sweet generosity and her determination that all would be well for everyone.

When he turned into the ward where Esther lay, he saw her perched rather precariously on the edge of Esther's bed. She had caught those roving hands in both of hers and was speaking to her with a gentle insistence and a determined lightness of tone that seemed quite heartbreaking. He stood at the door, unwilling to break in on the privacy of the moment.

And suddenly he saw that eager form, lean forward, crumple and cry out: 'Talk, why don't you?' she called out in anger and despair, 'why won't you talk? Why will you not be well? It is all so awful, so, so awful.'

In a few strides, Joshua was there to catch her before she fell to the floor. Finally it had all been too much: the fear about her little brother, the loss of the big one, the loss of home, the uncertainty, her father's unhappiness. Joshua sat on the floor, his arm around the slim young girl and simply let her cry. The nurses looked in briefly, saw what was happening, drew the curtains around the bed and draped a blanket over Nella.

Gradually the racking sobs allowed words to become clear, 'O Joshua,' she cried, 'where will we go? Where will we live? How will I speak to my mother so far away from the angel at her graveside?'

Joshua told her what he knew, that Adam had chosen a place in Kimberley near the schools for her and Thomas. It was not much, he knew, and not consoling, but it was what would be and she needed to know. She listened quietly and then sitting up with a sudden urgency, said:

'What about Janine? And what about N'tsa? She won't like it there. We can't leave, oh we can't leave!' She cried softly now, too despairing to call out, knowing there would be no answer, knowing that this change was inevitable and that she was powerless in it. Eventually, exhausted, she fell asleep. Joshua held her tight, wishing he could take her to Pniel or Wonderfontein where a white kudu might appear from the cracks in the rocks to console her.

But he was trapped here, beside the bed of a woman in a coma who had retreated and chosen to lie in this terrifying stillness in which only her roving hands moved constantly.

She had lain like that through Abraham's funeral, through the battle over the land, through the drought and through the rain which relieved it. For weeks, as the world changed around her, Adam buried her husband in a grave far from his mother's. She lay like that now as the only family she had known in her short life left the home they had known for generations, left the life they had lived for generations.

Joshua got up cautiously and carried Nella back to her father, saying a soft farewell to Esther as he went. When Adam saw him carrying her limply in his arms, he hurried over anxiously. But Joshua shook his head and smiled sadly as he explained what had happened.

Adam stroked her hair softly. 'It is good,' he said. 'It is good, she needed that cry and for me she always hides her tears.' Softly he kissed the top of her head.

Sharon left a month later, made more restless by the progress on the mine, and distressed by the changes being wrought on a landscape of which she had come to feel a part. She drove through the sticky heat of the day without stopping until she saw the grey, jagged skyline of Johannesburg reaching up through the choking grey from Soweto's cooking fires, and the fine endless dust blowing off the dumps.

It felt strange to be driving along those dangerous, fast, roads again, with overloaded taxis careening from side to side, hooting greeting or warning amid the sleek grey cars of the city's young professionals. She slid easily past the once beautiful station, under the grey concrete pillars, then past the planetarium and through the gates of the University of the Witwatersrand. Parking was easier here on Saturdays: some things did not change much she thought wryly, surprised at the happiness of this thought. She made her way to the dim corridors of the anthropology building and came eventually to the small dungeon room, which had been her domain for a while.

How odd to be back, to realise how much she had missed its dusty ugliness and the roots of the Jacaranda tree outside. She heard footsteps coming down the corridor and then the voice of her mentor and supervisor of her project.

'Sharon, how are you?'

She turned.

'You look exhausted. Have you organized somewhere to sleep? No? Why am I not surprised?'

And after barely a pause, 'Come. You're coming home with me. I still have that couch.'

Leaving Sharon no time to protest, she took up her backpack and left the room. Sharon followed, too tired to go through the ritual of refusing only to eventually accept with tarnished grace.

She left her car locked up in the carports of the university and drove with Professor Oelke out of the centre of Jo'burg to the leafy, quiet high walled suburbs, where a little removed from the highway, only the dogs barked and the creepy crawlies hummed, as ice clinked gently in sun downer glasses. Sharon was silently shown the bathroom and handed deliciously soft, clean towels. After so long in a caravan, the hot water, even the electric lights seemed a miracle of modern science and the bubble bath was close to ecstatic. She emerged feeling a new person in a borrowed bathrobe.

She joined Professor Oelke on the dark and leafy veranda for a glass of fresh mango and orange juice. For a moment both sat quietly and simply listened to the world settling for the evening around them. The joyful bark of dogs greeting owners coming home, the shout of children released briefly into swimming pools and the inevitable sound of TVs through open patio doors. They drank the cool sweet juice and chatted inconsequentially about the mine, which had of course been on the news already, and the many plans and opinions of how best to run a mine in the New South Africa.

Then Professor Oelke brought out two platefuls of steaming bobotie and a bottle of rich red wine. They ate companionably before they pushed back their plates, and in the flickering candlelight to avoid the many insects attracted by brighter lights, Professor Oelke finally asked, 'So what have you got so far, then, on this great and frustrating project of yours?'

'A story,' Sharon replied, shrugging hopelessly, 'a painting or two, land claims battles, people who are lost, the opening of a mine, a romance and a promise of rain for hearts in exile.'

'I would have thought that's enough to be getting on with,' the professor remarked dryly.

'But they're such fragments, they come from so far apart and yet they form a whole, I think. I sense a pattern, but I can't see it.' She paused, trying to gauge her professor's reaction.

'Or perhaps I only want it to be there and all is coincidence really.'

'Why don't you tell me what it is that they have in common?'

'That's just it – nothing that I can see . . . they simply all happened together, in the same place and some at the same time, but others years apart or even centuries. They're little rags, merely, from which I need to weave some kind of theory to make sense of the raw data.' Her professor watched her shrewdly as she spoke. She noted the signs of strain around the eyes and the brow too ready to frown. So she said, quietly, sensibly:

'Well, we will have to sort out then, which are synchronicities and which are simple chance and irrelevant.'

Soon it came to the time at which Adam signed the final paper, which sold the land he had worked for so long, and which he knew as a man knows a woman he has loved for a long time. He sold the land his son had hoped would be his one day, which he had cared for through tilling, through love and labour, through learning its names and places, through understanding how it worked in its seasons, through giving it labour and seeing with patience what it could give in return. It had truly been his, beyond any contract and so he could leave it, knowing it could not really be taken from him. But his children, he knew did not yet have that certainty and were leaving not only their home but also the meagre memories of their mother, and the whole world of their imagination, peopled with the wonders of Hendrik's stories.

Knowing life near Abelshoop would become unbearable for them without Pniel, he took his two children: his daughter of the sunny heart and his little changeling who had not been born his but had become so, out of the wilderness of Abelshoop and into the confusion of a growing city. For Thomas it would be a world no longer silent and perfect with the dazzle of quartz. Still, Adam took him, with the money, to a place where he would have to make sense and become part of the dreadful noise of the world. Nella too would go on to high school in Kimberley. She would be, he knew, bright and eager to take on the world, and still convinced that all the world loved her – as it did.

Kimberley Girls' High School, with its pseudo-public school business, suited Nella's high energy and thoughtfulness and she loved the choir, the music lessons and the infinitely better equipped art room. Her enthusiasm for exploration and discovery gained in scope. Her art teacher, who seemed to live in the art cupboard with a ghost she named George, was both terrifying and strangely familiar. The fulsome praise for felicitous experiments and the overwhelming tantrums over poor and unimaginative work, turned art into a battleground with oneself in daring and fear overcome, as one reached for unknown territory which turned into home as one explored.

'Life is a mystery,' her art teacher said, 'and our job is to paint that mystery.'

Thomas too discovered a world to be explored in talking to strangers in his soft, deep voice and asking questions. He was so consumed by his thirst for knowledge that school was transformed from something merely to be endured between time spent with his beloved quartz. Its purity had mirrored his silence and kept that threatened, unbroken wilderness intact in his heart. His favourite subjects soon became History and Religious Studies, which questioned most profoundly the simple perfection of his silent world, but offered also the hope at least of answers in a world so wounded by loss. An unexpected joy for one who had been silent so long was singing – softly at first, then gradually increasing in strength and range as he found his voice and all the places it could go.

Often in the evenings Nella would sit down at her mother's piano, playing the old Lutheran hymns of the missionaries, and Thomas would find the worn hymn book and sing – both prayer and gratitude for the wonders of an imperfect world:

Breit aus die Flügel beide
O Jesu, meine Freude
Und nimm dies Küchlein ein
Will Satan mich verschlingen
So lass die Englein singen
Dies Kind soll unverletzet sein.

Joshua left Abelshoop too, called off the project by project managers who would in their turn be replaced by mine managers, shift bosses, by all the ugly hierarchies and petty rivalries of the mining world. He fled from them gratefully, back into the quiet bush, the sand, the endless soil sampling of the hopeless exploration project, of science merely, unrelated to life, to people, to politics and its expediencies. These projects, pointless in a commercial sense, their only value lying in the brief moments of joyous discovery they might afford, were therefore also harmless, he felt – and safe. They left in their wake only graphs and well-marked maps and a dead place in the desert, where one's caravan had stood. No lives irreparably changed; no gaping holes in the bowels of the earth; no graves to mark the storm of a passing stranger.

In the rather beautiful empty riverbeds and kloofs around Zeerust, Joshua was glad to scramble along new, still unmarked grid-lines, glad to look up and feel that he was a stranger in a place merely unknown and so un-haunted by the familiar names with which man stakes his claim upon the earth. Ben, who liked to roam, came with him, but Josef decided to stay on Pniel and work again on a mine. He had found a home with Klaas and his family, as he had not known since leaving Grahamstown.

Joshua accepted no invitations to supper, briefly and swiftly drank the tea he was offered on the stoeps of various farmhouses, and was civil but remote. And it worked. The farmers simply shook their heads as they thought and talked briefly about another mad geologist who had parked his caravan at Oom Lourens' place and was achieving as little as all the others did. Sometimes Joshua found himself peering carefully at the shade beneath the acacias, longing to see there again a shimmering shape only partly of this world. He kicked himself for it but couldn't help himself. Ben watched and smiled but said nothing. The nights were long and empty here, the campfires small and fearful in the dark, and though the sky glittered, it was the cold faraway shine of the winter sky, like the sun pale and tired, bright but never truly warm.

Then one night he dreamed of Hendrik. 'Stranger,' he said, 'Stranger, you are now Mvundla, because you gave Thomas his voice back. Do not forget who you are.'

Joshua did not yet know what this meant, so he waited, and schooled himself not to wonder what Sharon, and Paul and Adam were doing.

'Let's have some tea to finish off and think about it for a while.' Professor Oelke took Sharon into the kitchen and talked of small domestic things for a while: her two cats and a play at her daughter's school in which she needed to be able to fly and was rather anxious about. When they each had a steaming mug of stern, unsweetened strong city tea in their hands, she led the way to her study.

'Now let's begin at one place only, don't think of it all. Tell me the story first – what is it about?'

So Sharon told the story of the white kudu again – almost word for word as she had heard it from Hendrik. Professor Oelke listened without interruption. She had once spent many an hour with the elders on the mission station in the old Transvaal where she had grown up, collecting their stories, recording them; then writing them and checking them again and again for accuracy. She listened now with some enchantment to this tale of rain and thirsty earth, of love impossible across the gulfs of strange worlds.

As Sharon finished, her eyes were filled with images of the place where the story belonged: she could see Witkopje, where both the star maiden and the white kudu had appeared. She could hear Hendrik's voice filled with the certainty of wonders to come, and she could sense Nella's breathing next to her as she had listened to the story. She thought she could feel the heat beaming off the sand, too.

Professor Oelke let her dream-think for a while as she leaved through the pictures and notepapers and found the careful copies of the rock paintings, which depicted the white kudu, legs delicately crossed as it stepped from the cracks of the rock, the round ears pricked forward in welcome and curiosity. She saw also others in which the kudu was waiting just inside the other world beyond the rock, while the tiny man on the other side of the crack in the stone was bent double, hands extended behind him in pleading, cringing almost, as !kia took hold of him and he writhed in agony on the threshold between the worlds.

Involuntarily her hand reached out to the little figure. She murmured beneath her breath the words from a nursery rhyme her mother used to sing to her, about a small deformed gnome who caused a child all sorts of trouble during the day and then at the end as the child kneels to say it prayers, the little hunchback comes again but asks only for the child's prayers. 'Liebes Kindlein, ach ich bitt, bet fürs bucklicht Männlein mit.'

She remembered crying over the little rotten creature, which yet asked for forgiveness, and which she now knew was a part of every human heart, which craven and full of random mischief, begs at the end of the day for redemption and a sharing of the light. And here he seemed to stand again: tiny, sinful mortal man on the threshold of the divine world – writhing in agony, but salvation was waiting just beyond the rock face, waiting to step into a ready heart.

Only occasionally in Kimberley did Adam's children speak of Abelshoop – recalling Hendrik's stories and most rarely of all, the presence of the white kudu. A shyness neither had known before, to remember these things and to speak of them, beset them both. It was impossible as yet for them to tell what it was, but in the silence of their hearts they both wondered often, for there remained, despite all the liveliness of their new home, an aching gap.

Adam saw it in his children and recognised all the signs of an exiled heart. He himself felt like a tree uprooted. The earth, tarred and hidden here, allowed him no connection to the secrets of the soil in which growing things softly whispered their songs of life and hope and yearning for the light. They were songs he had known, he had shared their harmonies – and he could not hear them here. He went often to the park near the monument, or sat beneath the palm trees outside the Kimberley hotel to hear the birds, at least. He missed the cry of the fish eagle and the bubbling of the vlei loerie. Songs he had hardly been aware of knowing were now a gaping emptiness in his mind. He felt lost without his land, his familiar routines and without his people. He found time to mourn all that he had lost: Miriam, Abraham, his land, himself.

He went one day to the McGregor Museum. He approached the red brick sprawling building with the steep Victorian roof and the rather dreary front patch of ground, which at the back was transformed into a beautifully green oasis of lawn with white iron garden furniture set out for tea and scones. He sidled shyly along the deep veranda to stand patiently at the door till he should be noticed.

Finally the young man at the desk looked up, 'Yes, can I help you?'

'Please,' said Adam, feeling as inept in this strange environment as Klaas would have felt, 'please, you have here a skeleton, from Abelshoop. I would like to see it.' He paid the entrance fee and was taken through the large rooms, which recalled dreamily the siege of Kimberley, the fashions of the early diamond rush and then darkened suddenly into a hall of nocturnal animals. Beyond all that stood the hall of religions, and right next to the door, as if waiting for a friend to appear, lay curled and peaceful upon carefully arranged sand, amid a few Kalahari grasses, the bushman skeleton.

The sated purring of the dishwasher told Elaine Shackleton that another day was achieved. Everyone had had food to eat, even the cats, and now all were sitting quietly going about the business of evening. A good day. And there it was again, the bleak endless void, not in the world, which was after all only itself, but within. The void declared all the peaceful, at times even beautiful routines of life, of survival, futile. She had contemplated this futility for a while – without beauty, without joy – and then stopped thinking about it and simply got on with it. For Sharon, she said to herself, but also because it was all there was to do. Her life had always been one of waiting: waiting for his return and now waiting for disaster. She had kept John where he belonged, she had won that battle, but she suspected it had been an empty victory. Futile.

She had become skilled at hiding this daily companion, from the eyes of the world at all times, and from herself, sometimes. Those long months every year when she had been alone with the child in a village where everyone knew everyone else's business and knew what to do about it so much better than oneself, and he had been away leading his "life of adventure" as he called it, in Africa.

She had played the role of patient wife and mother – and played it well. Keeping the home fires burning; taking care of his child; sending him chatty letters about the small events of their lives. The child's modest triumphs at school – she would never let their daughter get bigheaded – were her greatest joy to write of: hoping always that this would bring him home; would make him stay more readily.

It did not, but she had patience and service to offer and he was grateful to have a home to think of, a place which he called home, whether it felt so or not. It was something to show the world when the nagging voices of childhood asked, "well son and what have you made of yourself?" It was an answer to give Guilt, which streamed from his being in all directions, pleading; unforgiven. It streamed to the woman in Africa, and an experience of perfection denied and it swirled around him endlessly at home in the midst of the family and the traditional fidelities he had betrayed, though he honoured them outwardly.

To the world he presented a man of high achievement and ambitions unexpectedly realised, but within he was a worm that had neither been strong willed enough to forget moments of loveliness in a desert, nor man enough to choose freedom from empty obligations. On good days he could pretend to be a caged bear like Flaubert, lashing out with vicious wit at an uncomprehending world.

Sadly even he knew that this rather self-indulgent image was far from the truth and so he flung the remnants of his being at the rich and varied experience his standing in life afforded him: holidays in exotic places, painting and walking in Italy and the one brief, true consolation: singing. Everything else turned to dust in his mouth and the achievements of his life, obsequiously enumerated for him by the Uriah Heeps of the world, meant least of all. He felt hollow.

Elaine knew this, and the constant need for vigilance she had felt since his return from Africa sapped her love. Yet he became her all, her world – finally she needed him so much, she had to turn him into nothing. Then the last feeble embers of their love turned to ash and no glimmer remained to flare into sudden life, no surprises left in the brittle perfection. Was resignation better than despair? They never dared to ask.

'Professor Oelke, what is it?' faintly she heard Sharon's voice.

'Professor, you were looking at the drawings – what did you make of them?' She shook herself and quickly translated her thoughts into acceptable academic language. She began to speak, her voice gradually losing the softness of human and childhood memories and taking on the stern, well-projected voice of the lecturer. Sharon had missed it, and smiled.

'Of course these pictures represent a shamanistic experience. The little man here, bent so double, is in the grip of !kia. And the experience of liminality is treated with reverence by the San. It is an experience of ultimate personal union with the divine, achieved only at great pain, as can be seen from the bent figure and the supplication of his hands.'

'Yes,' Sharon said, 'that's what Hendrik said, too.'

'But in the trance dance this same experience becomes one of healing and social service and then in the paintings, which recall that experience, a cultural recording and self-expression and another sharing, a remembering of the place and time. The white animals of the rock paintings in Southern Africa, unusual in reality, are symbols of this experience, because the messengers from the spirit world often appear during !kia in the shape of an animal.'

'To us, to Westerners, this is hallucination because it seems so different from the accurate knowledge the San have of the animals, and their great skill at hunting.' Sharon put in, afraid to be lost in that world again.

'Oh, but to the San the two are not mutually exclusive – they are simply looking at things from different perspectives – from the world on earth, or from the stars, or from the world beneath the rocks.'

Sharon waited.

'The shamanistic union with an animal, !kia, is not a contradiction or denial of their carefully scientifically accurate and sophisticated observation and classification of animals in their habitat, on which their survival depends. It is an experience of a different order. The qualities of the animal observed take on symbolic dimensions in the realm of the imagination and the subconscious, where union with the spirit world becomes possible, real, and helpful to the community.'

Sharon moved to protest, but her professor stopped her with a hand.

'This process among us would often be dismissed as madness. Indeed, according to Joseph Campbell it mirrors the schizophrenic descent into chaos. But because the person experiencing !kia is not lost in the chaotic and unacknowledged symbols of his unconscious, but surrounded by symbols his religion has made real to him, it is not madness to be shut away or drugged. It's divine inspiration which serves – not threatens – society and becomes something to be feared – because of the pain and the risk of not returning – but also a gift and an honour. It is useful to the wellbeing of society because it brings healing and wisdom.'

Sharon smiled at her professor, grateful for the calm way in which she spoke the carefully chosen phrases and aware that beneath all that, flowed the current of a child's heart which recognized the experience beyond what the mind could do to explain it.

She took up the thread. 'And Hendrik's white kudu reveals all that longing to be in touch with one's greater self, represented by the star maiden, or the quartz – Jung's anima.'

'The stories and paintings of Hendrik's world are joining world literature now? There is my thesis: the gift of liminality to self and community.'

And Sharon wrote it.

Appointed Chief Geologist of N'osimasi Mine – so named by the people for its great promise of wealth and the unification of warring factions – Paul moved his office and all the paraphernalia of geologists into Adam's home as respectfully as he could. The walls were soon covered with the colourful science of geological maps, delicate pencil sketches of the planning office, architects ideas for the reception areas, the rec club and other buildings. Gradually they changed the wide, open horizon of Abelshoop: the slender grace and mournful music of the windmills replaced by the taller shaft heads and mine towers. Their whine seemed to silence the birds. Such hulking forms appeared more sinister, but of course more productive too. Over time their productivity bore visible fruit. The town grew, accompanied by the tamed beauty of landscape architects.

In its somewhat feudal way, the mine provided. There was a carefully laid out club with a swimming pool, golf course and restaurants. As well as a new primary school and kindergarten, there appeared the air-conditioned offices of the mine managers and their palatial tennis courted and swimming-pooled homes. All this had to be built, providing jobs in the process. The town became greener with that slightly frenetic aliveness that comes from living above a hollow earth, which shudders occasionally as it resettles into its changed contours and its emptiness.

So the people of the town and the area prospered – at a cost, but what choice did they have? The streets were no longer littered with the unemployed, and only the shanty town fell into disrepair. All was apparently well in this post-colonial piece of Africa: ecologically sound mining and politically correct employment policies in a large corporation. Who would have thought it?

The mine dumps had no time to look grey and mournful, but became almost immediately gently rolling hills with Karoo bush and Kalahari grass, with Cosmos and the lovely arches of the camel thorn trees. In carefully landscaped form, they surrounded the dam which had been near Ouma se Hek. Around the home dam on the other hand, the excavators had been put to such creative use that it now looked convincing as a lake, with softly sloping hillocks ranging from Witkopje almost to the doorstep of the mine reception area – Adam's old home. The quantities of water which the mine preserved or created meant that the weaver birds soon returned after their initial fright, flamingos came too and the bright jewels of the malachite Kingfisher could be seen alongside the red bishops weaving their flight above the water and among the trees.

A game reserve with a long and curving river boundary, as the Parks Board had promised was soon created. The tall game fences drew their shining lines across the veld where Adam's farm fences had been and the wide emptiness was now populated: Black and Blue Wildebeest, Impala, Gemsbok, Zebra, the Kudu and Springbok, and the Duiker and Steenbok that already lived there. Long lost game of the area was re-introduced to be viewed in amazement at wonderfully natural-looking watering holes – actually great feats of engineering and irrigation, and the finds of Johannes – from beneath the elegant lapas by visiting shareholders and tourists.

As far as Paul could see there remained only one problem he and the other managers had so far not managed satisfactorily: that was the "San heritage" of the area. Hendrik and his family had stayed on in his house behind the reception of the mine, and while not exactly an eyesore in its round and clean simplicity, it was a constant reminder of a job left undone.

Hendrik watched all that happened with golden eyes gone quiet and reserved. His son Dawid had gone to Kimberley, Hendrik did not understand entirely why. So he waited, knowing the white kudu had done his work, had worked his ambiguous magic, but had not yet gone home. Hendrik did not know what needed to be done still: the strangers had come, the rains had come and riches had bubbled up from the earth in unimaginable plenty. His people were respected: their names rang out again across this land in new and strange forms, formed by the tongues of strangers, which he found oddly beautiful. "So what is the matter?" he thought, "Why can I not feel the peace I should? I am tired – I want to go home."

Writing turned out to be not enough for Sharon. Professor Oelke sensed this and questioned her.

'Well,' clearly less comfortable in telling this part, 'the way Hendrik and Dawid told the story, there was a prophecy linked to the white kudu.' Sharon stopped, uncertain.

'Go on,' Professor Oelke said, 'what was the prophecy?'

'That, when strangers came, the white kudu would be seen again. He would be able to go home to the star maiden and the drought would be broken.' she answered wretchedly.

'Why so wretched? That makes sense, after all. The union of the longing heart with the soul makes life bearable again, the spirit feels at home and the world is renewed in rain. Why does this bother you so much?'

Sharon squirmed. 'Well, the geologist, Joshua, who found Kara/tuma was considered to be the stranger.' Sharon was not yet able to speak of her father in this.

The professor laughed, briefly surprised, then asked, 'And did the drought break, did the white kudu go home?' No trace of laughter now.

'Yes, we had quite a bit of rain and then, when the gold was found in sufficient quantities – that too was felt to be a kind of rain, a blessing – it bestowed an ability to live again on the land and not starve.' Her voice trailed away and then she turned. 'You don't think this is ridiculous?'

'No,' the older woman replied. 'It is how oral traditions work. Unlike written ones, they have reference points not only in the past, but incorporate living reality – the present.'

'There's more.'

Haltingly, she told the story of Miriam and John: the great intensity of failure that it had been, of the child Thomas, born of the union nonetheless – of the blessing delayed.

Almost inaudibly she added, 'John is my father. He was offered !kia – that same experience through love, the psychologists tell us – but he refused. That refusal halted the story, the prophecy, and the possibility of grace. He betrayed hope – for the town, for Miriam and for himself, because he allowed social convention to deny the reality of his experience.'

On the outskirts of Kimberley, just beyond Kamfer's dam with its joyful weight of flamingos, as one drives North to Klerksdorp and Potchefstroom, there lies a red building with a green roof. It's beautifully set among oak trees, with poplars lining an avenue that leads one unerringly to the Victorian lookalike colonial mansion. Within that building are kept those who lose their minds but are too rich to be truly mad, and so remain trapped forever in genteel disorder – waiting for release or disaster.

Esther Vermeulen was transferred there when her bullet wound healed. The hospital could do no more for her and she refused to leave off her staring. This blankness, this persistent absence, distressed Adam who was afraid of his desire to break it violently. So he placed her in this misplaced building for lost souls, unable either to live or to die.

Once in this building Esther, through bursts of inconsolable crying as well as tantrums of surprising and distressing intensity, gave the nursing staff to understand that she wanted a white room, with white curtains and a white bed. No cheerful colours of a spurious attempt at normality for her. Now she sat on her white wooden chair in her white room staring out past her white curtains, clutching her white clad doll looking at the green world outside, which was closed to her.

"What did she seek in this pristine world?" Adam wondered in the mornings, when, with Nella and Thomas safely at school, he would visit her. "A return to the quartz world of Wonderfontein? A still and frozen dream of the games of Nella and Thomas as they ran to the river and laughed for joy at the wondrousness of life – a childhood he knew she had never experienced?" He hated this refusal of hers. In her presence, he felt awkward, dirty with life, and helpless, as Miriam had made him feel helpless when she was pregnant with Thomas.

Miriam had made a choice which to him had seemed like refusal, until the singing beneath the trees at Abraham's funeral. Now he looked at true refusal. He did not like to be reminded of the past in this way, of his own failure to understand and of the repetition here. Still he went nearly every day to see her and then sought comfort with Kara/tuma in the Hall of Religions.

On the table before her lay a set of cards laid out for Patience. She played endlessly, patiently, and very well, the nurses told him with futile pride. She showed no response to how the game turned out, was never tempted to cheat, and never turned a card out of sequence. Endlessly the cards passed through her hands in threes, as she laid them on their piles or strung them out in the even perfection of alternating red and black.

O, the neat order of descending hierarchies, which the game does not allow one to question, and becoming meaningless as soon as one does. Watching her play with rapt attention and an expressionless face was profoundly moving, for the intensity of concentration suggested a searching a hope to find something meaningful. And yet the empty repetition, the rule bound treadmill which dealt with chance in the same way over again, held no hope of resolution. Whether the game came out was little influenced by the skill of the player, knowing what was needed on each of the seven lines of neat cards, and able to see, even create, the occasional possibility of sequence was all. Still the cards might come out wrongly and mostly did; and there were no wild cards, with which to take the game into one's own hands.

Adam would sit opposite her and tell her all the little pieces of news. Mostly he told her about his children while she played or held her doll and stared out of the window. She seemed not to hear him, but he would not give up. He hoped, and waited for a response.

11
Waiting

Tales of a white kudu began to circulate again. It hurt to see this creature as public property. No photos as yet, but beautifully imitated bushman paintings, imaginatively represented this rare creature in glossy brochures. Paul turned away sickened, knowing he should be glad. So much was good about this, beyond economy. Much had been restored – the names for example. Each mine shaft named for the five brief and wild seasons of the Bushman's year seemed an elegant way of offering the riches of the earth back to its lost people.

The Lost People, Paul mused, remembering the plans at the beginning of this venture. He would like to erect a museum or something to them. He would like to protect the many paintings that were scattered about the three farms more carefully. But he didn't know how to do this without being patronising or offensive. He was haunted by the story of the white kudu, of how John and Joshua had both become drawn into it and he found Hendrik's golden-eyed smile disconcerting.

Then two years later, just as the Abelshoop mine project was beginning to find its routines and regularities, he received a letter from that Sharon Shackleton, who had taken care of the skeleton for them. Was she John's daughter? And then he kicked himself for beginning to see the Bushman destinies and entanglements everywhere, going native he thought grimly – as John and Joshua had. Her request was to bring a group of students from Wits University to explore the rock paintings of the area, find some tools and speak to Hendrik, if he were still there.

Curious, and in response to a hunch he couldn't quite place, he invited her and her students for a week in September, and found himself looking forward to the visit. He tried to imagine how the place would look to her now, and wondered whether she would approve of the mine's inept attempts to protect a heritage they simply didn't understand. Luckily local folklore, and the awe which everyone felt for the white kudu, kept people away from the paintings; while Hendrik's stories and his fame as a trance healer were so widespread that he was respected and his hut and garden were left intact. In fact he had become in many ways a talisman of the mine and Paul couldn't imagine it without him. He felt it was a little like living in the presence of a saint – awe-inspiring but also unsettling. That was the closest he could come to defining it, anyway. Little did he know how troubled this particular saint felt.

As he awaited the arrival of Sharon, a plan gradually fermented, flashed into moments of brilliance and subsided again into unreadable blackness. But eventually he thought he had found a solution. He allowed it to rest in his mind and wrote several letters to head office before approaching De Wet, the mine manager, with a plan already formed and approved. He knew this was cheating, but thought it important enough to break the many unwritten rules of large corporations that were run by expatriates.

Eventually he spoke to De Wet whose hands were tied and could not prevent the project from going ahead. All Paul now had to do, was wait for September's brief spring and the archaeologist who would come then. She did not come. Things came up and the visit was cancelled.

Elaine's despair was renewed on the morning her daughter announced that she was going to Africa to complete her studies in anthropology and archaeology. She wished to study the San people and had been offered a place at Wits University in Johannesburg for her postgraduate research. It was a university, in a city, not the wilderness which robbed the heart and left it without all the usual bonds of decency. Elaine knew she should be glad of that at least, but the hollow place within shrunk in fear nonetheless.

John also was overwhelmed as he remembered that he was to blame for planting this seed in his daughter's heart. All his life he had been afraid of the potential realisation by his child of the faint glimmers of life within his heart, which lay only in memories.

And now she stood before him and wished to go in search of a people who lived differently. He had to let her go, but he knew that the time between this departure and her return would be one of waiting for disaster, of all his house of cards to come tumbling down about him again.

They took her to the airport with heavy hearts, smiling with the appropriate parental pride at their daughter. And they drove home in silence to wait for the long-unspoken words to come back to them, their daughter's eyes opened to the people they really were.

'Thank you! Thank you very much,' Adam said as the young man with the glasses and the pencils in his shirt pockets left him with Kara/tuma once again. The young man smiled at the courteous man in neat khaki and veldskoene who had become a familiar figure at the McGregor Museum.

'Hey old friend,' whispered Adam, as he did nearly every day – stepping close to the glass which shielded the lifeless display from the potential vandalism of the living. 'Now we are both here where we do not belong. Do you ache to be back in the open veld, to feel the stinging winds of August and the storms of December afternoons?'

'Do you miss the bark of the baboons and the howl of the jackal – even the insane laughter of the hyena? Do you think we can live here?'

His eyes searched anxiously over all the delicate bones, lying in that too clean sand in the ancient foetal position, hoping to see an answer, scrying desperately a future he did not, could not believe existed, because he could not imagine it. And a voice he had not heard in years, that he had longed for in all the nights of those years, came to him from many memories.

"Adam, do not let the time of the hyena come upon you now, here in the city. They would not understand its necessity and would not let you find the answers that you need in your heart's wilderness."

"But what must I do?" he cried, anxious to keep his mind here, not let it turn in frustration from her whirling metaphors, from her madness.

"Wait," she replied with the certainty of the dead. "Wait, be patient. Only be patient. Don't be too hopeful, it feeds despair, but do not despair entirely, either," her voice silvery in the slanted golden afternoon light in a hall where all the gods lived patiently together. Adam turned, expecting to see he knew not what, but saw only the dainty dance of dust motes in that light and took delight in it.

"Was I right to leave?" Adam could not help but ask of that golden light. But her voice had gone and he knew the answer, and knew he did not like it, for it was half truth and half lie, and the only possible answer: it was right at the time. Right to leave the place where his heart lay buried. All he could do now was wait.

The silence of the Highveld night, unbroken by the faintly swelling and falling hum of the highways around Johannesburg, held the two archaeologists spellbound for a while. Then Sharon went on.

'But he didn't know it, did he? Nor did Joshua. They didn't even know about any of this – until they were a part of it, until it was too late. They played parts. That's all. They didn't choose to hurt and destroy, but they did. When we are involved in these stories, they become simply accidental, random, without cause.'

'As gifts must be,' Professor Oelke said softly. 'Do you know that in German "gift" means poison?'

'No.' Sharon didn't know what to make of that.

And three days later, Sharon said to her mentor, 'Then the only question worth asking still is: How do we live with such gifts?'

Professor Oelke responded, 'In Abelshoop people will live more bearable lives now. You and all the individuals involved have had a very moving experience. All manner of things have been well.' Pause. 'And memories to make the daily grind bearable, at times even beautiful.'

'Is that the kudu?'

'Yes.'

'And what happens now?'

'You should write to your father.'

Sharon began the letter immediately, though it took the longest time to finish. It was interrupted by a knock on her study door. She opened and Professor Beard, head of their faculty walked in with a letter.

'What is it?' Sharon asked, a little surprised by his face.

'A request for the presence of an archaeologist – a job offer. A very good one.'

'From?'

'From N'osimasi Mine in the Northern Cape.'

'And you think I would be interested?' She was not sure whether to be angry or to laugh.

'No, we think you should go.' Professor Oelke stepped in behind him. 'It is your field of specialism. You know that area better than anyone.'

'But . . .'

'Go – they need a curator, someone to lead research projects. The universities need places in the field where students would be welcome, would be funded and would find things worth finding. Go! It is a gift.'

Sharon sat back down. 'How long have I got?'

'A month.'

'Thank you.'

She finished the letter to her father, giving her address as N'osimasi Museum, Abelshoop and placed it together with a copy of her thesis in an envelope and sent it that same day before she could change her mind.

Paul drove out to see the Radcliffe sisters. Rosalie and Cecilia had asked to remain on their land and had kept ownership of the piece with the river boundary, where the company was not allowed to mine for ecological, and other, reasons. They went about setting up a school for the children of mine employees with funding help from the mine. The school was to be built near the river, and Rosalie and Cecilia had taken a young teacher under their wing.

The message from head office to the mine managers was: get involved, support and fund. It will look good to the liberal shareholders. So Paul drove out to see the sisters to let them know he cared.

'Paul,' Cecilia cried, 'come and look at the plans for the building.' He was whisked off to be shown a series of delicate drawings of buildings in the veld, with the river just behind the graceful buildings. They had the rounded, soft shape of African huts, a little like the termite mounds which dotted the veld everywhere, or the tops of the camel thorn trees – no angles anywhere, only smooth flowing curves. 'Let's drive out to where it will all stand,' she suggested.

'Moira, dear, will you come?'

'Yes, of course,' and a slim form appeared in the doorway, with honey gold hair and a generous smile.

They took a leisurely drive out to the wide bow in the river's course. The day had all the clarity of the rainy season's mornings, when the previous afternoon's rains had settled and cleared the dust enough to reveal the subtle and delicate shades of the landscape: yellow and brown, red soil, and the shimmering white of the blades among the silver green leaves, the dark bark and the soft yellow balls of the blossoming thorn trees. Even the half people, strange lost forms, were blooming into a brief, though armless life. As they approached the river they could hear the occasional bark of a baboon outpost, informing his tribe of the things he was seeing, the soft melodious bubbling of the doves and the loud, wild chatter of the busy weaver birds.

Moira had brought the pictures and the plans and Paul was poring over her shoulder in admiration. Rosalie began pacing out the dimensions, while Cecilia held back, afraid of turning it even briefly into a building site. Hendrik arrived soon after. He'd been following the honey bird again, he said happily as he joined Cecilia, who was hunkered down by the river, watching dragon-flies dart across it and listening for the occasional plop of a curious fish.

'En toe?' Hendrik enquired, 'are you happy with your plans? I think the river will be happy to hear the chatter of the children. Alive: like the chatter of the gashemshe after the rain.'

Moira had come up behind them. 'Who are the gashemshe, Hendrik?'

'They are the little black rain birds.'

'Cecilia,' Moira called, 'Cecilia! Hendrik has a name for the school.'

After about a year, when he sensed that they were settled into their new lives, Adam would occasionally bring Nella and Thomas to visit Esther at the weekends. He hoped that their presence might stir something that his own could not. It didn't and she remained silent in her white world, in which only a speck of dirt, the nurses told him, would lead to any kind of a response from her. He explained to his two children, both of them slender tall teenagers now, 'Hers is a world intact and unbroken by any of life's threatening experiences. A world of repetition only, statistically vast variations no doubt in the 52 cards, but essentially the same patterns over and over again. A world in which her soul can rest in safety, like quartz used to be for Thomas.' His daughter's response shocked him to the core.

'No,' Nella said angrily, 'that is not what it's about. We should not envy her the perfection she longs for. We should pity her because she is afraid, and only does what she must. But the perfection of quartz it is not.'

'Why, Nella?' he asked.

'Because quartz is white not because it keeps away from the earth but because it belongs to the earth. It is white and beautiful because the earth made it so. It is the power of the earth transformed to perfection. It is not denial. It is pure, like alchemist's gold, not through refusing suffering, but through all the horrid processes in the earth's entrails.' Her eyes searched his face to see whether he understood.

'Go on.'

'It is like the gold they are finding there now – on Pniel. Look at the pain they cause the earth to find it, look at what they destroy in the process, but what they find has made life possible for the people, all the people of Abelshoop. It has made that piece of earth inhabitable for so many people, who struggled before. Abraham did not want that, he wanted to keep the land, even if it meant it would die. That is what she is living – Abraham's stubbornness.'

Adam looked at her vivid face, which had changed so much in the brief year – almost a young woman now, thoughtful and passionate as the child had been, but wiser now with loss and compromise.

It was the first time any of them had mentioned Abraham openly and it was a relief. 'Oh, Nella,' her father said, 'you are so right. But what can we do to help her?'

'We must wait,' she said with a conviction as strong as her dead mother's had been at the exposed grave of Kara/'tuma, though it was warm and golden with her young life.

They waited, all of them: some with patience; some of them impatiently; others merciful, or merciless with themselves, with or without hope. But wait they had to nonetheless.

Sharon's letter arrived early one morning, slipping innocuously through the door with bills and the odd card from friends holidaying in exotic places. Elaine picked it up while she was drinking her first cup of tea of the day, still in warm slippers and a bathrobe, not entirely ready to face the day. She took the pile through to the kitchen table where she could leaf through it in peace, wondering what the big heavy envelope might be. When she saw its postmark, she involuntarily caught her breath. "Pretoria, South Africa" she could faintly make out on the stamped circle and felt again the stab of pain, which had accompanied the arrival of the post for several months all those years ago.

She recognized her daughter's handwriting, and reminded herself that the dreadful woman was dead. Then she felt hurt that the letter should be addressed to him alone. She resisted the temptation to open it and carefully took it upstairs to him with his morning tea in bed.

John saw her stricken face as she came into their room. 'What is it?' he asked anxiously.

She tried to smile, 'A letter from our daughter at last.'

'Yes, it has been a long time hasn't it?' he tried to joke about it, aware of the ineptness of it. Though, when he held the envelope, he said with relief, 'Oh! It's her thesis. She promised to send it once it was complete and accepted.'

'Oh well, happy reading,' she said. 'I'll go and shower.' He opened the envelope, leaving his tea to grow cold as he read.

Dear father,
Here as promised, the thesis. No doubt you'll find much to argue about and I look forward to that. Also of course, dear aged P, thank you for making all this possible and for first awakening my curiosity for a very different world. I have discovered so much here, about the San and about myself.

He paused, smiling. So far so good he thought, realizing how much he missed the banter with his child. He read on.

I don't know how to tell you what I've discovered, but tell you I must for it has changed everything.

This time the pause was a stab of fear. He had known this moment would come. He had longed for it in many ways, the truth at last, but dreadfully afraid to stand so revealed before his daughter; no longer only daddy, but a flawed human being. He made himself read on as she described with vivid simplicity the skeleton unearthed, which had led her to Abelshoop and the events which had occurred there and her gradual piecing together of the meaning of it all.

Daddy, what you discovered here was beautiful and painful – leaving it must have been a torment. How you lived back home I do not know, how you chose between fidelities that were impossible, I cannot imagine. It must have hurt, especially after Miriam had died and Thomas . . .the sentence trailed off. I must forgive you, dearest father, but it would have been nice not to have to have been so alone when I discovered it.
Yours as always
Sharon

He stared at her name for a while, feeling naked and exposed, and thought of the ruthlessness of fate which had not, in the end, let him escape without choice. When he had thought he was simply following his destiny in coming back from the African interlude as he called it, he had been lying. And now he knew it. Life was not a path some god had designed for him and of which he remained somehow innocent, but a series of choices that caused a great deal of pain. He had not known how much he needed his daughter's forgiveness until it had been given.

Elaine came back, wet and steaming from the bathroom. And when she saw the look on his face, she knew without asking that that dreadful woman was back. Somehow, even from beyond death, she reached into their lives. How had her daughter become entangled in it, she wondered angrily.

There followed another dreadful conversation, accusations so old they barely hurt but that had become the very centre of their lives. With pity, he thought of his daughter standing alone on the brink of it, probably for longer than she'd realized.

'Elaine,' he said, 'Elaine, please stop,' taking her in his arms.

'I can't,' she sobbed. 'I don't know how.'

12
Return

Sharon was the first to return to Abelshoop arriving in October, just before the start of thuma. Hendrik and Dawid were at the airport in Kimberley to greet her, two small and dusty golden figures in safari suits with the kudu head logo of N'osimasi mine.

Hendrik smiled delightedly, 'Welcome back Kamiyo, child of the river who renews our paintings.'

'Oh Hendrik,' she said, taking that small frail form in her arms, 'will you never stop naming things?'

'It is through our names that we talk to each other beyond mere words. You needed a new one.' He answered.

'We all call you Kamiyo now in our stories about the finding of the mine.'

'Will you tell me my name story one day?'

'Of course.'

Paul, the chief geologist, whom she faintly remembered, had driven them in. He held back politely until she had stopped talking to Hendrik and then came forward, 'Welcome Kamiyo. I know no other name for you anymore. It's better than Sharon Shackleton,' smiling. And she was glad to lose her father's name. Then he became full of enthusiasm for the museum and the research projects there. Then when they had her luggage, he said, 'Do you mind if we go via town? My wife is just at her check-up.'

'Of course.'

A questioning look to Hendrik and Dawid, who grinned, 'A little soldier on his way.'

So they stopped at the hospital. 'I don't mind waiting,' Sharon said, 'I will catch up with Hendrik and Dawid so long.'

Hendrik looked old and frail now, though he seemed transparent with joy at seeing her.

'What has been happening? Tell me.' They told her of the Gashemshe School at the river on Wonderfontein and of the museum, at which they worked. They told her also of the shudders of the earth as it settled around the hollow tunnels beneath their feet. They told her of the failure of some of the projects, the reforestation of the mine dumps was tricky and the air had grown dim with constant dust much finer than the sand. They told her of accidents underground, of rock falls and people trapped for days. They told her also of the beautiful gardens, the lake with the flamingos and the game park. They told her that they had not danced in a year.

'Why not?'

'The white kudu has gone,' they replied, 'but he has not gone home. And we do not know how to dance the dances of a hollow earth.'

Paul returned and introduced Sharon to his wife, Moira.

Then they drove out to Abelshoop and Sharon became absorbed in the landscape, which hurt the eye in the dry, charged air. As they left Kimberley, gradually the smell of the peppercorn trees faded to be replaced by the faint trace still of winter burning acrid in the nose, and the ubiquitous dust.

Paul dropped first Moira, and then Hendrik and Dawid home. Sharon held Dawid back a moment.

'What's the matter with Hendrik?' she asked him.

'He has cancer – of the bone the doctors say. There is nothing they can do and there is no one whose /num is strong enough to dance for him.'

'Oh Dawid, I am sorry.'

'Yes . . . Thank you. Now that you are here, he will be ready to go, I think. He is tired.'

Paul drove Sharon to the rec club, where a room had been prepared for her. It felt odd to be back, and not back, in this way. To see Witkopje, to see it gleaming in the sun and then to turn and see not open veld but the luxurious garden around the rec club, with the golf course stretching to the river, where lapas marked braai places and boats were moored. Having unpacked briefly and washed the weariness of the journey from her, Sharon walked out for half an hour before the appointed dinner time with Paul and Moira. She walked quietly up Witkopje and came suddenly upon the face of the white kudu emerging from the rock, his ears pricked forward as he stepped towards her. Softly, she placed her hand on his neck.

'Hi, Ou Groote,' she said, 'here I am again.'

And so began a new phase of life for Sharon, who knew she was indeed now Kamiyo. And as Kamiyo she found herself once again in the gentle shade of Witkopje and knew it was her home. It was interesting work: setting up a museum, with Dawid as her assistant, of as much of the San culture as could be remembered. They spent hours taking photographs of paintings and discussing what they might mean and then with Hendrik's help thinking of ways to display them. The mine was generous in its funding, so she was able to buy many artefacts she knew were lying unseen in various other museums across the country. At the same time, Dawid and family, and Klaas and Mina were able to make for the museum beautifully painted and etched ostrich eggs, shell necklaces, karosses and the harp. Moira brought her Gashemshe pupils often to practise rock painting with paints which Mina showed them to mix in their little horn tip containers. Soon also enquiries about research projects came in and invitations to speak at functions and give lectures.

It was useful work, at times beautiful and the old restlessness faded almost entirely. Then one day a letter arrived from the

McGregor Museum in Kimberley. They were taking down their hall of religions, wanting to do a wider cultural spread and the space simply did not allow for the skeleton to be suitably displayed. Would N'osimasi museum like it to come back to the place where it had been found? All day she felt as if she had been given a wonderful gift and at lunchtime she shut everything up and she and Dawid took the letter and the news to Hendrik, who had become too weak to leave his hut.

Hendrik's faded eyes lit up when she read him the letter. 'Oh,' he said, 'this news is sweeter than honey. If Kara/tuma comes home to help you and see that all is well, the little whirlwind can come for me and take me to the fields of heaven's star flower.'

'Hendrik,' Sharon said, taking his light and wrinkled hand, 'must you?'

'Yes.' And turning with great difficulty to his son, he said, 'Dawid tonight you must dance – call everyone.'

'Pa,' Dawid said, his voice again that of a child, 'tonight?'

And so it was that there was once again a gathering around a bright fire on Pniel. This time it was just outside Hendrik's old hut, which had stayed where it was through all the mining and building of the past three years. Hendrik was sitting outside again for the first time in months. He sat wrapped in a beautiful kudu kaross on a bed of blankets banked about his body to keep the creeping winds out. But in the light of the fire his face was bright as it had not been in a long time and he called out to Kamiyo as she walked up, 'Come my dear, come sit here next to me,' patting the ground next to his blankets.

She sat on the warm sand, with her legs crossed and took his dear old hand in hers. 'Hendrik, it's good to see you up,' she said.

'Just wait,' he said, 'just you wait, the night is young – look how low the Southern Cross still is. It has a long way to go and the rain bulls have not yet galloped tonight.'

Sharon squeezed his hand and sat quietly holding it as she had so often in the past few weeks, while he told her his stories and she recorded them for a book.

A kudu was roasting in pieces on the fire, it sizzled gently now and again as the fat was squeezed from the lean meat by the hungry flames, which leapt about and sent their ashen stars into the night. Beer was sent around and the meat was hungrily eaten. Kamiyo watched that Hendrik ate, which he did, his eyes twinkling at her as his small pointed tongue delicately caught every last drip of the meat juice from his fingers. When he had finished, he sighed and leaned back. 'That was good. Ou Groote he said, thank your cousin for me, no? Klaas, that was good hunting.' Klaas leapt up and bowed lightly in Hendrik's direction and then cast his eyes briefly up at the stars, while his hand gestured gratefully to the meat.

Gradually the eating came to an end, children fell asleep on their mother's laps or nestled comfortably against their shoulders. Only the bottles of beer passed peacefully from one hand to another. The fire died down to a soft glow of embers as the moon rose, a slim boat sailing through a sea of stars, while on the horizon unseen in the darkness the rain clouds gathered.

Kamiyo glanced over at Hendrik. He smiled at her, his eyes quiet now, but bright and holding within them a secret joy. 'It is beautiful, no?'

'It is,' she agreed.

'You are glad to be living here?'

'Yes, Hendrik, Kamiyo is very glad to be living here.'

Then Mina began clapping, slowly, heavily at first. Gradually the other women joined in: first the heavy clap and then the soft shiver of the shell bracelets they were wearing. One by one the men got up and stamped their feet softly in the red sand. Again the shells of their anklets shivered a soft hiss after each stamp. The rhythm was soon mesmerising as the men began a shuffling line circling the fire. Only Hendrik remained seated, nor did he clap with the women, but his eyes danced as he watched with happy pride his family dance for him. Kamiyo clapped too, but her eyes were nearly always on Hendrik; he seemed beautiful tonight, radiant in the starlight.

The dancing continued its soft insistent rhythm, but remained calm, there would be no !kia tonight, only this soothing quiet dance and the longing in the voices of the women.

'Hendrik,' Sharon could not resist, 'what do they sing?'

'They sing for the stars to come and take my heart home,' he answered her.

Kamiyo could not see for the tears in her eyes. She had known it all along, but to have it said and said so calmly was heartbreaking. She could not now imagine the world without this tiny old man who even now seemed so much more alive than anyone else she knew.

He took her hand, 'Sjjt sjjt sjjt my kind,' he said, 'sjjt. It will be all right. I will be with you still. I am looking forward to long talks with Ou Groote and walks too across the fields of the stars.' And she looked at his face, on which were now the marks of great pain in the hollow places beneath his merry wrinkles. So she nodded, but kept his hand in hers as they sat quietly watching the dancers and listened to the song calling on the mercy of the stars.

A wind began to blow and Hendrik shivered with anticipation, the dance became more insistent, the song's pleading rose piercingly. Kamiyo looked up and saw suddenly coming across the sand towards them from the open veld a small dancing whirlwind. It spun and flickered as a flame might, it approached half shyly the old man whose soul it had come to take to the stars. It circled the fire and the dancers, who watched even as they kept to the rhythm of their dance and then it swirled through the fire and seemed to bow before Hendrik.

Hendrik smiled slowly. 'Old friend,' he said, 'welcome.' And the little wind blew softly around him, stroking his old head with lingering fingers, gradually enveloping him entirely in a gentle swirl of dust and ash stars caught up in its dance. Hendrik laid his head back on the blankets sighing and smiling. Then without letting go of Kamiyo's hand, he held his other one out into the wind he said, 'Let us go,' and the hand Kamiyo held went limp and soft.

She dropped her forehead on to it. 'Goodbye Hendrik,' she whispered to herself, 'goodbye.'

The dancers' circling slowed, the song lost its piercing sweetness, became softly melodious, mournful yes, but also joyful as the little wind took off towards the stars and they saw Hendrik's face, smiling – the hollows of pain smoothed and gentled. Almost imperceptibly the dance came to an end and the song quietened entirely. One by one the men sat down around the fire. In silence they watched the faint, almost invisible, blue flames run away across the glowing embers of the fire as the ashen stars settled and winked out on the sand around them. Then Dawid began to tell a story of Hendrik's childhood, how he had danced with the little black rain birds and fallen into the river and come up again holding a silver fish in his hands rejoicing. They sat all night recalling his life, telling stories and as they spoke the rain began to fall.

The next morning the museum remained closed. Dawid was preparing to bury his father and Kamiyo had gone to Kimberley to fetch Kara/tuma home. The curator had waited for her. Together they stepped up to the glass window behind which he lay curled upon the sand. He opened it and Kamiyo caught her breath on the dusty dead smell, which greeted them. She opened the box she had brought lined with horse blankets and tissue paper. Tenderly she picked up his bones one by one and placed them in the box, softly as if he were a baby. She wept for Hendrik and for these bones, which had lain so long in exile, for the story which she feared was ending in tears after all.

'Sharon, my dear, how are you?' the voice suddenly familiar in that rainbow silence of the stained glass window afternoon and the tread, soft but firm with that sure and certain weight upon the ground of a man who has walked on earth he knew and loved to its very bones: earth he owned and which knew him by his name, too.

'Adam!' she turned towards him, careful to place the bone in her hand down gently first, as the big man came to take both her hands warmly.

'What are you doing here?' she asked in delight

'Oh, I visit Kara/tuma a lot,' he answered lightly, too lightly. 'How are you all?'

'The children are well. Listen can I help you? What are you doing?'

'Kara/tuma is coming home,' she said. 'Adam you must come back with me perhaps. Hendrik . . .' she paused.

'I know,' he said. 'Hendrik is dead. That is why I wanted to see Kara/tuma. I will come back with you – just for the burial of Hendrik.'

Together they placed the light, fragile bones in their box and carried it out to her car.

Then they drank coffee in the museum teashop and talked a little of the old days, but there was much between them that lay silent and unspoken. They smiled through the silences, knowing what they meant.

Kamiyo went off to do the paperwork regarding Kara/tuma's move, while Adam went to fetch his children from school and prepare for a weekend at Pniel, in which they would bury Hendrik.

It was a simple ceremony in the end. Hendrik had asked that he would be placed in a shallow grave just beneath the painting of Ou Groote on Witkopje, among the playing children. And this is what happened. Dawid and Klaas dug the grave. Nothing was done to Hendrik's body, they left him just as he had died, curled in the position he wished to be buried in, the position he had held when first formed: foetal, curled about his heart.

They carried him out to Witkopje, placed him tenderly in the soft sand pit they had dug for him and Dawid spoke to him. 'Enjoy,' he said, 'enjoy the flowers of the sky pastures, and the gallop of the rain bulls as they follow the lightning across the sky. Enjoy the company of the quartz maiden and come sing for us occasionally on the wind.' Klaas and Dawid turned away from the grave and gathered the children about them.

Dawid picked up a quartz rock, edges smoothed and brightness dimmed by years of exposure at the earth's surface. 'Find lots of rocks like these to place on the grave, so that he will not be disturbed,' he said.

And they did. Adam and Sharon helped and found themselves as pleased as any of the children who grinned proudly when Dawid found the stones they brought acceptable. Soft murmurs of 'Oupa Hendrik will like this one,' and long, serious discussions about the merits of various stones turned the day's loss to grace as the mound gradually took shape. It was not big, not big enough to change the shape of Witkopje.

'So little,' Adam said to Dawid.

'Yes, so little his place of rest will be and unnoticed by the world, largely as his life was. It is right.'

Now Klein-Hendrik – Hendrik's youngest grandchild, shyly took out a hand sized flat rock from his pocket, 'Oom Klaas, may I put this one the pile?'

Klaas and Dawid looked at the stone, they smiled and nodded. 'Ja it will be the last.'

The child reached to place the rock with great care, balanced in the middle of the mound. Just then the earth shook greatly and both Dawid and Adam hunkered down quickly shielding the stone-mound with their hands. The child waited till the shuddering stopped and then placed his final stone.

They all stood quietly a moment, looking at the mound and then turned and went away for tea at Hendrik's hut. Adam was careful to keep up with Dawid, lest he should lose his way in this changed landscape, which had once been his.

When Kamiyo knelt to say a quiet word, she saw etched on that final stone a tiny rendering of the painting of Ou Groote in flight and she remembered the picture she had not yet given her father.

Moira and Paul's son was born that evening. When Paul came in to the rec club from the hospital, having left Moira sleeping with exhaustion, he was greeted by enthusiastic offers of drink. Even Kamiyo came out of hiding to have a round with all the others.

Paul said to her, 'You know we need a celebration, a proper one. Shall we have an opening for your museum? It has been a long time since we did all the openings of other buildings here.'

'Yes,' Kamiyo said, 'I think I would like that.'

'But not just a party,' Paul, drunk with happiness, became expansive now, 'a conference, and a week perhaps of people talking about what's going on here. Because this is an amazing place: a place where an old man dies and a baby is born and life is beautiful.' The others were gathering about him now, smiling, but he was unstoppable. 'A meeting, like you had for the land claims stuff – all the people who have been involved, let us talk about it – in honour of Hendrik and of Adam and all the other lost people of this place.'

He beamed around at everyone and his eyes slowly came to rest on Sharon, 'We should invite Joshua,' he said, '. . . and your father.'

The invitation lay on his desk among the graphs and grids, maps and notebooks. Every now and again, he paused in his work to play negligently with the wonderfully textured piece of card, run an index finger along the scalloped edging and then tap the whole thing thoughtfully against his forehead. He had laughed with derision at first, wondering what Paul could be thinking to ask him not only to come, but to speak about "the project". But the card had not gone straight to the bin. It had stayed nagging, its gold writing appearing again and again from amongst his work. He didn't like it; there was no rational reason to go. It was work he had completed and handed over. He was happy back in exploration, a stranger in a strange land with Ben for company and the night birds who were no longer so strange. He liked it that way and intended to keep it that way.

Nevertheless, he found himself heading into the Zeerust post office where no one knew him by name even now, and accepting the invitation in writing, quite formally. Even just writing the name Abelshoop on the envelope filled him with the familiar sense of foreboding.

Thus it was that, after three years in the deep bush of Groot Marico, Joshua found himself driving northwest out of Kimberley again with Ben, on a road he had half hoped never to see again. He felt awkward and anxious about coming into that shimmering, uncertain landscape again.

Leaving Kimberley just after lunch, he hoped to reach the N'osimasi rec club just as night fell, go straight to bed and come down as the conference began. In this way he could avoid Paul and not have to think too much about the past. But as he was driving on the endless road, staring out of the dusty window, he found himself half hoping to see again the familiar landmarks of that world. He was greeted only by the grotesque looming shaft towers which had replaced the slender elegance of the windmills and narrowed the wideness of the horizon, and yet had brought such prosperity to the town. He heard in his mind again the mournful sound of the windmills blades and had to swerve with shocking suddenness at the bray of a donkey that had wandered into the road. The screeching brakes brought a small figure out of the bush, all but invisible beneath its huge hat. It ran after the frightened donkey, consoled it as best he could and walked cheerfully on.

Joshua rolled down his window. 'I'm terribly sorry,' and was rewarded only with a huge grin from beneath the hat and a dismissive wave of a small black hand. But then the stance suddenly changed and the little hands began digging in the bag, slung across the donkey's back.

'Will you buy?' the voice wheedled now as the hands held out to him a 15 inch windmill 'Look it really turns,' he said enthusiastically. Joshua was only too happy to buy the neat little construction. Ben laughed at him.

'Ten more minute to the turn off,' he said. What had been an entirely nondescript farm gate was now an imposing entrance. Two pillars flanked a wrought iron gate on the bars of which hung the elegant shape of a kudu painted white. It was not Ou Groote he was relieved to see, for the creature had both horns, which reached up to the sky in graceful swirls and seemed to form a vessel as he peered through the gate within which lay the wealth of the mine beneath the cycads and the flamingos.

The dirt road had been covered over and lay neat and even on the ground, and lined with young trees doing their best in the heat. They had used native trees of course, so they managed all right. He had to follow the signs like a stranger, for the whole familiar world of Pniel was gone beneath the glamour of N'osimasi Mine: near the rec club, not far from where his caravan had stood, it was green and silent except for the distant humming of the shafts.

As he pulled up and got out of the car, the earth shuddered with the underground blasting. Joshua shivered. He closed his car, took his suitcase from the boot and made for the entrance beneath the waving fronds of cycads. With an apologetic smile, Ben rushed off to find Josef. Somewhere a water feature splashed softly. He found it all faintly but insistently irritating. The doors were automatic and moved with smooth silence. The receptionist was smiley and efficient from just beyond the pot plants and the computer, but an otherwise empty desk. She knew at once who he was and booked him in. She told him Paul had asked to be told when he arrived and proceeded to phone him. Joshua went to his room and was stopped short by another shudder so familiar to mining towns as the hollowed earth readjusted.

Half an hour later, before Paul could knock on his door to find him moping, he made his way to the bar and ordered a glass of wine, then went out to the patio. He stood a moment looking for a quiet seat, then found a remote corner under the bougainvillea, facing out into the garden.

'Joshua, I didn't think to see you here again.'

He turned in surprise and there stood Sharon. He leapt up to hug her, this stranger who had witnessed his defeat at the hands of Thomas, of Esther, of Adam, and of the mining world.

'Will you join me for a long drink?' he asked. 'I'm expecting Paul any minute.'

'Sure,' she said.

They sat looking out over the small artificial lake which adorned the park of the rec club beneath the sweeping fronds of the cycads and drowning in the whiteness of lilies.

'So. Tell me who you are now,' Joshua said.

'They have called me Kamiyo. It's one of Josef's stories, a kind of African Pygmalion really. A man is alone and carves himself a beautiful woman from a tree at the river. The statue is beautiful and he loves it.'

Joshua lifted his glass to her with mock chivalry.

'Do you want to hear the story or not?'

'Please go on.'

'The younger men of the village are jealous and steal her. He sends messages to her, asking back for everything he had given her as his wife. Finally he even asks for her life. She gives it and turns back into a wooden statue.

'The statue gradually falls apart and the pieces roll back down to the river – where the tree grows again.'

'A strange story. How do you feel about it?'

'Well, it's hopeful, isn't it? Rebirth. And Hendrik said that I breathed life back into their paintings. I prefer not to think of the infidelity in it.'

Joshua gave her a strained smile, 'The infidelity was not yours.'

'No,' she said.

They were both silent for a while. Joshua thought of Esther, of Miriam and John, and Gideon and Adam.

She watched his face and then said gently, 'Not everything can be redeemed.'

To distract him, she explained how she had taken on the job of N'osimasi museum curator and how the idea of this celebration had been born.

'Celebration?' he asked. 'I thought it was a conference.'

She laughed, 'Ag Mvundla, we did not think there would be any other way to get you here.'

And he too had to laugh at the truth of it. Then the silence grew between them, longer than was comfortable. He fiddled anxiously with a napkin and turned it round to read the words on it, then asked, mostly for the sake of saying something, how she felt now about the names the mine had used.

A grimace passed over her face, but then she said, 'You have to take what you can get, don't you? The San have been remembered and honoured. It is in many ways unpleasant: a politically correct sop to the local people to help them swallow this neo-colonialism, as well as the politically squeamish shareholders. It's one of life's stupid pointless ironies that now when the earth here is being entirely ruined, their names are suddenly remembered.'

'Like your new name?'

'Yes,' she said, suddenly understanding. 'Kamiyo – it's both past and future.'

She paused. 'The future does not quite fit us yet – our choices must shape it.' Then a little uncertainly, 'the names alone bring nothing back, but they're all we have left – and their paintings: diminished memory of a light and beautiful way of life. That is gone, irretrievably so, but the names may echo, even in this fake world of the mines.'

She drew breath, 'Now and again I get someone visiting the museum, who hears the names, truly hears them and finds in the paintings that moment of connection with a stranger from a different time, a far off place. And in that moment is restored the lightness of the life they lived and their delighted laughter is heard again, briefly.'

'Wow, Sharon, Kamiyo,' he half joked, 'are you practising your speech on me, then? What does Hendrik think of it?'

But there were tears in her eyes. 'What is it?'

'Don't,' she said, resisting his hand as it reached for hers. 'Hendrik died two days ago. We buried him this afternoon.'

Joshua's hands froze and the muted chatter of communal weaver birds echoed again in his skull. 'How, when?'

And she told him of Hendrik's long illness, of his happiness that Kara/tuma would be brought back to Pniel and their people remembered. 'He was grateful that the mine used the names of his language for things. That they would ring again across these kopjes, dongas and kranse . . .'

'Well the shaft heads, anyway,' Joshua interrupted.

'Yes, and often they seem so empty to me – just words without the life, the belief the customs and ceremonies, which gave them substance. And using them for this seems a terrible betrayal. But when life has done with us the words are all that is left. And perhaps we have a duty to recreate momentarily the splendour that lived once. It doesn't last, of course. All is barren again – they are not life. But they are all we have now with which to shore up our sense of ruin.'

'And ruins are beautiful too.' Paul had joined them.

'Mvundla,' he said, 'the news of your arrival has spread. Welcome to N'osimasi mine,' the joy of new fatherhood still fresh upon his face. Dawid and Klaas joined them.

'Haai, Mvundla,' they called. 'You give the kleinbaas his voice back, but you come in silence.' He smiled, spreading his hands, helpless as always in the face of other people's affection. And then the mood became celebratory.

"Why?" Joshua asked himself. It seemed so odd, so much was lost, why the joy – the bubbling wells of joy. "And I – am I to be Mvundla now?"

'Kara/tuma is being brought home by Kamiyo and Mvundla is there to welcome him' Dawid answered his unspoken question, 'that is cause for celebration.'

And Joshua saw again before his mind's eye the small curled form, half hidden in the sand, the look of absolute terror on Ben's face as he refused to go on excavating and then the arrival of Sharon, who had so tenderly removed the bones and taken them to a place of safety. Only to have her own existence, the solidity of her childhood questioned by this place. "The new names," he thought, "are strange now, but perhaps we will grow into them."

At that point Kamiyo got up. 'I have an early start in the morning,' she said. 'My parents are arriving. I need to fetch them.'

'What?' Joshua stood up with her, 'Sharon, Kamiyo are you serious?'

She smiled, 'Final skeletons, you know.' But her eyes belied the flippant tone.

As he had so often in the past, Joshua walked her back – to her room, this time, no caravan, no open sky, but still that same companionship.

'Goodnight, Mvundla,' she said. He liked to have her call him by that name.

'Goodnight, Kamiyo.'

As he made his way back, Paul caught up with him, 'Joshua, Mvundla,' he said, 'can I leave you to be here when Adam arrives – at about lunch time?'

Elaine had not wanted to come to see this place. The Crime Scene she called it in her mind, aware of the melodrama but unable to stop herself. But there had been about the invitation, propped up against the rose quartz paperweight on John's desk, something insistent, something undeniable. And finally John's tired assumption that they would refuse became unbearable. Everything she had fought to keep had slipped through her fingers anyway, even as she held it. She had known that she would go to that place ever since Sharon's letter to John had arrived, with her thesis, telling him, that she had discovered Miriam, too. But the consolation Sharon had found in the tales of the desert people left Elaine cold. Only fear gripped her heart again.

All the same, here she was on the plane heading for her husband's past, which had somehow become her daughter's future. John was staring in silence out of the window. The first flight had as always been long and tiring, with little sleep in the cramped space and the emptiness of his skull. And despite the anxiety about what awaited them, they were now both looking forward to landing in Kimberley after the four hour wait in the cold steel bleakness, which was Johannesburg International Airport, unrelieved by the loud and aggressively bright restaurants and bustle of people.

'Look,' John said unexpectedly, 'the Big Hole.'

She looked down across his lap into a huge gaping hole in the earth, a green deep sunken lake with steep impossible sides. She had never paid much attention to his work, playing the social side when she had to, but mostly she'd treated it as a necessary evil in his, and therefore their lives. It was an evil that had made their life possible. Now she stared in horror at this hole in which such riches had been found and taken, to leave the land so scarred – certainly changed forever.

'That is what you do?' she asked.

'No, I just make it possible for others to do that,' short, irritated that it came still as such a surprise to her.

The plane turned smoothly, gliding over the smoky valley of ashes, which was Galeshewe, circling back over Kimberley itself, the diamond sorting house, the park, the monument and on the other side coming down over the Elizabeth Conradie School for the Disabled towards Kimberley's dusty dry air strip and the glass block, which was the airport.

They stepped out onto the top steps that led from the plane and were instantly engulfed in the ever-present hot dry wind of eastern Kimberley. It carried faintly the smell of peppercorn trees and dust, with faint echoes still of the August burning of the fields. The October rains had just begun, John noted, surprising himself. They had been late and he could still tell.

Then the strangeness of all airports rescued him from the rising questions. The hot tarmac to be rushed across, waiting at luggage retrieval, the tired smiling companionship of fellow travellers who would never see each other again. All contained the return for him so it was not overwhelming. Finally they turned with their luggage and there she stood: their daughter.

She was wearing a white dress, clearly in honour of the occasion as the un-matching flat sandals showed, and the veld hat which she had at least removed and swung in greeting.

'Mum,' she said tenderly, taking her small mother in her arms. 'You must be tired come. We'll go straight out to N'osimasi where you can have a shower and rest, put your feet up, but feel yourself safely on terra firma.'

Softly, Elaine asked, 'Is it terra firma?'

'Oh mother,' she said, 'that I can't tell you. It is most of the time – though it's hollow and shudders with the mining.'

'Dad,' she turned to him, still a tall man, his iron-grey hair an unruly mop, his smile for his daughter now lopsided, half afraid. 'How does it feel to be back?'

'Strange,' he said.

She took them out to the car, stored their luggage and drove carefully out of the car park. Her mother sat at the back and closed her eyes, not wanting to see, afraid of the looks of recognition flitting across John's face. Sharon glanced sideways at her father. He sat upright, not relaxing his back against the seat of the Toyota company car that was too familiar for comfort. His hands were tense on his thighs. He wished he was driving, that he had something to do, anything rather than watch and admire his daughter's competence in a world in which he had failed, or thought he did.

'How is Tant Rina of the Kooperasie?' he asked, trying to be light.

'She's fine. It's no longer a Kooperasie though, it's a huge Pick 'n Pay Hypermarket, quite glamorous, really. We have a mall now – how scary is that?'

'I can't imagine it, sleepy little Abelshoop – a mall!'

'Oh yes: the march of progress. Only the off license is still the same and of course the stillte kerk, although the congregation is much bigger and it has competition now from an Anglican church – for the expatriates on the mines. Most of the metallurgists and the geologists are from overseas in one way or another. Quite an eclectic company really.' She was aware that she was babbling.

'And your little part of it.'

'Very small still. Dawid and me, really.'

'But the centre of this week?'

'Yes. The centre of this week. For Hendrik,' and they both fell silent then, thinking of the small wrinkled man with the honey gold eyes and the smile which lit up in greeting for even the smallest creature.

Elaine sat resting her head against the back of the car seat behind them and listened to them with dread, like a tight fist clenched about her heart.

"Why," she thought as she had a billion times, "why does something so far removed from their own lives mean so much to them?" She had never shared with them this love of the far away and unimaginable. She had always felt excluded when they talked like this, turning instead to the familiar forms of her own gentle life. So she turned now also to her own concerns. "Why am I so afraid? That dreadful woman is dead after all and the place John says is changed beyond all recognition. Why do I still fear them?"

And then she knew. It was not them she feared but the endless deep wells of loss in John's eyes when news of her death had come, knowing she could never fill them. That was what she feared, the echoing emptiness which this place might mercilessly expose.

Kamiyo turned in through the gate of N'osimasi, hardly noticing any more how out of place it stood on the edge of the veld before it swooped down to the river. John noticed and grimaced – though one still small voice inside him told him he was glad: the more different it all was, the less chance of memories of Miriam overwhelming him.

'You'll be sleeping at the Radcliffe place. They kindly agreed to help with the accommodation.'

'Oh good,' John said, 'Elaine, you'll love them.'

'They will have kept breakfast for you and then I thought we might do a tour then lunch at the rec club. That's where everyone will be assembled by then. Does that sound manageable?' Kamiyo asked, 'or would you prefer to rest first?'

'No, no rest – a good walk will iron the stiffness out better,' John replied.

'Do you mind if I just walk on my own?' Elaine said, to both and to no one in particular.

As John had said, Cecilia and Rosalie struck her as wonderful people. They were soon deep in conversation about gardens and jams as she found her way to the kitchen after a quick shower, to help with breakfast. Nevertheless, after they had eaten she took herself out to the garden alone. John and his daughter went off to the museum, she wanting to show him Kara/tuma, and Rosalie and Cecilia let them all go. They were after all expecting more company.

Soon enough, they heard another car drive up. It was Joshua with Adam and the children. He looked questioningly at Cecilia. She nodded.

'Oh dear,' he whispered.

'No,' she said, 'it will be good. It must be good. Elaine is out in the garden alone, by the way.' They brought their luggage in while Cecilia showed them the bathroom and made tea.

'Oh Cecilia,' Nella cried happily, 'it is so lovely; we visited you so much but we never got to stay with you really.'

'Well it was about time then,' Rosalie said briskly. 'Come and drink some tea?'

'Do you mind if I don't?' Thomas asked. 'I just want to walk in the garden.'

Nella could see the shock of his voice still in their eyes. She had become so used to it, and forgot how lovely it was some times.

'No, that will be fine, off you go. We might all have tea in the garden actually,' Cecilia decided. And he went.

Elaine had wandered restlessly in the garden, smelling the jasmine near the house and the subtler smell of the many roses. Near the kitchen the basil and mint had been almost overwhelming. She found a chair at the fountain and sat down, tired despite herself and unsure how to respond to the peace she felt here. She ought to be angry, ought to feel hurt. Some days, the wounds were after all still as fresh as they had ever been. Why did they not bleed now?

As she sat thinking, a young boy came towards her from the other side of the fountain. He seemed disturbingly beautiful, with pale hair and tall, slender form. The fountain behind him was making rainbows in the late afternoon sun, and his white hair gleamed like a halo. Then she realised who he must be.

She was afraid of this child, this proof of a love she had willed out of existence, but he came towards her, his narrow face lit with a vulnerable smile. He held something in his hand. He came right up to her ignoring all the others on the wide veranda. And she too could see only him, not the dark man behind or the girl watching, breath held. He stood before her, his face serious now, though the eyes remained soft.

'Hello,' he said, 'welcome to N'osimasi,' and held out his right hand. She shook it, not knowing what else to do, mesmerised by his familiar grey eyes so dark in that pale face.

Then, as if surprising even himself, 'This is for you,' and in his hand lay a small white object. She looked more closely. It was a bird, carefully, lovingly carved and polished from quartz. Moved suddenly by those tiny outstretched wings, which were nonetheless too heavy to fly, she picked it out of his open hand and nearly dropped it with fright as the earth began again that shaking. She clutched the child's arm while it lasted.

He smiled at her, 'Klaas says you get used to it.'

She examined the little creature and the boy went on in his melodious voice, 'In my mother's stories, many animals and one little bird like to sing to the stars.'

And for the first time in thirteen years, Elaine forgot to flinch at the mention of that person, 'What does it sing?' she asked.

Softly he took her arm, this awkward bony beautiful child and led her out, deep into the garden, leaving the others behind drinking tea. And more softly still he sang: *'Take my heart, my heart so small and frightened and without hope, take my famished heart and in the night let the star flowers bloom in my eyes, teaching me patience, waiting for rain.'*

'That's beautiful,' she said, and though she could feel her eyes brimming with the loneliness of years of anger and pain, she said, 'will you teach me that song?'

'It is just a little song from a children's story. It will not take you long to learn.' he replied.

'Thank you,' she said simply, as the tight fist about her heart relented at last in that clear air near the fountain beneath the apple tree, smelling of honey. Thomas straightened the chair for her then folded himself up on the grass at her feet.

'Did you carve this yourself?' she asked.

'Yes,' he said shyly. 'It is the honey guide.'

'A honey guide?'

'Yes, it shows Hendrik . . . used to show Hendrik, where the bees make their wild honey. It is the sweetest honey you will ever taste, though,' a grimace briefly, 'Janine used to make us drink it in hot toddies if we were ill.'

They talked for an hour about little daily things: lovely or funny but recognisable to both, though they had led such different lives. The acres of pain, which should have separated them, shrank as the deep grey eyes met hers as open and undefended as an animal's.

Adam had come out to find his son. They were due for lunch at the rec club soon and he found the new roads and strange buildings bewildering. He did not want to go alone. He paused when he saw him talking to the strange woman, realising who she must be. He watched and then slowly, heavily went on, knowing that a renewed meeting with John was only hours away. What was he to say to him? How does one put fifteen years of anger and jealousy away for a greeting?

'Thomas,' he called so they would know of his approach, 'it is time to go to lunch.' Thomas immediately uncurled himself and offered Elaine a courteous hand as she made to stand up. And they walked together back to the house.

Mvundla and Rosalie drove the party over to the rec club. The festive mood was growing stronger. He was puzzled by this and spoke to Rosalie about it on the way. 'Should we not be mourning Hendrik?'

'Well,' she said, 'I suppose this is a kind of wake for him.'

'But the mood is so joyful.'

'Yes it is. Is that wrong do you feel?'

'No, but it is hard to understand.'

'Then don't try. Hendrik would not mind. I think I can hear him laughing at you.'

Mvundla was silent then, not rebuked, but chastened in mind nonetheless.

John and Kamiyo meantime had been to her museum and had talked about the merits of the various possibilities for displaying Kara/tuma. She only had this afternoon to decide. Tomorrow would be the opening of the museum, and her speech and all needed to be in place for it. How she wished that she had Hendrik to advise her. It was lovely to have her father there but his mind was not on the same ghost as hers at all. She gave up. She turned to him, 'Father, I have something to give you.'

'What?' an anxious response.

'A picture. Thomas drew it while he was in hospital. He meant it for you.'

And she searched briefly in her desk and found the picture of Ou Groote flying joyfully to the stars. In silence she handed it to him. In silence he took it.

Then she said, 'Go, take it with you, I need to finish off here and you're only in the way.'

Stunned John wandered towards Witkopje. But it was only when he stood before the painting of Ou Groote at last that any memories awakened at all. And then they did with a vividness that brought him to his knees. He had to sit down, leaning his back against the rock. He left his hands hanging loosely on his knees and stared out at the changed world, but saw only the one he lost so many years ago. He remembered her last letter: "John, I have waited so long."

And John wept. He covered his face with his hands and wept as a child might weep – with sorrow and loss and waste: with abandon. Unseen, the faded shadow of Miriam sat impossibly by him. She longed to put a hand on his shoulder to reach again across the gulfs and simply say: "Enough, John, enough," even as his daughter called him to lunch.

But he stood up alone, waved his hat and called 'I'm coming,' though he was afraid of what he would say before them all and what he would say after all these years to Adam. He went with

Sharon and they sat on the patio of the rec club with long cool drinks as they waited.

Dawid arrived first and sat perched on the edge of the veranda, his golden eyes bright with an overflowing merriment. He hugged his knees gleefully as they waited. He sensed in all this what it was his father had meant when he had said in answer to his questions, 'we will dance again when all have come home.' He knew now that it was soon, but he also knew that being here was not enough: not enough for Adam, for John, nor really for Kamiyo and Mvundla.

They heard the cars draw up. Kamiyo jumped up and ordered cold water all round. John fluttered his hands unseen, Dawid sat dead still now, breathless almost. The others came out through the door. Elaine and Thomas together, both Kamiyo and Mvundla caught their breath at that, but then much was lost in the joyful greeting of Nella, who seemingly heedless, flung her arms about everyone and knocked two of the glasses over.

'Sharon, Kamiyo, don't you love your new name?' she asked breathlessly. 'It changes everything, doesn't it?' So everyone was kept busy with mopping and exclamations and no one but Dawid watched the two men, John and Adam, uncertain and awkward with the imagined weight of the moment, look up and see each other – while from the side gate approached another figure entirely.

'Xai kovadi,' Dawid thought, 'make me laugh – bring them together just so.' He chuckled inaudibly. John stood up as Adam approached. Now Adam lifted his face and looked up at John. Their eyes met. The fountain splashed on.

Elaine was looking down at the little bird nestled in her hand, recalling little wisps of the song the boy had sung for her. He had settled comfortably on the ground, his back leaning against the wall of the veranda, his hands resting loosely on his angled knees, while the others bustled about. Elaine diffidently stretched out her hand and brushed it lightly over her husband's son's hair. He turned briefly to smile at her.

Now the two men were about a metre apart, both slowly raising their hands, ready to shake, to be civilised, when what they wanted to do was to tear each other's hearts out with rage pent up for fifteen years. Mvundla watched, thinking how odd that the story should end here, where it had almost begun. It had been a failure and ridiculous, he thought, the sad waste of years.

Just at that point, a comical figure came around the corner of the building, singing loudly and tunelessly but with great enthusiasm: 'Hasi, hoekom is jou stert so kort, hasi hoekom is jou stert so kort? Wat het van jou stertjie geword?' (Little hare, why is your tail so short? What happened?). He swung buckets of kitchen refuse destined for the compost heaps rhythmically against his leg. The man was entirely unaware of the party on the patio, caught up in his own moment, blinking up into the sun to gauge the time and then going on noisily with his work. He disappeared, singing, with an unconcerned heart, the foolish and cheerful song about the shortness of a hare's tail.

Dawid could no longer contain himself, he whispered to Mvundla, 'Hey that is your song!'

'What? Oh yes,' Joshua-Mvundla remembered that Mvundla was also a hare. He laughed, shrugging in that moment into his new name. It was no longer portentous, simply a name, born from a story – and it fitted.

Dawid gleefully allowed his legs their freedom now and they dangled loosely over the edge of the veranda wall as he threw back his head, opened his mouth and let the laughter bubble out. Loud and warbling as a bird at sunrise, he laughed so hard he fell over the edge of the veranda. Thomas leapt up, giggling stupidly as the man fell. He called out, 'Dawid are you OK?' before collapsing with laughter over the wall above Dawid's wriggling feet. Nella too was laughing and Thomas turned smiling, trying unsuccessfully to hide it, with his back to the others, not sure all would find it a good time to laugh.

Mvundla winked at him and Kamiyo grinned, but Elaine looked up, deeply shocked that anyone should laugh at this point. She glanced anxiously at John and Adam and caught her breath, recognising the dreaded moment as she looked from one to the other, her eyes bright with tears. And then the two men, the cause of their strife long absent now, still seemed so foolishly caught up in the remaining momentum that she too laughed out loud. Shocked, John turned to her and as their locked looks broke apart, both Adam and John saw the others, all laughing now as the song of the short tail faded.

Both were embarrassed, aware suddenly of the absurdity of the song from the kitchen, and of their anger, sustained too long beyond its cause. Laughing too, Adam stretched out his hand now, 'John, welcome back.'

'Adam,' John replied, taking the proffered hand, 'Thank you.' And the moment passed safely through the world.

Kamiyo perched with Dawid on the ledge of the veranda wall and watched them all. She felt at ease about what she had done in bringing them here. She leaned back against a pillar and thought of the next day; of the speech she would give about Hendrik and about Kara/tuma and what they had meant to N'osimasi. She would speak also of that name, N'osimasi, and what it meant now: that the worlds could come together and not be destroyed by the meeting.

"What we have now," she would say, "are only traces of that time: of the wonder that it was," she thought. "We do not walk with gods, but they do still send us their rain – their blessing occasionally, even here in the desert."

They sat on that shuddering patio till late into the night.

Klaas said, 'Aish, it is busy tonight.'

'Yes,' Paul said, 'let us hope no accidents, then.'

But the others talked of the past amidst laughter and tears and no one had the heart to tell them it was closing time. The stars came out and the moon rose; the water feature, silent now, reflected their light as their voices carried out into the night and swirled around Witkopje where they made Hendrik smile.

At last Rosalie stood up and said, 'Time for bed.'

Adam, his children, Elaine and John rose obediently. Joshua and Sharon walked them to the car. And when they had gone they both decided without a word to walk up to Witkopje.

As they got to the top, Kamiyo clutched Mvundla's arm. 'Look.' she said, 'Look!'

'What is it?' Mvundla asked, peering in the darkness.

'The door is shut.' she cried.

They ran up the last few steps and the crack, which had run down the rock along the edge of the quartz intrusion had indeed closed – almost seamlessly – leaving only the head of Ou Groote. The rest was shut in by the rock.

'It must be the shifting caused by the mines,' Joshua said perplexed.

'Who cares what it is,' Kamiyo cried in distress, 'the door between the worlds is gone. Ou Groote cannot come back.'

And Mvundla, Joshua again, stared at the rock face, realising that she was right. He was filled with a terrible sense of loss.

But he crouched down to replace the rocks, which had fallen from Hendrik's mound and said softly, 'Kamiyo, Kamiyo listen to me. Ou Groote has gone home. It is what he wanted.'

'I know,' she said, her sobs lessening, 'I know, but we won't see him again.'

'No.'

They stood in silence at Hendrik's grave and looked long at the luminous painting.

'It is all we have now,' Kamiyo whispered.

'Yes, and memory.'

'It's not enough.'

Kamiyo reached for Mvundla's hand and saw mirrored in his eyes as he held hers for a moment, her own relief at the warm human touch. They walked back together as the first raindrops stirred the red dust, which lay shimmering with quartz in the floodlights of the mine.